Making her w... **laggie paused, an ac**... **s.**

Wet copper. Wa...

She stopped at th... hand flew to her mouth. Dark smears violated her cream-colored living room walls. They formed letters, the same letters over and over again. F. E. A. R. The four-letter word was written repeatedly across the room in various styles and sizes. But all in blood.

Only when her bottom hit the hardwood floor did Maggie realize she'd lost the strength in her legs. Was the intruder still in the house? How had he gotten in? Where had all of that blood come from?

The harsh ringing of the phone jolted through her. She crawled to the phone in the kitchen and pulled the receiver down from its cradle. With a shaking hand, she brought it to her ear.

"Hello?" It was barely a whisper as she gasped for air.

"Maggie," the cheerful voice said. "You got home safe, I see. And by now, you've learned tonight's lesson."

"Lesson?" She was pleased that her voice sounded stronger.

"About fear, of course. Did I scare you, Maggie? I believe I did," he said when she didn't answer. "I proved my point. But then, I knew you'd be an apt pupil."

"Why did you do this?"

"There is only fear. All other emotions are born of fear. You have to understand that before we move on to your next lesson."

The click of the receiver hummed in her ear for a long time.

The next lesson, the voice had said. And apparently she'd been appointed teacher's pet.

ANNE MARIE BECKER

is an award-winning author of romantic suspense. Her novel, *Only Fear,* won the 2009 Golden Heart Award for Best Romantic Suspense. She has always been fascinated with people and how they "work"—inside and out—which led to degrees in biology, psychology and counseling. Now, her roles as wife, mother, writer and domestic goddess continue to satisfy her curiosity. For more about Anne Marie, please visit her at www.annemariebecker.com.

Anne Marie Becker

ONLY
FEAR

CARINA
PRESS™

For Tim,
whose support, enthusiasm and love are boundless.

CARINA PRESS™

Recycling programs
for this product may
not exist in your area.

ISBN-13: 978-0-373-06264-5

ONLY FEAR

Copyright © 2011 by Anne Marie Becker

All rights reserved. Except for use in any review, the reproduction or utilization of this work in whole or in part in any form by any electronic, mechanical or other means, now known or hereafter invented, including xerography, photocopying and recording, or in any information storage or retrieval system, is forbidden without the written permission of the publisher, Harlequin Enterprises Limited, 225 Duncan Mill Road, Don Mills, Ontario M3B 3K9, Canada.

This is a work of fiction. Names, characters, places and incidents are either the product of the author's imagination or are used fictitiously, and any resemblance to actual persons, living or dead, business establishments, events or locales is entirely coincidental.

This edition published by arrangement with Harlequin Books S.A.

® and TM are trademarks of the publisher. Trademarks indicated with ® are registered in the United States Patent and Trademark Office, the Canadian Trade Marks Office and in other countries.

www.CarinaPress.com

Printed in U.S.A.

My deepest appreciation to Deb Nemeth,
for helping me whip this story into shape.
And to my agent, Jill Marsal, for believing in it
from the start, even before all the hype.

Thank you to Andrea, Danny and Tim
for their input. Their feedback was immensely helpful.
Dan and Carol, words of gratitude could never be enough.

I am grateful for the camaraderie of my cohorts
at NARWA and Kiss of Death, and my friend Julie. They
have been a wealth of information and encouragement. As
for my Ruby Sisters at www.rubyslipperedsisterhood.com—
I'm so lucky to be part of such a supportive
and fabulous group of übertalented women.

My admiration and gratitude goes out to John Douglas
for his books about his work on the cases that helped create
the FBI's Behavioral Analysis Unit. Also, to the men and
women who endeavor to find justice for victims of violent
crime, to prevent repeat offenders from claiming more
victims, and to help survivors and their families
find peace of mind, your work is so important.

ONE

THE COLD, HARD TILE of the ladies' room wall felt good against her cheek as Maggie attempted to regroup. Pushing up from the floor, she brushed off the seat of her pants and straightened her blouse, performing a mental body scan. Breathing back to normal. Pulse slowing.

Good news—she was going to survive.

Of course, she always did. If only her brain could believe it.

Knowing she had to get back, Maggie blotted her face with a wet paper towel and tossed it into the trash on her way out.

Her director shot her a look of concern as she strode into the radio station's production booth. Tall, lanky and in his mid-twenties, David Talbot had been her right-hand man since Chicago Great Lakes University had asked her to start a talk show nine months ago. A communications student, David had jumped at the chance to work here. With raised eyebrows, he silently asked, *Are you okay?*

With a nod of reassurance, she returned to her desk. Her portion of the studio was the sound booth, a small room just past David's area, separated by a wall of glass through which they could see each other. As David cued her, she took a sip of water with a hint of lime before speaking into the microphone in front of her.

"Welcome back to *Live with Levine.* I'm Dr. Margaret Levine." Her wilted confidence bloomed again as she pulled her theoretical therapist's cloak around her. "I've got Dan from downtown Chicago on the line with me. Before the commercial break, Dan, you were telling us about your personal tragedy. Your wife was recently shot and killed during a mugging."

"Yes." The man's voice clogged with tears. "I don't know what I'll do without her."

"It sounds like you really miss her." Maggie's heart tore for him as a flash of her brother's smiling face hit her in the chest like a battering ram. Her breathing hitched and her pulse rate picked up as the image was quickly replaced with one of Brad lying in a pool of blood.

"Tell us about your wife," Maggie prompted gently, focusing on her breathing. As Dan from downtown talked through his tears about his wife of five years, she struggled against the urge to flee and curl up in that bathroom stall again. The details of Dan's tragedy were so similar to hers. She couldn't help but think about it, and the remembered images threatened to overwhelm her.

Especially today, of all days.

"Thank you, Dan, for sharing your story with us. It takes a lot of courage to face each day as you have." She knew that firsthand. "I'm so sorry for your loss. Check in with us and let us know how you're doing, okay?"

The man drew in a shaky breath and blew it out. "Okay. Thanks for listening, Dr. Levine."

"Anytime." She looked at the board in front of her, lit up with lights, each one representing a person who needed a listening ear, and picked the next one in the queue. It had already been a long night in the city of Chicago, and still there were people who needed to tell their stories.

Maggie glanced at the computer screen, skimming David's notes on the caller. "Hello, Frantically Frustrated, how can we help tonight?"

A woman's voice answered. "My mother-in-law is insane."

Maggie's lips twitched. Now here was something that wouldn't make her think of her brother. Or panic attacks. "How so?"

"She wants to move in with us. And *that* would totally make *me* insane." Through the glass partition, Maggie saw David chuckling.

"And what does your husband say about this?"

The caller sighed. "Nothing. He refuses to worry about it. And he won't, until she shows up on our doorstep with luggage in hand." There was a slight pause. "I've been dreaming about giving him an ultimatum. Her or me."

"It's the Fourth of July, so I'd expect a few fireworks tonight, but be careful. Don't say things you can't take back."

"I wouldn't actually confront him. I can't even talk to him about it."

"Can't or won't? Don't be afraid. Try just sitting down and talking to him first. Calmly. Tell him how you feel. What you fear."

There was a pause on the other end, but Maggie didn't rush in to fill the silence. Waiting a person out usually paid off despite the moments of dead air. When the woman spoke again, her voice was subdued. "I'm afraid he'll close himself off from me. Or, worse, choose his mother."

"That's good. Name your fear, decide to face it head-on, and it can't control you. But you'll never know what your husband's thinking if you don't ask. Let him in. He can't read your mind. I'm sure if you talk to him, he'll see how important this is to you. Communication is power. Your fear is eating away at that power. Don't let fear win."

She glanced at the clock on the wall, noting it was two minutes until midnight. Almost Tuesday. Her shift at WGLU was almost over. "I see our time has just about drawn to a close." Through the glass, David held up one long finger and pointed toward her computer screen. She selected the one he'd highlighted for her. "But we have time for one more quick call."

At least, she hoped it was quick. She was eager to get home to Sigmund and curl up with him and a good book before sinking into a few precious hours of sleep. Too soon, the holiday break would be over and it would be time to return to the university to teach her summer-school psych classes. The new session began on Thursday.

Maggie pushed the blinking button. "Hello," she said in a husky voice—the one the station manager threatened to trademark. "You're on live with Dr. Margaret Levine. What's your question?"

A familiar low chuckle filled her ears. One side of her mouth quirked upward in a half smile of recognition. The night just got more interesting. And perhaps more tedious. She never knew what this man was going to say.

She sat forward in her chair. "Happy Fourth of July, Owen. It's been a while." A few weeks, anyway. That was a long time to go between calls from Owen. He wasn't a stranger, but he could be strange. There was something about him, something that mocked the world and its general populace. An inflated sense of superiority she found amusing.

And he was usually good for some excellent banter.

"I've been around, listening. You missed me." The words weren't a question and were deep with intimacy, as if it were only the two of them and not most of the university and half of Chicago listening.

Maggie rubbed her arms against a sudden chill. She had her boundaries, and she wouldn't let this man cross them. She reminded herself that she was in a radio booth, probably miles away from her caller. He couldn't even see her. Didn't know what she looked like. But then, she didn't know him from David, either. She wouldn't know if she passed him on the street.

"What can I help you with tonight?"

Another chuckle filled her ears. "You've got it backward. It is *I* who can help *you*." His pretentious tone grated. She ignored the stab of annoyance she felt at the thought he might be mocking her. Owen had a tendency to get preachy, which was not the object of her show.

"Help me? Regarding what, exactly?" Mentally, she reviewed the night's conversations.

"What you said about fear, and being afraid. It was wrong."

She raised an eyebrow as he chuckled again. Her temper, too often annoyingly consistent with the stereotype about redheads, flared at his condescending tone, but the psychiatrist in her controlled it. After all, she preferred to think of her hair as auburn. Drawing on her clinical demeanor, and adding a healthy dose of curiosity, she continued. "By all means, enlighten us."

"Don't be afraid," he mimicked in a singsong voice. "I can't believe you're telling the public that. Fear is what makes our blood pump through our bodies. It doesn't take away our power. It *is* power."

"Well, fear is often accompanied by an adrenaline rush and can make you experience things differently," she acknowledged. "It's the fight-or-flight response preparing our bodies to face something or someone down or to flee. But fear can also paralyze us and make us reluctant to face things." She knew that all too well.

"Everything, every action every person takes is related to fear." The tempo of his voice picked up in his excitement. "We can't live without it. It's what makes our blood flow. It's what motivates us in everything. Anxiety, for instance—"

This time, Maggie forced a chuckle, wincing when it

came out sounding nervous. "Oh, come now, Owen. Anxiety can be thought of as a type of fear, but it doesn't make the world go round. We'd all be a bunch of neurotics."

Her gaze went to the clock. The show was almost over. She balked at him going down this road with her on the air, especially in the final two minutes, when she couldn't delve deeper. She didn't want to leave her audience on an awkward or confusing note. It would be irresponsible.

"And yet—" Owen's voice took on a condescending ring "—people are anxious because they are afraid. And rightly so." He sounded quite proud of himself.

"Some would say that's just nature, not fear. That we're wired to thrive on stressors of various kinds."

"We're animals at heart, Maggie." He switched to her nickname with such ease, prickles of alarm crept across the back of her neck. Callers respectfully called her Dr. Levine, or Dr. Margaret. Only friends and family called her Maggie. It was one of those boundaries she'd so carefully erected and maintained. "And animals thrive on fear, not anxiety. That's what makes predators so powerful. They sense the fear in their prey. They use it."

"You sound like a scientist." Maggie covered her unease with another husky laugh as David signaled her to wrap things up. Something about the way Owen's voice had turned cold and hard when he spoke of predators set off alarm bells in her head, and her instincts were usually right.

Well, they used to be.

"Don't mock me," Owen snapped, his voice no longer simply hard but solid and cutting as a diamond. Maggie's chilled blood turned downright icy. "You think you know everything, but you have much to learn. Perhaps I could teach you a thing or two. I've dedicated years to this subject, Maggie, and I know it's one that's close to your heart."

What did he know?

A hard knot of pain formed behind her breastbone, pushing until she felt as if her heart might be expanding in her chest. The notes written on the papers in front of her blurred and swam.

Not now. Please, not again. Maybe she shouldn't have stopped taking the anxiety medication. But she'd been doing so much better, before today.

"I'm an avid student of the human psyche." Owen laughed, but it was no less frightening.

Through the window that separated her small room from the production booth, David cast her a worried look. She shook her head, signaling him that she would handle it, even as she felt a shiver rack her body. She gritted her teeth against it, forcing a deep breath, focusing on things that were real. The pounding of her pulse at her temple. The tightness of her neck from her rigid posture. The almost minuscule electronic whir of equipment and an open mic. The lingering acid taste of the soda she'd had with dinner, combined with the taste of fear.

I am in control.

"Interesting theory, Owen." She forced her clenched teeth to relax enough to get the words out. She pushed the button to take him off the air before he could say anything more. "But that's all the time we have left tonight. Join me, Dr. Margaret Levine, tomorrow night where my focus will be depression. In the meantime, treat yourselves gently."

After her signature sign-off message, Maggie removed the headphones and sat back in her chair, uncertain her shaky legs would carry her to the break room across the hall. David rushed in with his usual long strides, running his fingers over the top of his buzz-cut dark hair. As a graduate communications student doing his internship at the station, he worked sixty hours a week, thriving on caffeine and nicotine. It was no wonder he was skinny as a flagpole. But he was sharp. And right now, he was excited.

"Owen again. I thought he'd be a good way to end the show, but man, I'm sorry. That guy's missing some cookies from his jar, isn't he? He sure knows how to get our listeners stirred up, though. After that show on personality disorders, we had more people calling in to respond to his comments than ever before." David paced the small room. Two steps were all he could manage before he ran out of space and had to pivot. "I should ask Sharon to come in tomorrow and help man the phones."

The station's undergraduate intern, Sharon Moss, worked about twenty hours a week. A vibrant, hard-working girl, she enjoyed working on *Live with Levine*. More important, David clearly liked her and relished an excuse to be with her.

Maggie bit down hard on her bottom lip, resisting the urge to rub the growing ache in her chest. When her breath hitched in smaller and smaller increments, she knew this wasn't going away soon. First, Dan's mention of his wife dying by a violent hand, and now Owen's tirade about fear.

Twice in one night, after months of nothing.

But then, this was no ordinary night. Today was the first anniversary of Brad's death.

I am in control, I am in control, she chanted to herself. But it was obvious to her she was not in control.

"Excuse me." She suddenly pushed up from her chair and walked as quickly as she could to the bathroom down the hall. Trying to suck a decent breath of air into her frozen lungs, she stumbled into the first stall. She slammed the door closed and slumped against it, then sank to the floor and rested her head against the wall. Again, the coolness seemed to help. After suffering from similar episodes for the past twelve months, she knew what to expect. And what helped.

The shaking took over then, and she chanted her mantra through gritted teeth until she felt her color return, her pulse slow.

I am in control. She'd say it until she believed it.

Oh God, Brad. What I wouldn't give to speak to you today. And every day for a full lifetime.

A knock came at the ladies' room door, followed by David's hesitant voice as he slowly pushed it open a crack. "Maggie? You okay?"

She pulled herself up from the floor and was grateful when her legs supported her. "Yeah. Just a stomach bug or something. I'll be right out."

After splashing water on her face and holding a cool paper towel to the back of her neck, she examined the damage. Eyes dilated. Cheeks flushed. But nobody but a doctor would recognize the symptoms. Or they would mistake them for some passing ailment.

"Fake it 'til you make it," she muttered to herself.

She balled up the paper towel, then tossed it with more force than necessary into the trash bin. Angry now that she'd allowed herself to become upset again, she embraced the increased adrenaline. The sooner she could wrap things up at work, the sooner she could get home to familiar, safe surroundings. To Sigmund, whose purring would soothe her fears.

Fear. Anxiety. The very words had her wanting to sink to the floor again. Of all the things she'd said in the past hour, why would Owen pick that as a point of contention? Did he know about her panic attacks, or had he just followed the news last summer, like everyone else within a hundred-mile radius of Chicago, and made an educated guess?

She found David waiting for her in the break room, concern etched in his forehead. "You're sick? Why didn't you take the night off? We could have played a tape of an old show."

She shrugged and attempted a smile. It came off weak, she knew. "It kind of hit me at the end. I'm fine now."

He looked closer, but she turned to the fridge to grab a can of juice. Adopting a lighter tone, she strived for normalcy. "Got any plans?"

"For tonight?"

"It is the Fourth of July in the big city. Even past midnight, there's got to be a party somewhere."

After a shrug, he seemed to decide she was back to her usual self and smiled. "I didn't, but now I think I'll give Sharon a call and fill her in. She's usually up late."

"Gives you an excuse to talk to her." His crush on the girl was evident to everyone within fifty feet of the pair. She wondered if Sharon knew that he flushed bright red all the way to his ears whenever anyone so much as mentioned her name.

God, sometimes she felt so old. When was the last time she'd had that zing of new love? College? That had been years ago. At thirty-three, she'd given up feeling that kind of electric connection again.

Brad had been in love. Her younger brother had even talked engagement to his longtime girlfriend before... Well, it was best not to go down that road now. Not unless she wanted to spend some more quality time in the ladies' room tonight, slumped against the wall.

David grinned. "Exactly. We could use her help anyway, right? If Owen calls back, we'll have a big show on our hands tomorrow night, just like last time. We'll be golden."

She frowned. "Not everyone was happy about his opinions last time."

"Yeah, he set off several nights of angry response calls, not to mention the letters."

That he'd upset people was putting it mildly. In fact, his discussion about personality disorders had almost sparked an all-out war of words with her listeners. And Owen had clearly enjoyed it. She'd responded to every one of the calls and letters.

"But Steveroni was happy," David added.

Since he was turned away, pulling his usual post-show energy drink from the fridge, David missed her eye roll. The station manager, Steve Marconi, was not her concern. Technically, he was her boss, and therefore should be important to her, but she'd lost respect about the twelfth time he'd "bumped" into her. The not-so-innocent brushes of his hand were usually followed by an invitation to "dinner." She couldn't get much clearer than *no,* other than maybe *hell, no.* But she strived for professionalism and she couldn't let herself say that to him. She was *not* interested in making Steveroni happy.

"Maybe we can encourage Owen to call again, maybe even more frequently." David popped the top to his drink and took a gulp. He paced the room as he had before, excitement reddening his cheeks so that the freckles that dotted them almost disappeared. "I'd bet we can increase listener numbers by double, maybe triple." Maggie blanched. Seeing her negative reaction, David hurried on. "I'm not saying you don't already have a large audience. You've become the most popular radio personality in Chicago." He misunderstood her scowl, and continued to press his point. "I've heard Steveroni grumble that you would leave if some other, non-university station offered you more money." That was news to her. "It's only that if you had a regular verbal exchange with Owen, more people might tune in."

She didn't want the popularity. She'd rather be an unknown. But she wanted to help people, and her radio show was the best way she knew how while still protecting her... boundaries.

"I mean, he loves to talk with you. He can be a jerk about

it, but your topics seem to challenge him. He almost can't resist calling in to argue."

Maggie cocked her head. "And you want to create a stalker out of him."

It was David's turn to blanch. "No. That's not what I'm talking about. Oh God, Doc, is that what you thought?" He shook his head adamantly as one finger picked at the tab at the top of his drink. "I would never encourage that."

"And yet that's exactly the characteristics I hear in Owen." She rubbed her arms to ward off another sudden chill, then rose. "Look, let's just let things lie for now, shall we?"

Shamefaced and deflated, he nodded solemnly. "Whatever you say."

Maggie felt as if she'd kicked a puppy for licking her face. Kicked him hard, with steel-toed boots. David was always supportive, always upbeat and a great production director. He was also filled with the naive idealism of untested youth.

She sighed. "I said for now. We'll talk about it later."

He tossed a glance back over his shoulder, his mouth curved upward. "Okay. Let me close up shop and I'll walk you to your car."

It was their usual routine, but tonight Maggie welcomed the company more than other nights. Entering the dimly lit parking lot in the wee hours of the morning was always a bit scary, but after her odd conversation with Owen, she wouldn't leave anything, especially her safety, to chance. The lot was on campus but on the edge, and a dark, weed-choked empty lot bordered it on one side. There were bushes over there large enough for a grown man to hide behind.

"All set," David said fifteen minutes later, poking his head into the break room where Maggie was reviewing her notes for tomorrow's show. Depression was always a topic that hit home with a lot of people. She tried to touch on it every couple months.

After gathering her things in the soft leather tote her family had given her when she graduated from med school, she went with David down two flights of stairs to the ground floor, then out the double glass doors. Her heels clicked on the pavement, and she wished she'd thought to change into running shoes. Just in case.

A sudden boom made her jump, but the streak of red and white that lit up the sky was innocent enough. Someone in a nearby neighborhood was doing some late celebrating of the nation's birthday. It was now July fifth, but the sound of Black Cats pop-popping in the distance told her more than one person was planning to continue celebrating.

David, apparently unaware of her nerves, sent her a smile as they reached her car. She'd parked in her usual spot, not too far from the front doors—as close as she could get—and under the dim orange light of the parking lamp. The light was hazy, the air thick with the humidity that proclaimed a summer storm was in the making. They needed the rain after the heat wave that had seized hold of Chicago the past few weeks. But the heat kept burning off the clouds.

Not wanting David to think she was totally paranoid, Maggie resisted the urge to look under her car. Instead, she hurried to unlock the door to her old, practical Volvo while help was still nearby. Closing herself in, she locked the doors and rolled down the window, smiling in relief at her companion. "Have a good night. I'll see you tomorrow."

"Sure thing." He turned to leave, but hesitated and turned back to her. "And don't worry, Doc. What happened before will never happen again."

Maggie ignored the prickles that stabbed her skin at the thought of the past. Why did he have to bring that up now? She sucked a breath through her nose and blew it out through her mouth. "I know."

"I mean, what are the chances? That was a one-in-a-million type thing."

There was a time she wouldn't have thought it could have happened at all. She'd been young and foolish and had believed if she was good to people, they'd be good to her. Nearly a year later, she was all too aware of the lengths a person could go to if pushed.

"Good night, David." She tried to soften the stern tone with a tight smile.

He thumped the roof of the car with his knuckles. "Good night."

As he walked away, she immediately checked the backseat to be sure nobody was hiding there, and turned the key in the ignition. All before David got too far away. He could still hear her shouts for help at this distance, if need be. Or, there was always the panic button on the car alarm she'd had installed. Thankfully, however, everything was okay. She was alone.

Within minutes on the drive home, her grip relaxed and her knuckles regained their pink color. She'd chosen the shortest of her three routes home today. She usually varied her route a bit. But short was best today. She longed to be home, behind familiar, solid walls and the protection of a state-of-the-art home security system.

Pulling into the two-car garage of her modest home in Wilmette, a pleasant older suburb a short drive from the university, she closed the garage door behind her. She sat, watching it descend in the rearview mirror before getting out of the car.

"Here, kitty," she called as she entered the house and flipped on a light. She moved to the wall, quickly punching in the code to rearm the security system.

Sigmund usually met her in the hallway between the garage and the rest of the house, skidding down the polished wood floor before recovering his dignity and weaving between her legs. The chubby orange-striped cat, who reminded her of Garfield except for his shorter hair, could move impressively fast for an overweight beast. But tonight there was no sign of him.

Maggie switched on another light in the kitchen, dropping her bag on the countertop. The warm glow of the lights soothed her shattered nerves.

"I'm home, baby." She tossed her keys down next to her satchel before moving back into the hall. Maybe the cat was napping on her bed. Still, he usually met her at the door, wanting his dinner. He'd adapted to her late hours months ago.

"Are you hungry?" Making her way toward the living room, she paused in midstep, an acrid smell burning her nostrils. And not the lingering scent of the dinner she'd cooked before she'd left for work that evening.

Wet copper. Warm pennies.

She stopped at the archway into the living room and flipped on another light. Her hand flew to her mouth. Dark smears violated her pristine cream-colored living room walls. The smears formed letters, the same letters over and over again. *F. E. A. R.* Splashed and dripping across the long wall over the couch. Letters six inches or three feet, cursive or block. The four-letter word was written repeatedly across the living room in various styles and sizes. But all in blood.

Only when her bottom hit the hardwood floor did Maggie realize she'd lost the strength in her legs. Her eyes swiveled down the hall to the alarm, noting the red light that marked it as armed. It had been armed when she walked in, too, hadn't it? Yes, she clearly remembered the red light being on when she'd punched in her code. Was the intruder still in the house? And how had he gotten in to begin with?

And, *dear God,* where had all of that blood come from?

"Sigmund!" she called past vocal cords strung tight with fear. The sound of panic in her voice had her breath coming in short bursts for the third time this evening. *Damn it.* She should have taken a pill after the last time. She carried one with her at all times, just in case. But she'd foolishly thought she could control it. On this, of all days.

"Sigmund!" she called again, but it was more of a pathetic croak as she couldn't muster enough air into her aching chest. Whimpering, she slid backward until her spine hit the wall, then hugged her knees to her chest. A large ball of orange fur bolted from somewhere in the back of the house, skirted the edge of the living room and leaped into her arms. Maggie gasped in relief, then ran her fingers through Sigmund's fur, holding on for dear life as her muscles shook, fighting for control.

The harsh ringing of the phone jolted through her. Holding Sigmund to her chest with one arm, she crawled her way to the phone in the kitchen, unwilling to trust her legs to support her. Jerking the cord to pull the phone down from its cradle, she ducked to avoid it hitting her head. With a shaking hand, she managed to bring the receiver to her ear.

"Hello?" It was barely a whisper as she gasped for air.

"Maggie," the cheerful voice said. Owen's voice. "You got home safe, I see." He chuckled as her grip tightened on the phone. "And by now, you've learned tonight's lesson."

"Lesson?" She was pleased that her voice sounded stronger. Stronger, but not strong enough.

"About fear, of course. Did I scare you, Maggie? I believe I did," he said when she didn't answer. "I proved my point. But then, I knew you'd be an apt pupil. After all, you earned the highest marks in all of your classes in medical school."

"Why did you do this?" The man was insane.

Again, Owen's voice flipped from thrilled to threatening in the space of a stuttering heartbeat. "*There is only fear.*

All other emotions are born of fear. You have to understand that before we move on to your next lesson."

The click of the receiver hummed in her ear for a long time before she loosened her hold enough to let go. Even then, it felt like an eternity passed before the grip of her panic lessened enough for her to act.

The next lesson, Owen had said. And he'd apparently appointed her teacher's pet.

July Fourth was Ethan Townsend's least favorite day, and it was finally over. As his red-rimmed eyes bypassed his reflection in the mirror behind the bar, they found confirmation that it was indeed well past midnight—nearly two in the morning, actually, according to the clock high above the bottles of liquor that lined the wall. He tipped the final drops of Scotch down his throat and welcomed the burn as he silently toasted a welcome to July fifth.

He wasn't unpatriotic. It was just that the day everyone else in America was consuming vast quantities of beer and apple pie and setting off small explosives to celebrate the birth of the nation, Ethan was recalling fireworks of his own. And the life that had been lost three years ago because of them.

The bartender announced last call, which was a joke because Ethan and only one other customer, who'd nursed his drink for a good hour now, were in the godforsaken place. It was a dive, but it had what he needed on the one night a year he truly needed it. Solitude and alcohol.

His gaze rose to the mirror, again skipping over his own image and resting on that of the man in the corner, whose eyes were on him. Apparently interpreting the eye contact as an invitation, the man stood and wove his way unsteadily around empty chairs and tables to join him. It seemed his precious solitude was about to come to an end.

"I knew it." The man's breath stank of stale beer and cigarettes as his beady eyes peered at him. His jowls shook as he nodded vigorously. "You're that guy. The one from the TV a couple years back. The one that got that little girl killed."

Grief twisted Ethan's gut. "You've got the wrong guy."

"No," he insisted, stabbing a finger at him through the suddenly charged air. The bartender watched them warily from the other end of the bar. "It was all over the news for weeks. You are that guy."

Ethan's jaw, stubbled with a day's growth of beard, slid to the side. Of all the rotten luck... His hair was longer than three years ago, skimming the collar of his shirt, and his eyes were red with exhaustion, yet this guy recognized him. *Fuck.* He didn't want to explain or make excuses. Not to a stranger. He couldn't even explain it away to himself. And there were no excuses.

"You don't know what you're talking about. I didn't kill anyone." He felt the lie fall from his lips like lead. The thump of it echoed in his head as it settled in his stomach. "It wasn't my finger on the trigger."

"Yeah, but," the guy began, taking a step toward him, his finger still pointed accusingly.

Ethan's hand clenched around his glass. If the man touched him, so help him God...

Probably sensing trouble, the bartender brought his tab then, and Ethan quickly signed, rising off his barstool as he did so. At six feet, he was a good six inches taller than the other guy. And a good thirty pounds heavier. Thirty pounds of muscle. The fight wouldn't be fair, and this guy wasn't worth a visit to jail.

"Night," he said to the man, interrupting his attempts to bring up the past. On steady legs he walked out and crossed several blocks at a brisk pace, trying to clear his mind. Attempting to muddy it with liquor had obviously not helped. Maybe focusing on something else would.

But a sweet face continuously thwarted him. Innocent, trusting brown eyes. Tendrils of soft blond hair curling around cheeks still plump with youth—cheeks spattered with blood.

Cursing, Ethan picked up the pace. His cell phone rang. Not many people would call him at two in the morning. He knew better than to ignore this call. "Yeah?"

"We're meeting. Seven in the morning."

"I'll be there." The other person hung up just as abruptly.

Ethan turned down another street. Downtown Chicago at night wasn't the wisest choice for a stroll, but he was itching for a fight. For release. For something that would take his mind off a baby-doll face and enormous, sightless eyes.

A meeting at the Society would provide that. In the meantime, however, God help anyone who came across his path tonight.

TWO

"YOU'VE GOT TO HEAR THIS." Becca Haney bounced in and perched on the edge of Ethan's desk, a small stack of folders clutched to her chest. She countered his pointed look with a wide grin, swinging her bright purple-stockinged legs and black Mary Janes as she continued with exuberance. "Come on. You could at least *act* the teensiest bit curious."

It was really too early in the morning for this. With her sprightly manner, petite body and delicate facial structure, the girl—who was actually in her mid-twenties—reminded him of Tinker Bell. She pushed her rectangular, no doubt chic, black-framed glasses up on her nose. Her short, bleached-blond hair was spiked with purple tips today—to match the stockings, no doubt. One never knew what look Becca would choose. It changed with her mood, which ran the entire gamut—from happy to perky to exuberant. How anyone with such a small body could contain so much energy was beyond him.

Resigned to setting aside his crossword puzzle—which had really only been a poor attempt at a diversion for his pounding head until the meeting began—for a few moments, Ethan leaned back, his hands interlaced behind his neck as he studied her. "I'll listen if it'll get you off my desk."

Ignoring his sarcasm, she leaned forward. Her body practically vibrated with enthusiasm. "We've got a new case."

"So I gathered," he drawled as she waved several red

folders in his face. "Why else would Damian have called a meeting so early the day after a holiday?"

She shrugged as if he expected an answer. "Mr. Manchester could just want to check in. Or there could have been a break in a case."

Not likely. The entire team would have been called in right away in that event. So far, Ethan had only seen Becca and a glimpse of one other team member heading down the hall. Since Ethan hadn't wanted human contact until absolutely necessary, he'd hidden out in his office. But Becca had other plans.

"It's been weeks since we've had a new case," Becca continued.

"And you're excited about this one."

Every case they had at the Society for the Study of the Aberrant Mind, shortened to SSAM or the Society by its employees, dealt with serial murderers or other violent criminals. Each one was interesting in its own way. Challenging, yes, in that the usual channels of law enforcement hadn't solved them yet.

But they weren't fun.

Then again, Becca had only had to deal with technology and administration issues and had thus far been removed from danger while she was in training for the more serious assignments. As the newest, and smallest, employee at the Society, she was too young and innocent to face the grim reality, anyway.

Ethan had faced too many hard truths in his thirty-eight years. Some days, like today, he felt ancient.

"Oh yes. It involves one of my favorite celebrities."

He rubbed his temples to ease the ache there, to no avail. "A celebrity?"

"Dr. Margaret Levine." When he continued to stare at her, unimpressed, she rolled her eyes. "What, do you live under a rock? She's got a radio show, here in Chicago. Chicago Great Lakes University hosts it."

"And she's a serial murderer?"

Another eye roll. Jesus, his head throbbed. He fumbled in a desk drawer for a moment, then thumbed off the lid to a bottle of extra-strength Excedrin and tossed a couple pills in his mouth, swallowing them dry.

Becca didn't miss a beat. "No, of course not. She's a *psychiatrist*. And she's worried about one of her callers."

Fucking great. *This* was what he got called in early for, to babysit some full-of-herself *celebrity* with a full-blown case of paranoia? He could be home right now, licking his wounds and wallowing in guilt. "Sounds like Damian's doing someone a favor."

Still, his interest was piqued in spite of himself. It was unlike SSAM's founder to play favorites. They dealt with serious cases.

Serious, shitty cases where the body count of innocent victims sometimes reached into the teens or twenties.

Ethan frowned, ignoring the way it pulled at his temples, making his head throb even more. This Dr. Margaret Levine was probably an old friend who was getting a bit batty. After all, Damian Manchester was well into his sixties now—fit and healthy but, like the rest of them, getting older every day. Of course, Damian was far from batty. He was the most unnervingly observant, uncannily intuitive person Ethan knew. But his friends could possibly be older and much battier.

"He's ready for us," Lorena Castro said from the doorway.

So, a mindhunter was assigned to this one, though what an old celebrity needed with a profiler was beyond him. Ex-FBI and in her mid-forties, Lorena was a tough woman in many ways. Tough to get to know. Tough to beat. Tough, period. In a time when few women were FBI agents, and even fewer were becoming part of the FBI's elite Behavioral Analysis Unit, the exotic dark beauty had persevered. No, she'd excelled. She'd become a mindhunter, a highly trained profiler who could analyze a crime scene and extrapolate the criminal's behavior. Hell, she could probably predict if the guy wore boxers or tighty-whities based on how he committed a crime.

Following Becca and Lorena into the conference room, Ethan saw Damian alongside someone he recognized from a previous case, Detective Noah Crandall of the Chicago Police Department. Ethan took a seat, nodding a greeting. Despite the early hour, Damian was impeccable in his expensively tailored dark suit and tie. But there were also telltale signs of a rough night. He'd seen them on himself in the mirror just that morning. Tired eyes, drawn cheeks, tight mouth.

"Becca, could you pass out the folders?" Damian asked. "The information was rather hastily put together—thank you, Becca—but I think you'll find it a sufficient start."

When Damian opened his folder to the first page, the others followed suit. Dr. Margaret Levine's name jumped out at Ethan as he skimmed.

"The Voice of Reason?" He was unable to keep the disbelief from his voice.

"That's her nickname," Becca chimed in. "And she is. The voice of reason, that is. I've listened to her for months now, and she's a genius. She really helps people."

Damian gave a small smile, which was the only indication of happiness anyone ever saw from him. His gray eyes were always shadowed, and Ethan suspected the wrinkles around his mouth and across his forehead were due more to worry than age. But then, with Damian's history, Ethan didn't know how the man sucked in each breath or got out of bed in the morning, let alone ran a successful private business dedicated to catching serial murderers and other violent repeat offenders.

"Yes, she does." Damian reached his hand into the breast pocket of his suit for the reading glasses he kept there. "She's also a professor at Chicago Great Lakes University, so this case will be on our own turf. No extensive traveling."

A professor at the university. *Jackpot.* That had to be the connection between Damian and this woman. She was some colleague there, from when Damian had taught business courses years ago.

"She graduated top of her class at Columbia, with a medical degree, then earned her certification in psychiatry before returning to Chicago. Worked at a state institution as well as teaching at the university before she became a fulltime professor."

"And she's worried someone's following her?" Ethan asked, itching to get to the meat of the current problem, and why it required his expertise in personal security. "Is there any proof? What threats have been made?"

"I wouldn't have brought you in if there wasn't proof." Damian leaned back in his chair. "Detective Crandall will explain further."

The sandy-haired, sharp-dressed detective next to Damian cleared his throat. "There were no overt threats made. However," he continued when Ethan opened his mouth to speak, "there's no doubt in my mind that Dr. Levine could be in danger."

"Perhaps you could start with the caller at the radio station," Damian suggested, shifting back in his chair to give Noah the floor again.

"Dr. Levine does a radio talk show on weeknights from eleven until midnight. It centers around psychological issues, and she invites listeners to call in with questions and stories." Noah rapped a finger against one of the pages in the folder. "In here you'll find a transcription of the end of last night's show. Her final call was odd, and Dr. Levine reports she was a bit alarmed by the caller's tone and message, but you'll see she handled it smoothly."

Ethan's eyes scanned the first few paragraphs of the transcript, noting the caller's preoccupation with fear. "Couldn't this Owen just be a scholar itching for a fight over semantics? It's almost like he's correcting her grammar. Granted, it is about fear, but I still don't see a threat."

Damian's lips twitched. "You always did rush forward, Ethan. Allow Noah to explain further."

Ethan attempted to hide his impatience. "Please, by all means."

Noah flipped a few pages ahead in his packet, then turned a photograph so that it faced Ethan. His nerves prickled at the obscene scrawl of the word *fear* repeated across white walls. The letters dripped, as if they'd once been wet. *Blood?*

His gaze flicked up to Noah's. "I assume this is Dr. Levine's home?"

The detective nodded. "Her living room. She called the police at about one-thirty this morning."

"After she called me and I helped her get in contact with the authorities," Damian said.

And this woman had thought to call Damian Manchester first, of all people. Ethan filed that tidbit away under Interesting. Maybe Ethan and his fellow SSAM employees had been wrong about the man's apparent lack of a social life. A man had needs, after all, and Damian had been alone and single—in that order—for a long time. Rumor had it his marriage had crumbled under the weight of painful events, leading to an unsurprising divorce.

"So you think the same guy who called in to the show is responsible for the vandalism."

Noah nodded again. "They had just finished discussing

fear on her show. It's too much of a coincidence. Besides, he called her after she got home and discovered the message he left for her."

Message? The man acted as if it was a grocery list left out on the counter by a roommate or something. *Please pick up eggs, bread and butter at the store.* No, this was so much worse. Ethan was ashamed he'd questioned the existence of a threat at all. They were lucky the old lady hadn't had a stroke when she'd walked in.

"Why would anyone do this to Dr. Levine?" Becca asked. "Her objective is to *help* people."

"She's the sort to attract this kind of attention, unfortunately," Noah said. "And Owen, a fairly regular caller to the show, is a bit strange."

"What do you mean, 'she's the sort to attract this kind of attention'?" Ethan asked.

Damian responded. "Public personality, practically a celebrity, intelligent, attractive."

Ethan almost choked. *Attractive?* Well, perhaps the man with ironclad emotions had a woman friend after all.

Damian motioned to Becca. "If you're ready to play it, Noah was able to obtain a recording of last night's conversation from the radio station manager, Steve Marconi."

Everyone waited quietly, intent on Becca as she opened a laptop and pushed a couple buttons.

"Happy Fourth of July, Owen. It's been a while," a female said as the recording began. With the first few words, Ethan leaned forward, the husky voice bringing goose bumps to his skin. Was this Dr. Levine? Christ, the woman's vocal cords alone could arouse a man. He reminded himself she was older, at least in her fifties if she knew Damian, and forced himself to listen to the content, not the voice. But it was damn hard.

"I've been around, listening. You missed me." The smooth male voice spoke with confidence, just a bit mockingly.

"That's Owen," Noah pointed out. Ethan nodded, wanting to hush the man. He just wanted to hear more from Dr. Levine.

What followed sounded like friendly banter on the surface, but something wasn't right. And the doctor knew it. Her words were normal to the average listener, but Ethan, who was trained to pick up on anything odd in his surrounding environment, detected a thread of nervousness beneath the calm exterior.

Leaning forward, he closed his eyes to absorb the nuances that underlay the conversation. The mention of predators and prey brought his eyes open again.

When the so-called Owen snapped back at her, saying, "Don't mock me," Ethan saw the concern on Damian's face for his friend, who was beginning to sound scared. Dr. Levine covered it well, but to those who had been trained in studying behavior, fear was simple to detect. A sharply indrawn breath, a slight waver in the voice.

"I'm an avid student of the human psyche," Owen continued with a laugh, his mood apparently turning on a dime.

And then Dr. Levine was, wisely, closing the discussion for the night, signing off with a tagline about treating yourself gently. Christ, what kind of feel-good nonsense was that?

At a nod from Damian, Becca closed the laptop. The mood of the room was somber as each person processed the conversation.

"I'd say we're looking at a stalker," Lorena offered, finally speaking up.

Sighing, Damian gave a tight smile. "I was thinking the same thing. This man has called the show on several occasions."

"And he called her Maggie, trying to put himself on intimate terms with her. Is she certain she doesn't recognize the voice?"

"Yes," Noah answered. "Other than the other calls he's made to her show. According to Maggie, Owen has called in dozens of times over the past year, always expressing fairly strong opinions."

"Tell them the rest, Noah," Damian urged.

"We think this isn't the worst he's done. His reaction to her topic of fear, combined with the way he desecrated her apartment last night, was similar to crimes that have remained unsolved. For a decade."

"Crimes?" Ethan prompted, but the hair on his neck was already rising. From the look on Damian's and Noah's faces, he knew these were no ordinary *crimes*.

"We believe Owen may be connected to three murders in this area that occurred a decade ago."

"Fearmonger?" Lorena asked, leaning forward suddenly. "You think Dr. Levine has lured *Fearmonger* out of hiding?"

Noah nodded. "She may have. We're not jumping to conclusions yet."

"What ties them together?" Ethan didn't recall those murders, but then they would have been well before he moved back to Chicago and joined SSAM.

Lorena absently shoved her ink-black hair over her shoulder. "First, the victims were all from Chicago Great Lakes University, where Dr. Levine happens to teach. Second," she added, tapping her pen against the photograph of Levine's living room covered in the word *fear*, "each victim was found in her apartment with the words *fear me* written in their blood on the wall."

"But this man, this Owen guy, didn't kill Dr. Levine. He didn't use her blood. Was it even blood?" Ethan asked Noah.

"It was definitely blood," the detective responded. "But

we don't know where it came from. Could have been human or animal. The lab's analyzing it now."

"So the guy breaks in and vandalizes her home simply to reinforce his point?"

"He didn't actually break in. We didn't find any evidence of forced entry, and the security alarm was engaged when Maggie got home."

"So this has to be someone she knows, someone who had a key and the code?" Ethan's head hurt but he ignored it. A psychiatrist who knew a serial killer. It was a small, scary world out there.

"Or he was simply proving how smart and powerful he is by getting the code. There was a spare key hidden near her back door. It was still there, but we're testing for prints just in case."

"Did you ask her who had access to her house?"

Noah narrowed his eyes. "Yes, of course. But it was the early hours of the morning, Dr. Levine was exhausted and on edge, and she insists the only people who had her code and copies of her house key are family and a couple friends. We'll be in touch with them all."

"In the meantime," Damian said, "we'll be taking this case. Ethan, I want you in charge of protecting Dr. Levine. You know the drill. Secure her house and worksite. Teach her about personal safety—"

"I think she'll be an easy student there," Noah interrupted.

Damian nodded. "You're right. She's been through this sort of thing before."

"What?" Becca and Ethan asked simultaneously.

"With Owen?" Lorena asked.

"No. The other perpetrator is locked away."

"For good, if I have anything to say about it," Damian bit out. "Maggie was the victim of a stalker. She's a strong woman, but she's become a bit of a recluse since a patient of hers attacked her a year ago." His gray eyes flashed molten silver, revealing more emotion than he probably intended. "The woman was brutal to Maggie."

"A *woman?*" Ethan echoed in disbelief.

"Her name is Deborah Frame, and she was obsessed. Someone close to Maggie died because of it, which is why Noah is on this case. He worked the prior homicide, so I called him. I figured Maggie would be more comfortable with someone she knows and trusts."

The victim of two different stalkers? Ethan felt a pang of sympathy for the woman. What were the chances and why had they targeted her? Was she one of those old women people thought they could take advantage of? It didn't really matter. Apparently, he was in charge of making sure the second stalker didn't get to her like the first had.

An image of a child angel with brown eyes and blond hair arose, but he quickly closed it off in a corner of his mind before it threatened his confidence. Or his sanity. After all, he was no longer Secret Service, guarding the vice president's family. Not that Dr. Levine's life would be any less valuable to him, but he'd learned from mistakes at the highest level. He wouldn't be making them again.

"How can I help?" Becca asked the group, pulling Ethan out of his thoughts. He frowned at her, but she was ignoring him. She had been looking for a way to get her feet wet in the field for weeks, now that her training period was over.

"You can back up Ethan."

"Sir," Ethan protested. Becca was too young, too fragile. *Too blond-haired and brown-eyed,* the voice in his head said. *Too innocent.*

"She has to gain experience somewhere." Damian's tone brooked no argument.

"Besides," Becca said, practically bubbling over in her

excitement, "with my communications background, I can fit in at the radio station, and I'm young enough to pass as a student on campus."

"We all have things to do." In clear dismissal, Damian rose. "Noah will keep us apprised of the police investigation, and vice versa. Lorena, I'd like you to review the evidence in the Fearmonger cases, as well as the file on Dr. Levine's previous stalker, Deborah Frame. Noah will help you gain access to that information. Becca and Ethan, you have your assignments." The eyes he turned on Ethan were somber, his face lined with fatigue. "Protect Maggie. She's important to me."

Becca and Ethan hung back as the others left the conference room.

"Important?" Becca whispered in awe, echoing Damian's words. "I didn't think he'd let *anyone* become important to him."

Ethan had been thinking the same thing. "It had to happen sometime, didn't it? He's been alone for a long time."

Becca mulled that over for a minute before looking up with a smile. "My first case, and it will be important to Mr. Manchester. It's the perfect chance to prove myself to him."

Ethan's face went hard. "You'll do nothing of the sort. You're still wet behind the ears. What are you, twenty?"

The always-smiling pixie scowled. "You know I'm twenty-five. And I've been trained in self-defense, handling a suspect and use of weapons."

So she'd been training with SSAM's resident experts. That was one for the Pro column. But the Con column was still much longer.

"The real world is a whole other story. If we're dealing with a serial killer here, you'd better bring your A-game at all times. No getting so starstruck by Dr. Levine or Damian

Manchester that you lose focus. And, most important, no disobeying my orders."

Becca snapped to attention, clicking the heels of her Mary Janes together as she saluted him. "Aye, aye, Captain."

"This isn't the friggin' Navy, Tinker Bell." Ethan swiped his folder from the table and stalked from the room.

"What do you want me to do first?" She followed him into his office and stood at his desk, awaiting instructions.

"Call Dr. Levine. Find out if she's home and tell her to stay put, that I'm coming over. I assume Damian told her SSAM would be involved."

"Got it. Anything else?"

He spared her a glance. "Change into less conspicuous clothing."

"Say no more."

He had to give her credit, she didn't even pout about it. Maybe she *was* ready for the field. He pinched the bridge of his nose as his headache suddenly reappeared, full force. Hell, nobody was ready for the field. Too much real world could kill a person.

Maggie pushed her wobbly shopping cart with a little more force than was necessary. Her jaw hurt from grinding her teeth together. She wasn't just mad. She'd moved beyond mad and into full-out fury. Someone had invaded her home.

No, not some*one*. Some *thing*. Some *monster*.

The anger kept the panic at bay, but not always. When she'd first called Damian Manchester—the first person she could think of who would have a clue about how to deal with something like this—her chest had been aching so badly she had to force herself to draw a breath so she could speak.

And thank God Damian had answered her early-morning call for help. Otherwise, she'd probably still be slumped against her living room wall, holding poor Sigmund in a headlock.

Damian had kept her on the line while he called the police for her, asking specifically for Detective Crandall. She knew Noah. He'd been the detective in charge when Brad had been murdered.

And she *so* did not want to think about *that* right now. Not unless she wanted to end up curled up in a ball on the floor of the household-products aisle, waiting for her heart to stop pushing out of her chest and her breathing to return to normal.

It had been sometime after dawn, as she sat at her dining room table and watched Noah and his partner, Maria Santos, along with a team of Chicago Police Department crimescene technicians, comb her home for clues, that fear had shifted into anger. This creep wanted her to feel fear. Well, to hell with that. She chose anger.

"Can I help you, ma'am?"

Maggie turned to find a young woman eyeing her with concern. "I'm sorry?"

The woman was dressed in the forest-green apron that marked her as an employee of the grocery store. She gestured to the wall of cleaning products that Maggie had been staring at, probably for several long minutes. "Are you looking for something in particular?"

Peace of mind? Security? Sanity?

A super-mega-strength padlock for every door and window in the house?

A bubble of hysterical laughter threatened to escape. Maggie cleared her throat instead. "Bleach, I think. Whatever will take bloodstains off of walls."

The woman paled, her dark hair standing out all the more against her white skin. "Um" was all she could manage, glancing behind her for help.

Maggie shook her head at herself. She was obviously exhausted and not thinking clearly. And not fit to be out in public, apparently. "Thank you, but I think I can manage on my own."

With a smile of relief, the employee scurried away.

Way to go, Maggie mocked herself, selecting a bleach cleanser from the shelf. She'd feel better after some physical exertion. And after she cleaned the mess from her walls. Noah had given her permission to do so. The criminalists had gathered all they could from the scene.

Rubber gloves. Sponges. A sturdy bucket. Hell, what else would she need? She threw in an assortment of other products. She'd probably end up repainting the whole room, anyway. In the meantime, scrubbing would do her some good.

Putting Owen away for a long, long time would do her better.

Maggie took out her cell phone as she headed to the checkout lane.

She felt a stab of guilt as she dialed David's number. It should have been her parents she called, and a lot sooner than this. But what could she say? *Gee, Mom and Dad, looks like I picked up another fan along the way. Yeah, he might be dangerous, but what are the chances of losing two people you love to stalkers?*

They would descend on her like a giant bubble force field and try to protect her. And they'd probably get hurt. Like Brad had.

The reality was they were all powerless. It was best to keep them far away.

"Yo," a sleepy voice answered. It was close to noon, but David kept late hours. Maybe he'd managed to meet up with Sharon after all.

"Sorry to wake you."

"Doc?" The crisp rustle of sheets followed. "What's up?"

"I thought you should hear this from me first."

"You're not quitting, are you?" Alarm tinged David's voice. He was clearly awake now.

"No." Not yet, anyway. She'd taken the teaching position and the talk-show job to start a new life. Theoretically, she was supposed to have gotten away from the clients who might, say, turn to stalking their therapists. Clients like Deborah.

"No, I'm not quitting. But something happened last night. You may hear about it and I didn't want you to worry." Maggie smiled at the cashier as she accepted her change.

"Hear about what?" David asked through the phone at her ear. "What happened?"

"My place was broken into and vandalized." She pushed her cart through the sliding glass doors and out into the bright sunshine. Surely the sun shouldn't be shining so brightly on a day like today. She squinted as she fumbled in her purse for her sunglasses. It was then that she noticed her hands were shaking, which made her all the angrier.

"Oh, my God. Were you there? Are you okay?"

"No." To both questions. "But there's more. Owen is responsible."

"What?" David's response was almost a shout. "How do you know?"

"I'll explain later. Or the police will. I just wanted you to know that I got a call from a woman named Becca Haney. She's from a place called the Society for the Study of the Aberrant Mind, and she's going to be helping with the case. She'll probably be coming by the station this afternoon to check things out there."

"Check what things out?"

Feeling a trickle of sweat slide between her shoulder blades from the oppressive heat, Maggie began loading things into her car. Her eyes scanned the parking lot. Was

Owen watching her even now? He must have been observing her habits for some time. Anyone could guess she'd hidden a spare key under a rock near her back porch, when she'd foolishly thought the alarm system would be enough of a deterrent to break-ins. But he'd discovered her security code. How he'd accomplished that was still a mystery, unless he'd guessed she used the digits of the date of Brad's death. "Security. And maybe whether Owen's calls are traceable."

"They're not. All I know is they're local." There was a pause. "Wait. Security? They're worried about Owen coming to the station? And what? Mowing us down in a spray of bullets?" David was probably pacing by now, fumbling for a cigarette or shoving the fingers of his free hand through his short hair.

A spray of bullets? The scenario wasn't unthinkable, but she doubted it was Owen's style.

"Jesus, Doc," David breathed.

"Yeah, I know." She shoved her cart in line with the other empty ones in the corral and climbed into her car. Drew a breath and blew it out. "Just be careful, okay."

"Yeah. Shit. Yeah, you, too. So, you'll be in tonight?"

"Yes." Unless Owen had other plans for her.

THREE

As BECCA HEADED OFF to the campus building that housed WGLU to analyze possible security issues, Ethan drove to Dr. Levine's home to do the same. The home was a tidy one-story ranch-style house in Wilmette, a five-minute drive from the university. Walking up the path to the door, he noted that a small patch of grass, not thick and lush, but mostly green and well maintained despite Chicago's current heat wave, surrounded the house. A terra-cotta pot full of cheery red geraniums greeted him on the front porch.

And pumping '80s rock music made the door vibrate under his knuckles when he knocked. The volume, set to teeth-rattling, actually lent some relief to the throbbing of his head. Or maybe his headache was simply outwailed by the guitar solo.

Who was this woman—psychiatrist, professor and radio-talk-show host—who listened to angry rock bands from decades past? And not as many decades past as Ethan would have thought. Folksy '60s music would have been more in line with his image of the good doctor.

He tried the doorbell, but didn't hear it chime over the music. Perhaps it was broken. When nobody answered, he stepped off the porch and peeked in the front window. Bingo. The living room. Large red letters were emblazoned across otherwise pristine cream-colored walls, just like in the photographs he'd seen that morning.

His attention was swiftly captured by a sight that had the

corners of his mouth lifting into a smile of masculine appreciation. A woman in gray jogging shorts and a white tank top that hugged her soft feminine curves bent over to dip a sponge into the bucket at her feet. Yellow rubber gloves encased her hands to her elbows. Steam drifted to meet her face, where moist tendrils had clasped onto her forehead and neck. The sides of her dark red hair had been tucked up under a triangular kerchief, but the rest hung in waves down her back to her shoulder blades.

Dr. Levine hadn't wasted any time hiring someone to perform the unpleasant task of scrubbing the blood from her walls. And a beautiful someone, at that.

Uncomfortable that he was basically spying on the woman, Ethan took a step back and was about to return to the porch when the woman turned. A nearby oscillating fan rotated her way and she shifted to expose more of her face and neck to the airflow. In profile, the woman's features were that of a statue of a Greek goddess, and probably would have had the same alabaster tone had her cheeks not been tinged dark pink from both the heat of the day and the steam from the bucket. His lips twitched as she stopped scrubbing a moment to play air guitar. Wide, full lips moved to the lyrics as the guitarist's solo ended and the lead singer picked up again. He choked on his smile as her hips shook to the beat.

Rousing himself to action as the song ended and another began, he went back to the door and pounded harder, using the side of his fist. A moment later, the music was turned down and the woman's muffled voice called through the door. "Who is it?" Firm, but wary.

"Ethan Townsend. I'm here to talk to Dr. Levine."

A series of beeps sounded, disarming the alarm system. A bolt slid open and the door swung inward. Her golden-brown gaze slid over him in careful study.

His earlier attraction cooled like a hot stone dropping

into a bucket of cool water as irritation took over. She was the maid, not security for the Queen of England, for Christ's sake. His annoyance grew under her overt perusal, but he bit back the smart remark that rose to his lips. Instead, he treated her to his own careful study. Tit for tat.

The heat of the water and her activity had pinkened not just her face, but her neck, chest and upper arms, which glistened with perspiration. A droplet slid from her collarbone down her chest, disappearing beneath the edge of her tank top between what appeared to be ample and nicely formed breasts. Quickly lifting his gaze, he was equally enchanted by a light dusting of freckles across the bridge of her nose.

"Do you have some credentials on you?" she asked when his eyes finally met hers. A spark of something flickered in their liquid honey depths—amusement? Attraction? He wasn't sure.

"Credentials?" He barked out a short laugh. Where was Dr. Levine? Hadn't Becca called ahead? He could usually count on her, but...

She began closing the door on him, and his hand shot out to stop it, even as his mind registered disbelief. She was going to dismiss him. And why did that irritate him? He should be applauding this woman's caution after what had happened in this home.

"Wait a minute. I have creds." One hand reached into the front pocket of his jeans as the other remained on the door, his anger building at the woman's nerve. He slipped the SSAM identification badge through the small opening in the doorway. "I'm an agent from the Society for the Study of the Aberrant Mind. I'm here to help. Dr. Levine should be expecting me. I realize she's had a difficult time, but if I could just talk to her..."

Her surprise evident, the woman looked up from her examination of the identification Ethan had presented. As her smile slowly widened, Ethan's chest squeezed tighter and his breath caught. That reaction, and the way her eyes suddenly glinted like red topaz, threw him off guard.

She pulled the door open wider, moving aside to grant him entrance. "Come in."

He noted the keypad for the security system on the wall, and the location of windows and doors in the front rooms as he followed her to the rear of the house and the dining room–kitchen combo. A hallway led to what he assumed was the garage, and he noted another alarm keypad farther down on that wall. She sank down in a chair, waving a hand toward another to suggest he do the same as she resumed her evaluation of him. He got the feeling he came up lacking, and felt absurdly defensive. He didn't owe this woman anything.

"You're the security specialist?"

"Yes," he said, no longer trying to keep the irritation from his voice. "Look, is Dr. Levine here? I really need to go over some things. After what happened last night, I'd think she'd want to start as soon as possible."

Her eyes clouded. "Yes, she does."

Ethan scowled as suspicion gnawed at him. It couldn't be. This woman had to be in her early thirties. Surely she wasn't Dr. Margaret Levine. Margarets were aunts and mothers and grandmothers. Nuns. Old ladies with multiple cats. *Weren't they?* As if in response to his unspoken questions, a loud purring came from the floor where a well-fed orange cat wove between the woman's legs.

"You're Margaret Levine, the *psychiatrist?*"

She picked up the cat, effectively placing him as a physical barrier between them. Ethan wasn't the only one who could be defensive.

"I am."

That voice. When she dropped it just a bit, so it sounded

huskier—sexier—than it had when she first opened the door, he recognized it. He should have noticed before, but he hadn't been looking for it. He'd let his expectations color his perception. And that had been damn sloppy of him.

"And this is Sigmund." She lifted her cat so she could rub noses with it, then gave Ethan a small smile. "You seem surprised."

"You're not what I expected."

"Neither are you."

His jaw slid to the side. "What's that supposed to mean?"

She studied him a long moment, then shrugged. "Nothing." Setting Sigmund down, she moved to the kitchen. Despite his irritation, he couldn't help admiring her graceful walk, much like a cat's itself. The long legs and feminine flare of hips were hypnotizing. "Would you like something to drink?"

"Water's fine. We really should get started. The day's half over already."

She paused in reaching for a glass and raised an eyebrow at him.

Damn, again. He'd sounded so annoying. "I mean, I want to teach you as much as possible before I have to leave."

Dr. Levine returned to filling two glasses with water from a refrigerated pitcher. "What did Damian tell you, exactly?"

Damian. They were on a first-name basis. Ethan filed that away under Interesting, too.

"About what?"

She handed him a glass and took the seat opposite him. "About my past." Her eyes clouded again, and Ethan found himself reluctantly intrigued.

"That you're a radio-talk-show celebrity. And a professor at the university." He paused, knowing what she was really asking him. "And that this isn't the first time you've acquired a stalker."

She pursed her lips, drawing his attention there. The huff of laughter surprised him into meeting her gaze again. "*Acquired*. Interesting choice of words, Mr. Townsend." She studied her glass before continuing. "But of course, it would be important for you to know that part of my history. After the first time, I took a course. I've learned some things about self-defense."

"Good for you. Then, hopefully, this will mostly be refresher material. I may, however, have a few new things to add."

"I'm always open to learning more about staying safe." She sat back and rubbed her hands up and down her arms, as if warding off a chill. "And I assure you I take my own safety, and that of the people I love, very seriously."

"You live alone." It was a statement, not a question.

"I do. Unless you count Sigmund."

"Depends. Would Sigmund sink his claws and fangs into an intruder?"

Her mouth twitched. "No."

"Didn't think so."

She let out a sigh. "If you're asking if I have anyone who can come stay with me, or who is willing to protect me, the answer is no. Not anyone I would call on, anyway. I wouldn't endanger the people I love."

"You don't have any family? A boyfriend?"

"I have family. As I said, however, I won't endanger them."

He cocked an eyebrow. "They might not see it that way."

"You're probably right."

She wasn't going to budge. The woman was as stubborn as a mule. She'd rather put her own life at risk than accept help. Still, she *had* called Damian. She needed help. And it was Ethan's job to see that she got it.

"I can take care of myself." The quiet way she said it lacked the confidence Ethan would help her find.

"Do you own a gun?"

"No, but there are other ways of defending oneself."

He smirked. "Like kicking a man where it hurts most?"

Scowling, she shifted in her chair. "You mean the instep of his foot? Or a solid clap to the ear? Now you're insulting my intelligence."

So she had paid attention in her self-defense class. "Still…"

Her expelled breath lifted a curl from her forehead. "I have pepper spray in my purse. And I know how to shoot a gun, if that's what you're asking. I don't own one and don't particularly care for shooting," she added under her breath, "but would I if I had to?" She met his gaze unflinchingly. "Absolutely."

The truth of her words was evident in her expression.

"Okay. Let's start with an assessment of your home. Walk me through it."

As she took him on a tour of her small home, Ethan analyzed the strengths and weaknesses. She'd done a good job securing the windows and doors, but there were things even she, as cautious as she seemed to be, had missed. Things such as choosing an everyday item in each room of the house that could be used as a weapon, should she be trapped there with an assailant.

He reached around her as they stood in her master bathroom, his arm brushing the creamy skin of her bare shoulder as he lifted her can of hairspray. He caught the scent of her hair. Something flowery, but also earthy and subtle. Whatever it was, it had his body responding in a way it hadn't since he was in high school—quick and shameless. Accidental contact with her had almost brought him to his knees, so he didn't mind when she quickly stepped away, putting distance between them, though the bathroom was small. She didn't get far.

Heat seared the bare skin of Maggie's shoulder where Ethan's body grazed it. It had been so long since any man had touched her, let alone a man as attractive as the security specialist Damian had insisted she speak with. Wanting Damian's help, she couldn't refuse, no matter how hard it was to let a near-stranger into her home.

Into her home? Heck, the man was standing in her bathroom.

Her reaction to Ethan Townsend was a surprise. Taller than her by a few inches, and wide enough through the shoulders to make her wonder if he'd ever played football, he made her bathroom seem more like a coat closet with the two of them filling its space. And here he was handling her personal-care products. The things she used every day. There was something unbearably intimate about it, especially after so much time alone, and the thought brought a rush of heat to her face.

Seemingly oblivious, he lifted her bottle of hairspray. "Ever get this in your eyes?" he asked. She nodded. "Doesn't feel good, right? And it won't feel good to an intruder, if he happens to corner you in the bathroom. Spray it in his eyes if you can. It'll impair his vision—hopefully, long enough for you to make an escape."

"Sounds like you know from experience."

He shrugged. "I've been trained on what to do if I'm sprayed with pepper spray. Or hairspray. Or a couple other things that I'd rather not ever face again. My eyes still water when I think about it. But it taught me some valuable lessons, such as how to focus on taking my target down while enduring incredible pain."

He gestured for her to lead him out of the bathroom, and she exhaled a breath of relief. Some space between her and this man who smelled faintly of coffee and some mouthwatering spice—she thought maybe it was cinnamon—was definitely a good idea.

He led her to the kitchen where he selected a large knife from among others in the wooden block she had on her counter. Any spark of attraction she'd felt was quickly squelched as he held it up. She backed up a step. He couldn't know about her aversion to knives. Even Damian didn't know the full extent of that terror.

As her breath hitched, Maggie tried to focus on Ethan's mouth instead of the weapon, watching his lips form words. His mouth looked strong, yet soft when one side quirked upward into a semblance of a smile. She wondered what it would be like to kiss that corner. Would it taste of whatever spice scented his skin?

Ethan turned the knife over in his hand. "Don't go for the obvious—the knives. Too often, they can be turned on the victim and make a bad situation that much worse." He put the knife away and she sucked in a breath of relief. "Do you have a fire extinguisher nearby?" She nodded, opening the cupboard under the sink. "Use this on him, either as a club, or spray him and run. Or, use a good ole frying pan."

"You're kidding."

"Not at all." He touched her shoulder, his fingertips brushing the flesh exposed there by her tank top. She felt it catch fire from his heat. "You do whatever you have to. Fight him. Your life could depend on it."

She nodded.

His voice softened. "I know you've been through something like this before. I don't know the details." He hesitated, as if waiting for her to supply the story.

No way was she going there. Her feelings were too fragile after the past twenty-four hours.

"It could impact how you handle a crisis situation." He

paused again, but she didn't take the bait. He shrugged and moved away, his hand gone from her skin. She felt cold where a moment ago it had been hot.

They moved into the living room, where the red-brown letters stared down at them as Ethan spent another hour showing her basic self-defense techniques. It was a review for her, but she was grateful. After Deborah's brutal attack, she'd needed to feel in control again and the YMCA had offered a basic course that helped her regain some sense of security. In fact, she prided herself on how careful she was, both in public and at home. So she found her patience slipping as Ethan went over several home-safety issues yet again.

"Satisfied?" she asked, irritated when he'd pushed her through yet another round of questions about how often she changed her passwords, alarm code and the lightbulb on her porch.

His jaw slid to the side. "Cockiness can get you killed."

She sobered. He was only doing his job, after all. She knew better than to bite the hand that was feeding her. "I'm all too aware of that, Mr. Townsend."

"Call me Ethan. Can I call you Margaret?"

She laughed. "God, no. Call me Maggie."

The husky waves of her laugh flowed over him like a stimulant and a balm all at once. It made him want to reach out and touch her again, even if only to brush back that stray wisp of hair from her forehead that kept escaping from her kerchief.

He opened his mouth to say something when the ringing of her telephone interrupted. As she turned to the kitchen to answer, he looked around the living room, his eyes tracing the harsh strokes that formed the letters over and over.

F. E. A. R.

She'd scrubbed about half the living room, but there was more to be done. The smell of bleach permeated the air, yet she didn't risk opening a window. Did she find removing the message herself was cathartic? Or was she punishing herself for some unknown sin? Why would she put herself through it?

After seeing her level of privacy and security, he wondered if she just didn't want anyone else crossing the threshold of her sanctuary. It was obvious she lived alone except for Sigmund, who'd stuck close during his tour of the home. Her bedroom had been decorated in shades that weren't exactly feminine, but gave the impression of…softness. Comfort. The second bedroom was a home office. The third, which many people would have made into a guest room, stood completely empty.

He heard Maggie's sigh and turned back to her. "No, Mom, really, I'm okay.…Yes, I'm sure Agatha told you all about it."

Unabashedly listening for clues as to her relationship with her family, Ethan stepped into the kitchen and leaned against the counter. Her slender fingers reached to tuck away the lock of hair he'd been tempted to touch back into her kerchief. A tiny furrow formed between her eyes. Then she looked up and crossed her eyes in a way that had him smothering a laugh.

"Yes, the police were here. I'll tell you about it later. I've got company right now.…No, he's here about the break-in, so I have to go.…Love you, too. Bye." She crossed the kitchen to replace the receiver. "Sorry about that. My neighbor apparently observed the chaos this morning and couldn't wait to inform my mother. They used to be bridge partners, when my parents lived in this house."

"Why didn't you tell her what happened?" Ethan asked, puzzled that she'd told her mother she loved her, but hadn't called her when something of this magnitude had occurred. His own mother would crucify him if he'd left her out of the loop. Despite the overwhelming testosterone that he, his three brothers and his father had brought to the household, it was definitely a matriarchy.

Maggie hugged her middle as she shrugged. "She would have worried."

"She's a mom. She's supposed to worry. It's in the job description or something."

She turned away, clearly wanting to end the discussion. "I'd like to get back to scrubbing the living room, if we're done here."

He didn't answer for a moment, studying the rigidity of her spine, the stony set of her shoulders. The woman was holding it together. Barely. Dr. Levine struck him as an intensely private woman. It was obvious she wanted her privacy now.

"We're done. For now. You're not to go anywhere alone."

She turned back to protest but seemed to think better of it and pressed her lips together instead. She nodded. "Okay. How am I supposed to get around?"

"Limit your activities to what you absolutely need to do."

"And let him win?"

"And survive," he corrected. "Your safety is my job, so listen to me and you'll stay alive. Work, home, grocery store. That's about it."

"I could ask David to go with me, I suppose." The furrow between her eyes was back.

He didn't know who David was, and until he passed Ethan's stringent security check, the guy wouldn't be allowed alone with his client. "I'll accompany you, or Becca will."

"Becca? The woman who called earlier?"

"She's new at SSAM, but she's good." He hoped. "She'll pick you up for work tonight."

Snapping her rubber gloves back in place, she muttered

something under her breath and grabbed the sponge from the bucket.

"What was that?" he asked, perversely wanting to see the flare of heat in her eyes once more. He wasn't disappointed.

"I hate being babysat."

"But you like being alive."

She looked as if she was about to object to that, and he raised an eyebrow expectantly, but she only turned back to the wall and began scrubbing. He strode to the door and stood with his hands on his hips, waiting for her attention, but she was engrossed in her work. Allowing himself the luxury of watching her for a moment, he took in the slim line of her body, the slight part of her lips as she blew out a breath. His body stirred in response.

"Maggie," he said, frustration making her name sound like a growl.

She turned, her face flushed. That pesky tendril had escaped its confines again, curling across her cheek. "What? You can't find the door? It's right behind you."

He shook his head in disappointment. "Did you listen to anything I said today?"

"What?"

"The alarm? You need to set it behind me. Immediately. And I hope you changed the code since this guy somehow knew it."

Jesus. If this Owen guy was Fearmonger, Maggie had to be more careful. Didn't she know that? But then, he hadn't told her yet about the possible serial killer connection. He hadn't wanted to worry her until he had more evidence the break-in was linked to a murderer. As long as she was taking proper security measures, it wouldn't matter anyway. A stalker could be just as dangerous.

Looking sheepish, she rose immediately, tossing the sponge in the bucket with a small splash. "Right. Sorry. I promise I'm usually very good about that, and I did change the code this morning. I just got mad and forgot."

"And stirring your emotions to the point of distraction will be exactly what Owen is counting on."

She whirled on him and before he could stop himself, Ethan took a surprised step back. "Right now *he's* not the one pissing me off. I told you I forgot, but I promise you I would have remembered as soon as the door shut. I assure you, I don't want to go through anything like I did before ever again."

He stared, intrigued by the pulse pounding at her slender throat. She spun away and waited, her fingers poised on the keypad of the alarm. She cast a pointed look over her shoulder at him, as if to say, *Are you leaving or not?*

"Becca will be here to escort you to the station tonight. In the meantime, don't go anywhere." He left, pausing on the other side of the closed door until he heard a series of beeps, followed by a blast of music as Maggie apparently resumed her attack on the vandalized walls.

Good. Let her take her anger out on something other than him. She didn't like feeling like a prisoner? Too bad. It was his job to keep her alive.

When the living room was restored and her anger had faded with the onset of fatigue, Maggie double-checked the alarm and the locks on the doors and windows for the tenth time. Satisfied that she was safe for the moment, she sank into an armchair with a glass of pinot and rested her head against the cushion. And tried not to look at the wall where Owen had left his gruesome message. Though the letters were gone, they were still a vivid image in her mind.

The phone rang. Sighing, she dragged herself up again. She didn't have to look at caller ID to know who was calling. It was only a matter of time before Julia and Nancy

Levine joined forces in the crusade to save Maggie from herself. It was a familiar, and tired, cause. "Hello, Julia. I guess Mom called you."

"Well, she can't very well talk to *you,* now can she?" Only because she knew her younger sibling so well did Maggie hear the concern beneath the irritation. Still, she winced. Direct hit.

"There's nothing to tell." She hoped. Why worry them when they had no leads on Owen yet? "Someone broke in, wrote a strange message on my wall, and that's it."

"*That's it?* Are you that jaded?"

That was putting it mildly. "Maybe."

"We just want you to be safe," Julia said, her voice softer now. "And happy."

"I am safe. Working on happy." Not really, but Julia didn't need to know that. "Safe" was taking up too much energy, anyway. After what she'd been through in the past year, Maggie would settle for normal and boring, if not happy.

"You need someone," Julia continued. "If not us, then someone else. Someone to talk to."

Maggie thought about Damian Manchester, perhaps the only person she knew who would understand her fear of monsters—because yes, they did walk the earth. And then there was Noah Crandall, who seemed a competent detective and had been so understanding after her brother's murder.

But it was Ethan Townsend's face, with its hard lines and strong jaw softened by his warm green eyes and lopsided smile, that hovered in her mind. "I do have people I can talk to. They'll help me. They'll find this person."

"Come stay with me."

She squeezed her eyes shut against a wave of emotion. "That's sweet, but I have to be close to work. It's the one stable thing I have right now."

And it might be a way to find Owen. The idea had nested

in her mind after Ethan had left that afternoon, and it had grown in strength as she'd scrubbed letter after bloody letter from her walls.

Her walls. *Her* home. She wouldn't let Owen scare her away.

"I'm sorry, sis, but I have to get ready for work."

An exasperated sigh filled her ear. "Fine. But come see me sometime, okay? I miss you. And after yesterday, well…"

Yeah. The anniversary of Brad's murder had surely hit them all hard. "Definitely. We'll go shopping." Keep it light, she told herself. Now wasn't the time to break down. Besides, that might lead to another panic attack, and she was determined to avoid that at all costs.

There was a knock at the door, saving her from further pleas to reconnect with the family. Didn't they see that she was responsible for the misery they were all in? Letting them in during this latest crisis would only lead to more hurt for everyone. "I have to go. Someone's at the door."

"Fine. But we're going to talk soon."

"Of course."

"I mean it. I've had enough of your excuses." Julia paused. "You're not the only one hurting here."

The knock came again. "I know. But I really have to go." With a goodbye to her sister, she hung up and went to the door.

"Who is it?" she called, eyeing a short woman through the peephole. The blackness of night had fallen like a curtain but the porch light was bright against the woman's platinum blond hair.

"Becca Haney, from SSAM."

The sides of Becca's short hair had been pulled back into barrettes, and delicate glasses perched on her slightly upturned nose. What both surprised and reassured Maggie was the hint of sparkle that glinted off a tiny stud in the woman's nose. The piercing was so small as to be almost unnoticeable but it made Becca seem somehow more human. Quirky. Maggie was immediately comfortable with her. Disengaging the alarm, she swung the door open.

"Dr. Levine?"

"Please, call me Maggie." She waved the agent into her house and locked the door behind them, arming the security system. Seeing Becca watching her, Maggie pulled a face. "If I wasn't already cautious, Mr. Townsend hit me over the head with the lesson several times today."

"Well, Ethan does know more than any of us about security," Becca said, then smiled. "And about beating a lesson to death. But he's my mentor at SSAM, so don't tell him I said that."

Maggie grinned. "My lips are sealed."

"And I want you to know I know how to do my job. I've been trained by the best."

"I'm sure of that."

Becca looked around with curiosity. "I'm also not supposed to tell you that I'm a huge fan of your show."

"Lots of rules at the Society, aren't there?"

Becca's sigh showed just how much the young woman was struggling to find her place there. "'Fraid so." In an instant, her demeanor was cheerful again. "But I love it there."

"Did security at the radio station check out?"

"Since it's on the very edge of campus, the parking lot will be a nightmare after dark, but otherwise it looks safe enough."

Safe enough. But not totally safe. Nothing was ever totally safe. "I'm all set to go when you are." Maggie ran a quick hand over Sigmund's back when he came to say goodbye. At Becca's nod, Maggie grabbed her satchel and reengaged the alarm before pulling the front door shut behind her.

The young woman kept up a steady stream of conversation as she drove, which was fine with Maggie. The light chatter was like a soothing background hum while other parts of her brain were preoccupied with thoughts of Owen. Would he call two nights in a row? She was almost certain of it. He'd want to taunt her further, especially after last night.

At the station, Becca entered the production booth behind Maggie and surveyed the small room beyond the glass, where Maggie sat during her show.

David's forehead creased as he studied Becca. Leaning into Maggie, he dropped his voice to a whisper. "*She's* your bodyguard? She's smaller than you."

"And I'm sure she packs a wallop. And if she doesn't, her gun does." She eyed the small bump under Becca's suit jacket where her gun was nestled in a shoulder holster.

Instead of smiling as she'd intended him to, he frowned at her. "Are you really okay? Maybe you should take a night off. Sharon and I can field calls and replay an old show."

"And miss a chance to talk to Owen again?" She shook her head. "Not a chance." She wouldn't have believed it possible, but David actually turned a lighter shade of pale.

"I'm so sorry I got excited about him calling the show and that I suggested he should call more often. I never wanted..." He stopped and gulped. "I just don't like this."

Me, either. "We'll get it all squared away soon enough. We've got people helping us this time." She smiled at Becca before turning back to David. "It's almost time. Everything up and ready?"

"All set, boss."

Becca followed Maggie to her seat. "You sure you want to do this? David's right. Nobody would be too upset if you took the night off."

"Except Owen. I think he's out there somewhere, just waiting to call in."

"But you'd be so much safer at home."

Maggie arched a brow. "Where, despite my alarm system, Owen broke in?" She shook her head. "I'm not going to hide at home. Besides, you'll be right there by the door, right?"

"Yes, of course." Becca stiffened her spine, straightening to what had to be no more than five feet four inches.

Maggie smiled, putting her headphones on. "Then I'm not worried." A jolt of adrenaline shot through her as she thought of the night's program. If Owen thought she would just roll over and take another hit, he'd be sorely mistaken. She spoke to David through her microphone. "If Owen calls, give me some kind of signal, okay?"

He raised a finger to the side of his head and twirled it in the international sign for crazy. "How 'bout this?"

"That'll work. Then we'll make him wait."

"What?" David sputtered. Becca's face mirrored his concern.

"I want to see what kind of patience he has," Maggie explained.

"You want to intentionally provoke him?" David clearly thought that would be a bad move.

She shrugged, but she had plans for Owen. Let him be angry for a while. No, let him grow furious, as she was. "I need to test his limits. And if he's angry, maybe he'll drop his pompous attitude and all this nonsense about teaching me a lesson, and we'll get to the heart of the matter. What this is really about. Or, better yet, maybe I'll get a clue to who he is."

David shook his head. "You're the doctor."

"Am I late?" Breathless, her long brown hair flowing around her as she rushed in, Sharon Moss entered the production booth like a whirlwind. And David's scowl evaporated.

Sharon stuck her head through the doorway that joined Maggie's area to the production booth. Her flawless face was flushed. Despite the darkness that had fallen on the city at this late hour, it was still hot as Hades as the acres of pavement released their grip on the day's heat.

"I thought you might need me. David told me that Owen called last night." Sharon's eyes softened in sympathy. "And that he trashed your place, Dr. Levine. I'm so sorry." Trashed her place? Apparently, David hadn't told the girl everything, for which Maggie was grateful. "Are you okay?"

Maggie nodded. "I'm fine." And that would piss Owen off all the more.

"And Sigmund?" the girl asked with genuine concern. She had served as pet-sitter for the cat when Maggie attended a professional conference in Seattle several months ago. Sharon and Sigmund had formed a fast friendship.

"He's fine," Maggie said with a reassuring smile. In reality, the image of what she'd thought when she'd first seen the blood on her walls—that it had been Sigmund's—set her teeth on edge. She turned to Becca, who was observing Sharon with interest. "And this is Becca Haney, who's also here to help."

Sharon extended a hand to meet the SSAM agent's. "Cool. You'll like working with Dr. Levine."

David cleared his throat from the doorway. "People, it's almost eleven o'clock. Let's get moving."

Maggie found Becca's worried gaze on her and gave a nod of encouragement. Becca took up a post by the door like a sentry. She would be watching. And listening.

David gave her the usual cue through the glass. "Good evening, Chicago," Maggie began as she took her seat. "Welcome to *Live with Levine*. Tonight, our focus is depression." She intentionally left out any comments about yesterday's brief discussion of fear. Sensing Owen would like credit for his stunt—to put it mildly—she refused to acknowledge it at all, hoping it would push him to call in. Now the waiting game began.

Several minutes later, when David gave the signal that Owen had called, then held up two fingers to indicate which line he was on, Maggie ignored the hitch in her breathing. *Showtime*.

FOUR

THE PUNGENT SCENT of candles burning in the small alcove off the main church filled Damian Manchester's nostrils. His knees ached, but he forced his brain to ignore the pain. He still had a lot of praying to make up for, but he and God had come to an understanding several years ago.

Damian didn't blame God anymore for the horrors of the world, and God helped him destroy monsters.

And there was no doubt about it, monsters walked the earth. Twenty years ago, one had stolen his thirteen-year-old daughter away.

Shifting his weight from one knee to the other, he mentally recited the Lord's Prayer, letting the pain remind him that he was still alive. His daughter was not. And someone had yet to pay for his trespasses.

Deliver us from evil, amen.

When, years after his daughter's abduction, Damian had finally emerged from a haze of hate and despair, he had set about using his money and his mind toward something worthwhile, creating an organization populated by the best of the best. The Society for the Study of the Aberrant Mind had been founded in his daughter's memory. Its mission was to catch the worst, most violent offenders of society by working with law enforcement and various other special groups. In the twelve years it had been running, the SSAM team had managed to put numerous killers behind bars. In the meantime, the organization had started programs to educate the public and law enforcement officials in an effort to protect more innocents.

Innocents like Samantha.

The thought of his daughter brought the familiar itchiness to his throat and tightness to his chest. Damian focused on the throbbing in his knees instead, offering up the pain for his daughter.

The gentle sound of high heels clicking against marble resounded in the empty church, but he didn't turn. He knew that sound, and knew to whom those footsteps belonged. After all, she was the only one who would dare to approach him when he got like this.

"You know this isn't our guy." Lorena Castro's slim form took another step into the alcove and came to stand beside his small pew. "Fearmonger isn't Sam's killer."

The sound of his daughter's nickname spoken aloud was a painful echo in his heart, but it was no longer the agonizing black void that had once pressed on his chest day and night. It had only taken a couple decades to numb himself to that.

Ignoring the creaking of stiff joints as he shifted to a sitting position on the bench, a rush of tiny pinpricks traveled down his legs as the blood flow resumed. He sat back, sliding over to make room for Lorena.

"You're sure he's not the same guy." He'd already come to the same conclusion. The killer's signature, the way he performed a crime to meet his deviant needs, didn't match that of Sam's killer. But hearing the confirmation from his senior mindhunter didn't make the knowledge any easier to take.

Lorena's slender fingers wrapped around the fist he'd unconsciously formed on his thigh. "About as sure as I can be in this business. The crime scenes just don't match up." She shrugged. "Killers can change their MOs, but they don't usually differ that much."

Damian nodded. "But this guy—this Fearmonger—did kill people." Innocent people like Sam.

She squeezed his hand and his gaze was drawn there. Her caramel skin was smooth and warm against his. "Yes. And finding him, bringing him to justice, will bring peace to others." Her voice softened. "But not to you."

No. Not to him. Not entirely, anyway. But each monster they put away brought that peace just a little bit closer.

They sat in silence for several moments, and his eyes were locked on the crucifix that hung on the wall between two stained-glass windows. Her fingers were still draped across his fist, and he resisted the temptation to turn his palm to hers. He wasn't ready for that level of comfort from another person. He hadn't forgiven himself enough yet.

"You think it helps?" He couldn't keep the edge from his voice.

"Prayer? Couldn't hurt." There was a trace of amusement in her reply.

"No. I suppose not." And it did give him a brief measure of solace.

She tilted her head, her blue-black hair shifting over one shoulder as her expression softened. Her midnight eyes considered him. "Is this about Dr. Levine?"

"I'm worried about her."

"She's got you, and the Society, in her corner now. And Ethan's good at his job. I know I had my doubts at first..."

Damian chuckled, and it echoed in the silent church. "You gave him the cold shoulder for weeks."

She scowled. "That was before I knew more about what happened. The press made it sound like he'd made a horrendous mistake that had cost a girl her life." She shook her head. "But I've reviewed the information a friend at the FBI got for me. Ethan had to make a choice, and even if he doesn't believe it, he did the only thing he could at the time. The press may have crucified him, but he's proven himself at SSAM."

"Maybe he's proven himself to you, but he still hasn't been cleared by the most important person."

Her eyebrows knit in confusion. "You?"

"No. Himself. He needs to forgive himself." He sighed. "Maybe I'm wrong to push him now, though. He's still rough around the edges. Maggie needs someone she can depend on."

"Because of what she's already been through?"

"Yes, but not in the way you're thinking. This isn't just about her previous stalker. There's more to her past than you all know. And it'll make her all the more vulnerable to Fearmonger."

Owen was still waiting on line two. And he'd been waiting for twenty minutes now. Was it enough?

Maggie pressed the button. "Owen." She forced her voice to be calm as, out of the corner of her eye, she saw Becca straighten from her position against the wall. "How nice of you to join us again. Two nights in a row. An honor, indeed." It was her turn to act pompous, and she laced her voice with sarcasm, hoping to goad the man into revealing something about himself that would help them track him.

"Once again, you disappoint me, Maggie." At the sound of his voice in her headphones, tingles began at her nape and trickled outward, up to her scalp and down her spine. "You knew I'd be calling tonight." The chuckle again. How had she ever thought it sounded warm? It was like someone dropping an ice cube down the back of her shirt.

"*Hoped* is, perhaps, a better word."

"Hope is pointless. Did you learn nothing?" He made a tsk-tsk sound of disappointment. "I thought you'd be smarter than that. But then, the pupil pushes the teacher to adapt, to come up with more innovative ways of teaching. I can appreciate that."

More innovative than smearing blood on her walls? *Dear Lord.* She resisted the urge to cross herself as her mother always did in the presence of something evil. "Do you have anything of value to contribute to our discussion today, Owen?"

"Depression is for people too spineless to face their fears. They mope about instead of taking control. Instead, they'd rather other people take control for them, and then they complain when they do." Maggie opened her mouth to object, but Owen continued. "But that's not why I called. And I don't think it's what you want to talk to me about. You would much rather know about last night, and why I had to teach you a lesson, wouldn't you?" She could hear the grin in his voice. "Yes, Maggie, there is much to learn. I think, since we'll be spending so much time together, you'd better start calling me by my real name."

Her heart beat faster, knocking against her chest. "And what would that be?"

"Fearmonger."

"Fearmonger?" Becca signaled with her hands to keep him talking, even as she pulled her cell phone out of her pocket and began dialing. Maggie snapped her attention back to the microphone.

"I know that's what the police must be thinking after they saw your house. If they have half a brain among them, that is." There was a pause as Maggie tried to digest this. "Oh dear, maybe I gave them too much credit. Or maybe they just didn't fill you in."

Maggie ignored the anger that was rising within. Had the police known who this man was? Had Ethan, who she was just starting to trust? Either way, she wouldn't let Owen take control. "What kind of name is Fearmonger?"

"Fearmonger is just what he sounds like. He lives for other people's fears. He exploits them. He uses their fears to bring their lives new meaning. He's also suspected of murder."

Maggie pushed aside her breathlessness. There was no time for panic now. Had everyone been keeping this from her? Something this huge about the man who had broken into her home? "And did you? Kill someone?"

"Now that would be absurd of me to confess, wouldn't it? Especially on the radio, for all to hear. But I believe it was more like three someones—according to the Chicago PD, that is. As for me, I'm happy being Owen. Let's just say Fearmonger and I both know a lot about fear."

"So you said yesterday."

The voice hardened. "And you still doubt me?" There was a significant pause. "Even after last night?"

Ignore the pain. Focus on breathing in and out. In and out. She pictured her heart beating wildly, then gradually changed the mental picture until her heartbeat slowed to a normal pace. "No. I don't doubt you believe you're an expert on fear." And he seemed fear*less*. He was basically confessing to breaking and entering—and hinting at a whole heck of a lot more—on public radio. But everyone feared something. She'd just have to figure out what made Fearmonger afraid.

Stay calm. Make him the angry one. Maybe he'll reveal something more.

"Is that why you identify with this Fearmaker person?"

"Fear*monger*," he snapped. "An apropos euphemism, I suppose. I do seek fear. I study it. I create it. So trust me, Maggie, when I say I *know* fear. The look in a human's eyes just before their life is snuffed out like a candle is proof enough that fear is the basic component of life. Without it, we cease to exist."

The pressure in her chest threatened to crush her lungs,

but Maggie was too stunned to give in to the panic. Owen spoke as if he indeed *knew* what those last moments were like. But then, he tended to be melodramatic. Perhaps he was yanking her chain. She cleared her throat, determined not to let the man have control. She began to ask him more, but David signaled to her that Owen, or Fearmonger, had hung up. Damn.

"I think it's time for a short break," Maggie said into the microphone.

As the beginning jingle of a commercial sounded, she whipped off her headphones and rocked back in her chair, looking toward the production booth.

Her heart stopped. Standing in the doorway, scowling through the glass window so hard she thought his jaw would break, was Ethan Townsend. David and Sharon both leaped to attention as Ethan barked something to them, then waited as they left the room quickly. The entire time, his eyes were on Maggie.

He turned the knob and entered her domain. Becca followed him in, her nervous glance meeting Maggie's as she peered around Ethan's towering form. Anger seemed to simmer in the air around him as he took a few steps farther into the small room, bringing him within two feet of her. It was then that she noticed his clothing wasn't dark, as she'd originally thought, but wet. His hands were on his hips, causing his shirt to cling to his shoulders and biceps. His hair gleamed like polished mahogany as water dripped down the sides of his face. The storm had finally broken free of the heat's powerful grip.

Ethan continued to scowl at her, but spoke over his shoulder. "What were you thinking," he asked Becca, "letting her poke this guy with a stick?"

"Well, I—" Becca began, only to be cut off again with a raised hand.

"Save it. It's my fault. I knew you were a rookie. You can go."

Behind Ethan, Becca flushed red to the roots of her platinum hair, turned on her heel and left.

"Are you insane?" Ethan asked once they were alone. Water drops at his hairline collided together and formed a rivulet that traveled down his chiseled jaw before making the six-foot drop to the floor.

"You're wet." Maggie almost winced. What an inane thing to say. Still, her blood pumped harder at the thought he had hurried through the rain to her side. She licked her suddenly dry lips and the heat in his eyes seemed to flare in response. But then, it could have been her imagination. The man was, after all, furious with her.

"Yeah, *wet* tends to happen when it's raining outside and someone has to haul ass *through the rain* to stop someone else from doing something stupid." He waved a hand around in the air as he spoke. "Excuse me. I mean, to keep someone from *continuing* to do something stupid. Something that could get her killed. So, I repeat. Are. You. Insane."

"Not clinically, no." She crossed her arms to stifle the urge to reach out and shove him. Or maybe she was trying to resist the urge to brush off the drops of water that still clung to his eyebrows.

"If you're not insane, then you must be—"

She raised a hand to stop him, gritting her teeth together. "Don't say it."

"Say what?"

"Stupid. I'm not stupid."

"Reckless, then. The very thing we discussed earlier today. How to protect yourself from a stalker."

"Yes, exactly. A stalker. Not a serial killer."

"They're both dangerous." He dragged long fingers over his face, dislodging the water droplets she'd been eyeing.

"Damn it, Maggie, if this wasn't stupid, it definitely wasn't smart."

She matched his angry glare as she stood toe-to-toe with him. "Yes, we discussed personal security earlier, but there are some things you left out of our little chat, aren't there? Some things that might have been helpful to know."

Something flashed in his green eyes, all the more vibrant and dangerous in the low light of her sound booth. "I told you what you needed to know."

"According to *you*. Perhaps you didn't think it important for me to know that *my* stalker—the guy who broke into *my* house, bypassing *my* alarm code—is a *serial killer?*" Her voice raised to a fever pitch as David shuffled back into the production booth, looking warily through the glass from one to the other of them.

"Commercial break is about to end," he warned through the intercom before moving back to his seat.

"I have to get back on the air. But this isn't over."

A muscle in his jaw jumped. "No, it damn well isn't." He paused and dropped his hands from his hips to his sides, fisting them. Maggie thought maybe he was going to reach out and touch her, but then he swore and spun on his heel.

She tossed a final comment over her shoulder as she sat back down. "And you owe Becca an apology." The poor woman had been near tears when she'd left.

She scowled as Ethan walked out of the room, muttering something under his breath before he closed the door behind him. She could have sworn he'd said, "Therapists." And not in a good way.

"Overbearing jerk," she mumbled to herself before pulling the microphone in place. But even as she said it, she knew he'd been concerned. And why not? Her safety was his job, she reminded herself. She was nothing more than that. Any sizzles of attraction she'd imagined between them were better left to fizzle out.

There was one good thing about their argument, however, and that was that he'd made her forget her panic. His anger had fed her own, and she hadn't had time to focus on the ache that had begun to build in her chest as she talked to Owen. Or Fearmonger.

That she could get angry was, in itself, a miracle. She'd spent so much time being afraid. Then, with the anniversary of her brother's death and Owen—or whoever he was— stepping into her life, the fear had reared its ugly head again. Ethan helped her diffuse it.

Or at least gave her an alternate target for her anger.

"Welcome back," she said, forcing her attention to her show. "We've been discussing depression tonight, and we've heard one person's views on fear. Shame on you, Owen, for trying to scare us." She conjured a good-natured chuckle. "He's trying to prove his point."

Sharon, Becca and David had returned and were now crowded into the production area. Still, Ethan's anger seemed to fill up every empty space.

"But Owen's wrong," she said to her listeners as her gaze held Ethan's. "We don't thrive on fear. Perhaps animals do, but humans are beyond that. Yes, fear is the basis for many other emotions. Anxiety, for instance, can be thought of as the fear that something will or won't happen. Or that we won't be able to survive some perceived disaster in our life. But as humans, we have the power to find ways to cope with this, and to master our fears. Owen's view is not the only view. Some people thrive on fear. Others thrive on love."

As she closed out the show, her inner thoughts kept flashing back to Owen. She'd be damned if she was going to let him win. Been there, done that. She would not be a victim again.

The ending music swelled and Maggie pulled off her
headphones and made her way to the production booth.
"Good show," David said, as he always did, and he quickly
squeezed past everyone, making himself scarce as he disappeared across the hall to the break room. Sharon left close on
his heels. She gave Maggie a wry smile before hustling away.

"Nice job," Becca said, but the spark of excitement had
been extinguished. Ethan had obviously chastised her. Maggie felt sorry for the energetic, carefree woman who'd accompanied her that night. She wondered if she'd get that
inner fire back under Ethan Townsend's grave tutelage.

"I'll escort Dr. Levine home," he said, glancing around
as if unable to meet Becca's eyes. Perhaps he felt bad about
his earlier rebuke, after all. "I'll touch base with you later."

Becca nodded and, with a small, halfhearted smile for
Maggie, she left the two of them alone.

"I really can get myself home." She went back to her
chair, gathering her notes and stuffing them in her satchel.

"Do you have a car?"

She'd forgotten about that. Becca had driven her here. She
huffed out a breath. "No. Guess you got me there."

He reached out and took her arm, his touch surprisingly
gentle as he turned her to face him. "I'm just trying to do
my job. Keep you safe."

The air fairly crackled with his sense of chivalry and she
sighed. How could a woman refuse when a handsome man
wished to guard her with his life?

"Let's get going, then. It's been a long day."

He walked her out and, for once, she didn't feel the need
to constantly survey the parking lot. Her bodyguard did that
enough for the both of them. He kept a hand at her elbow,
his heat at her side. Though she was taller than the average
woman, his large frame made her feel almost dainty.

Earlier, the daytime temperature had risen high enough

that now, even after the relief of the brief but intense rain and the cover of dark, steam rose from the puddles left on the ground, reflecting orange in the glow of the parking lot lamps. The smell of rain still permeated the thick air, increasing the feeling of intimacy surrounding them. And yet, she knew next to nothing about the man to whom she was entrusting her life.

"You were Secret Service before, right?"

At her quiet question, his head whipped around to face her. It was a moment before he answered, returning his attention to their surroundings as they approached his car. "Yes."

A man of few words. They were usually the most interesting type, and a challenge this particular mental health professional couldn't resist. She prodded him. "Why did you leave?"

He opened the passenger door of his car and motioned for her to get in. She waited until he was settled in the driver's seat beside her, but he still didn't respond. Instead, he kept his eyes on the road, away from her.

Maggie liked to see a client's eyes when they spoke. That was one thing she missed now that she was on the radio. Nonverbal cues provided a valuable subtext to the words one spoke. Still, he wasn't her client. She didn't really have the right to pry, though something urged her on.

"Is it too painful?"

He shot her a grin that took her by surprise and made her mouth go dry. "You don't give up, do you? Like a pit bull."

"I've heard more flattering analogies, but no, I don't give up." Her voice softened. "Not when it's evident there's something there, under the surface, that needs to come out."

His jaw clenched, the easy grin gone now. Perhaps she'd pushed too far. "Don't psychoanalyze me, Doctor."

"I wouldn't dare. We don't have enough time," she added, arching a brow at him.

His short laugh surprised them both. "No, you probably don't." His smile died away again as he looked straight ahead. "You're right. I don't want to talk about it, though."

"I can respect that," she murmured, her heart going out to him as he nodded briefly. The therapist in her longed to help him. And so did the woman in her.

As her home was illuminated by his headlights, the dread inside Maggie grew. She'd angered Owen again tonight. What price would she pay this time?

Ethan seemed to read her thoughts. "Noah's had an unmarked police car patrolling the neighborhood all evening."

She shot him a grateful glance. "That was thoughtful."

He shrugged. "Fearmonger seems to be targeting you. You're our best bet for catching him."

Ouch. So she wasn't the center of everyone's world. She knew that. How indelicate of him to point it out, though. In this whole insane mess, she was well aware that her pride mattered little.

He walked her to her door and waited as she disengaged the alarm, then turned on the inside lights. She froze, unable to go any further. But Ethan was already stepping past her with a quick hand signal to wait there for him. He took his gun from its shoulder holster and held it with both hands. And then he was gone.

Several moments had passed when she heard a thump, followed by a crash as something shattered within the depths of her house. A groan and a muffled curse met her ears. Worried, she took a step into the small foyer.

"Ethan?" As her breath caught in her chest, Maggie forced air into her lungs and mentally counted to avoid giving in to panic.

"It's okay," he finally called.

She'd only had to count to five. She blew the breath out when he reappeared in front of her, holstering his weapon.

"All clear." He grimaced. "But you'll need a new bedroom lamp. Maybe I was wrong about enlisting Sigmund as an attack cat. He jumped out at me from under the bed and wrapped his claws around my ankle. Surprised the hell out of me."

"He's been through a lot." Her words retained a tremor of the fear she'd felt.

Ethan's gaze was piercing as he examined her face, probably noting her paleness. He reached out and laid a palm against her cheek, his thumb lightly brushing the corner of her mouth. She trembled under his delicate touch. "So have you. But you're okay now."

She caught a whiff of laundry detergent along with Ethan's masculine scent, no doubt heightened by the humid night air and the dampness of his clothes. Thinking of the dampness reminded her that this man had run through the rain to get to her earlier. Because he'd been concerned for her safety. She felt herself leaning forward, as if drawn by some unseen force. Her gaze flickered to meet his, and she sensed a war being waged within.

"It's okay. You can kiss me," she whispered.

He stilled, his palm warm against her cheek as she brought her arms around his waist and held on, feeling his muscles bunch and tense beneath the wet shirt at her fingertips. She imagined the warm skin that lay there, just under the thin cotton fabric.

Her words hung in the sudden quiet for several long seconds before she felt his exhale of breath against her face. "I can't." A look of regret clouded the dark green depths of his eyes and he dropped his hand from her cheek. She removed her hands as well and took a step back, struggling to hide her disappointment.

"I can't," he repeated, his voice thick. "It's not..."

God, he was going to make stupid excuses that she didn't

want to hear. She forced a smile. "No problem. I understand. This is, after all, a job."

"You've been through so much." She couldn't stand the softness in his voice. The understanding. The *pity*.

She stood by the door with her hand on the knob, both dreading the moment he would leave her in this house alone, and welcoming it so she could recover from her embarrassment. She'd practically lain down at his feet. But then, Ethan was a sexy man. He was probably used to stepping over women who threw themselves at him.

And there was always the possibility someone waited at home for him. But he had the appearance of a loner. No, she doubted this man had anyone with whom to share his burdens.

"Noah and I are just a couple quick phone calls away."

She swallowed and avoided his gaze. "Okay, then."

"You'll be okay," he said, and again she had the uncomfortable feeling he was reading her thoughts. "Noah's got an officer stationed in a car across the street. Get some sleep. We both could use some. Neither of us is operating on all thrusters." Great. Now he was making excuses for her behavior. "I'll be back in the morning to check on you." He turned to go.

"What about Becca?"

"She'll be otherwise engaged."

Poor girl. She was trying so hard to impress Ethan and Damian. And it really hadn't been her fault that Maggie had provoked Owen. "It wasn't her idea for me to engage Owen in conversation. She didn't expect any trouble. And there wasn't any."

He had crossed the threshold of the door and turned back. At her words in Becca's defense, he shook his head. His whole demeanor seemed to darken somehow. "But you couldn't have known that. Usually the worst harm comes when you least expect it." The shadow that seemed to pass over his face mingled with the night's true darkness as he turned. He walked across the porch, calling back over his shoulder, "Set the alarm."

She closed the door behind him and took a split second to compose herself, to shake off her reaction to the raw pain she'd seen in his expression. Exactly what had happened to Ethan Townsend? She made a mental note to find out.

Sigmund wove between her legs, meowing his standard greeting. At least she wasn't completely alone. A small voice, one that had been growing louder in recent weeks, told her that living for her job and her beloved pet wouldn't be good enough.

Not for much longer, anyway.

The blade of his bowie knife flashed in the moonlight, setting off an answering flash like gunpowder igniting in his blood. The energy of it pumped through him, her fear driving it.

"Pretty, isn't it?"

He didn't expect an answer from his victim as he showed her the knife. Her mouth was bound with duct tape the same silver of his blade. But he saw the fear screaming in her eyes.

That was satisfying. Soon, he'd remove the tape and hear her screams.

That was always even more satisfying.

And dear Maggie would know what it was to fear. Truly fear. That would be the ultimate satisfaction.

He looked with disgust at the prey before him. She wasn't Maggie. She was only a teaching tool and always had been a means to an end. But someday…someday it would be Maggie. She would no longer doubt him or question his wisdom.

He'd have her respect.

For now, however, he had to settle. He shrugged. Might

as well perfect his craft before the ultimate prize was captured. And giving Maggie something to think about would heighten the final pleasure. He grew hard thinking about it, about sinking the knife into Maggie's creamy flesh.

She would be his. Soon.

"I'm going to dial," he told his present student. "When she answers, I'll remove the tape. And I want you to scream like you mean it."

His victim's wide blue eyes filled with hope. She thought she'd be able to yell for help. That she had a chance.

He smiled, running a hand over her glossy brown hair. The blossoming of hope always led to the greatest screams—when they realized all of that hope couldn't trump fear.

He dialed Maggie's home number, waiting impatiently as it rang. She'd better be home, or this next victim's life would be a prolonged hell. Of course, it was four in the morning. Where else would sweet, solitary Maggie be?

"Hello?" Her voice, husky with sleep, aroused him further. He imagined it screaming for mercy.

"Maggie," he exclaimed with the exuberance of a friend long parted.

"Owen?" she asked, suddenly awake. The sheets rustled through the phone as she sat up.

Excellent. He'd surprised her. Her reactions would be open and honest. And he wanted a reaction. She thought she could discredit him on public radio, that she could hide her fear behind big, tough words. But he would have the last laugh.

"I told you, I'm Fearmonger. Call me by my name. Owen isn't my real name, anyway, as you probably already suspected." He paused, watching his chosen victim's eyes widen with the revelation. She'd had no clue who he'd pretended to be, or who he really was. He smiled. He'd always loved seeing his own image reflected there in the dark pupils of the victim's eyes, along with the fear that made them dilate. It had been way too long since he'd enjoyed himself this much.

"It's time for another lesson," he said into the phone. His victim whimpered as the tip of his knife caressed one cheek.

"What? I don't need another lesson." Fear laced Maggie's voice. So, the doctor was familiar with the emotion after all. Anxiety wouldn't be far behind. Too bad he wouldn't be there to witness one of her panic attacks. The thought of plunging his blade into a heart pumping hard with fear aroused him still further.

He chuckled, watching a drop of deep, rich blood trickle down the creamy cheek before him as he nicked her with the blade. His victim whimpered and tried to pull her face away, but there was nowhere to go. She was strapped down tight to the cold, hard table.

"I have a friend here who would like to explain how wrong you are about fear," he said to Maggie. "It really does motivate everything."

With a rip that took flesh off his victim's lips, he removed the duct tape. She screamed. A rush of adrenaline singed him from nerve ending to nerve ending. She was too afraid to think clearly, or she might have screamed for help, or at least given her location. Instead, the sounds were filled with pain. And fear.

But it wasn't enough. He could hear Maggie shouting questions to the victim, not crying out in horror.

"Where are you? Who are you? Tell me where you are. I'll get help." Maggie was breathless.

He ripped the phone away from the woman's blood-speckled lips and laughed into it. "No, no, dear Maggie. That's not how we play this game. We have to get to the lesson."

"You bastard! Don't touch her. Don't…" Her declarations ended on a sob.

Ah-ha. *Success*.

"Fear always wins." He dropped the phone onto the nearby table, still connected so Maggie could hear the victim's screams as they echoed off the walls. He brought the knife across the woman's tender palms, her cheeks, her breasts and, finally, across her tender naked thighs to the point where every woman's animal instincts reigned. When her screams stopped because she'd passed out from the pain—and the fear—he slit her throat, reveling in the gurgle that came with her last breath.

He picked up the receiver with hands slick with blood. A smile curved his blood-spattered lips as he heard the sobs of his student. He'd gotten her attention.

"Maggie. Maggie!" he said more sharply when she continued to sob.

"I'm here." He could picture the good doctor as she tried to pull herself together.

"That was lesson number two. An extra one, for daring to contradict me on the air today, in front of everyone." He clucked at her with his tongue. "I expected better from my star pupil. You have so much yet to learn."

FIVE

AS THE LINE WENT DEAD in her ear, Maggie's eyes darted to the bedside clock. Four in the morning. She'd finally drifted off to sleep, after an hour of tossing and turning, only to be awakened inside her worst nightmare. Though deep down she knew what she was experiencing was real, she hoped it was some sick game. She prayed, for that woman's sake—whoever she was—that Owen was not some serial killer, and that he was just pushing Maggie's buttons.

Finding Ethan's card on the bedside table, she fumbled with the phone.

Shit. Her hands shook so badly she had to hang up and redial before she got it right. In the meantime, precious time was wasted.

"Yeah?" His sleepy voice sounded like heaven to her.

"Ethan?" She winced as the tightness in her chest threatened to cut off her air.

"Maggie?" He was instantly alert. He cursed as something thumped into something else. "What is it?"

"He called. He…" She gritted her teeth to stop them from chattering.

"Who called? What happened? Are you okay?"

No, I am not okay, she wanted to scream. Definitely not. Not in any way, shape or form. But some woman out there was a whole heck of a lot worse.

She took a deep, rattling breath. "I'm okay, but he… I think Fearmonger killed someone." Lord help her, she actually hoped the woman was out of her misery. The screams of her pain still echoed in Maggie's head.

"I'll be right there. I'll contact the officer parked outside and make sure he's keeping an eye on things until I get there."

The officer outside. She'd totally forgotten him. Her first instinct had been to get to Ethan. He would know what to do.

"Don't open the door." His voice was muffled for a second, and she imagined he was pulling a shirt over an expanse of bare chest. "Not to anyone but me." She heard the sharpness in his voice, knew he was trying to break through her terror, but she couldn't answer. She could only numbly nod her head. "Maggie, do you hear me? Do you understand?"

She forced breath from her lungs, past her vocal cords. Made her throat work. "Y-yes."

"Hang in there. I'm on my way."

Dropping the phone to the bed, she pulled her knees to her chest and hugged them. *That poor woman.* She could still hear her screams of terror. They had seemed endless, but Maggie hadn't wanted to hang up. What if the woman yelled something important? But in the end, she had no more information than before.

And she had heard the gurgle as the victim released her last breath.

Ethan knocked on Maggie's door only fifteen minutes later. Record time, considering he lived almost a half hour away, even at four in the morning. But those minutes had felt like an eternity as his mind replayed the panic, the sense of utter desolation, in her voice.

A quick check-in with the bleary-eyed but alert officer still parked across from Maggie's house revealed nothing. He hadn't seen or heard anything unusual all night. Ethan scowled at the front door when she didn't answer his knock, then tried peeking in the living room window. This time, however, the drapes were pulled tightly closed.

Alarm coursed through him and he pounded on the door, every second feeling like a century. He fumbled in his pocket for the spare key he'd insisted she give him earlier. Once through the door, he quickly punched in the new code he'd seen her use only a few hours ago, when he'd brought her home from work. He was relieved to see the red light that indicated it was armed. However, Fearmonger had been able to bypass the alarm once before. That mystery still stumped him, and he knew it worried Damian, too.

Cautiously, his gun in his hands, he moved down the hall to the master bedroom. Soft light spilled into the hallway. There was no sound.

No, wait. *Humming.* He heard humming.

Silently, he crept forward until he could see into the bedroom. He lowered his gun.

Gaping at him, Maggie ripped the headphones from her head. "I'm sorry. I must not have heard the door."

"Guess not," he said around a jaw still stiff with tension.

"I thought it would take you longer, and I needed a distraction." She gestured to the laptop resting on her outstretched legs. The headphones were connected to the computer.

He sucked in a breath as his initial tension subsided. She was a vision, her mussed red hair in stark contrast to her soft white nightgown and sky blue sheets.

"Are you okay?" He moved beside the bed, tugging the edge of her nightgown over her knees, covering the creamy white skin there. Pity.

Her mouth pressed into a tight line as a shudder racked her body. He wanted to reach out and pull her to him, but he didn't trust himself not to take it further, to claim the soft lips she'd offered him earlier.

"No," Maggie replied. "I kept hearing her final gasp for air." She gestured to the headphones again, and he understood. She'd needed to block the sound, even if only for a little while. She looked up at him and his heart melted at the frustration he saw there. "I'm not okay, and I won't be until he's dead." Determination mixed with the fear in her eyes, making them sparkle like sun on gold. At that moment, he had no doubt she meant what she said.

He nudged her aside to make room for him to sit next to her. Resting his head against the headboard, he gestured to the computer. "What are you doing?"

"Listening to old recordings of the show David gave me earlier, at work." She shrugged. "I couldn't just sit here, waiting for you. I was hoping Owen, or Fearmonger, gave a clue to who his victim—" her eyes hardened with the word, then filled with tears before she could continue "—to who the woman he took is. Or where he took her."

He wished he could reach out and comfort her, run a hand over her silky, tousled hair. She looked like a kid, her eyes wide, her gown rumpled from sleep. But when he caught sight of the gentle curve of her breasts, the shadow of a nipple, the bareness of her lower thigh where her nightgown had ridden up again as she'd shifted to make room for him, all images of a child were wiped from his mind. Instead of reaching for her as he wanted to, he crossed his arms, tucking his hands into his armpits.

"What can I do?" Her voice echoed the misery she must be feeling. The mattress shifted as she swung her long legs over the side and rose from the bed. "I should have been dressing. What was I thinking? We need to go find this woman. Maybe she's still alive."

His gaze tracked her as she went to her closet, then to the master bathroom with an armload of clothes. "You weren't."

"What?" she called from the other room.

"You weren't thinking. You were reacting. And there's nothing you *can* do." He knew what that kind of helplessness felt like. It was an itch that crawled under your skin and picked at you until you couldn't stand being immobile anymore.

A moment later, she stood in the doorway in jeans and a T-shirt, her hair loose and flowing about her shoulders like licks of fire. Her fists met her hips. "Are you saying I'm useless? I refuse to accept that."

He rose from the bed, shifting uncomfortably to hide his arousal. God, she looked like an avenging angel, ready for a fight. "I'm just saying, you're not in the most rational state of mind right now."

"I can't just sit around." She bit her lip and looked away. He couldn't resist reaching for her any longer. She came into his embrace easily, without resistance. He held her against his chest as she trembled, his hands entwined in her glorious hair. It was like silken threads sliding between his fingers.

"You're not. You're doing what you can." He pulled back enough to look into her eyes. There, he saw anger and frustration. Not weakness or self-pity, even after all she'd been through. He admired the hell out of her. "Right? Most people in your situation would be cowering in the corner."

"Been there, done that." Her response was a whisper across her dark pink lips. She'd been chewing on them since he saw her last. He longed to stroke his thumbs—or his tongue—over them and soothe their rawness.

"I've called for reinforcements. Becca is tracking down the source of the call. Noah has been informed and has alerted the other police on this shift to be on the alert for anything unusual. We'll find her."

"But in what state?"

Her cheeks were flushed with emotion, and this time he didn't prevent his thumbs from swiping over them, cooling the heat there. She didn't seem to notice the action, but touching her did strange things to his gut. Skin-to-skin contact with her tugged at something deep inside. He wanted to pull her further into his arms but was thankful when she pulled away. He felt the loss immediately, but *damn,* what was he thinking? There were boundaries here he couldn't cross.

"We'll hope for the best," he said, inwardly groaning at how pathetic the words sounded.

"And expect the worst." She tugged her hair into a loose ponytail and stalked down the hallway. He and Sigmund followed.

"Where are you going?"

"Coffee. Want a cup?"

It was only five in the morning, but he sensed that she needed something to keep her active, and they weren't going to get any more sleep anyway. "And then I need you to tell me what Fearmonger said. Are you up to that?"

Her jaw set with determination, she turned and gave him a brief nod. She was tough.

"Anything to get this bastard." She recounted the brief, horrific conversation as she went through the motions of making coffee. Sigmund meowed and she automatically moved to fill his food bowl by the refrigerator. "He thinks he's invincible."

"Sigmund?" Ethan had been watching the sway of her hips, and the way her ponytail swished against her T-shirt as she moved back and forth, fetching mugs from the cupboard and spoons from the drawer.

Her husky laugh warmed him. "No. Fearmonger."

"Most serial killers do. They pride themselves in fooling the police, in proving they're unstoppable." He leaned against a countertop near her, unable to stay across the room. "But he's not. He is *not* invincible."

She sighed. "I know. But neither are his victims, and they're the ones who'll suffer."

The ringing of his cell phone had him moving reluctantly away from her. What was with this constant need to touch her whenever she was near?

As he answered the phone with a gruff greeting, Damian's voice filled his ear. "Noah located the victim."

He tensed, already sensing from Damian's tone what the answer to his next question would be. "And?"

"She's dead." Damian's voice was calm but Ethan sensed the man's frustration. "And the son of a bitch didn't make it easy."

Blowing out a breath, his gaze swiveled to meet Maggie's. She was hugging herself, her mug of steaming coffee untouched on the counter. "Where?" he asked, trying to keep his voice neutral so as not to alarm her. There would be a time for that soon enough.

"The university," Damian said. "A janitor on his early-morning shift found her and called the police." As his boss paused, Ethan's gut ached. There was more to this, and it wasn't good. "The woman's mutilated body was in Maggie's classroom."

"In her *classroom?*" Forgetting to keep his voice neutral, or to resist the desire to touch Maggie, Ethan moved close again and reached for her hand. He squeezed her cold fingertips, hoping the simple gesture reassured her that everything would be okay when it certainly wasn't. And wouldn't be. Not for a while, anyway. This bastard was making things way too personal. "We'll be there in twenty minutes."

"Ten," Maggie interrupted, pulling away to dump her steaming coffee in the sink.

"Make that ten," he echoed to Damian before hanging up.

* * *

"I'm sorry we can't let you any closer, Dr. Levine." Detective Maria Santos, Noah Crandall's partner, seemed a nice woman. Her brown eyes were as warm as they'd been a little over twenty-four hours ago, when the pair had come to Maggie's house to investigate the break-in.

Maggie clasped her shaking hands tightly together. It was the only way she could keep from rubbing at the ache in her chest. She'd been sitting this way, outside the psych building, since Noah had asked her to take a look at a photo of the victim's sliced-up face and—*dear God*—it was Sharon. Young, innocent, vivacious Sharon Moss, to whom she'd just spoken hours before. Except her beautiful face had been sliced in several places. Sharon's screams echoed in Maggie's ears as she imagined how much she must have suffered. Maggie bit her bottom lip hard enough to make herself focus.

"You know you can't go in there." A lock of sandy-blond hair fell onto Noah's forehead, concealing the lines of concern there.

"I understand. It is a crime scene. I just thought, maybe…" What? That she would have more luck than the police? Her lips trembled and she pressed them together. This was entirely her fault. All of it. And now Sharon was dead.

She jumped to her feet, wanting to walk until she ran out of sidewalk. But she couldn't. She owed Sharon justice. So she ended up standing there, feeling useless.

"I provoked a serial murderer. What was I thinking?" She shouldn't have prodded him. It hadn't led to anything helpful. "I'm responsible," she whispered, horrified.

"You didn't know." Ethan's voice came from behind her, his comforting hand suddenly there, a warm weight on her shoulder, anchoring her. She resisted the urge to lean into it. But she remembered how he'd grasped her hand earlier, in her kitchen. His support—however brief—had kept her from crumpling into a heap on the floor. "You didn't know he was a serial killer. I didn't tell you until afterward."

"Still, I sensed something strange." Pressing her fingertips to her stomach in an effort to stifle the sudden nausea, she swayed. She felt a hand at her waist, steadying her, and looked up to find Ethan taking her weight against him. "I killed Sharon. Maybe not with my hands, but…"

He nudged her gently back down onto the concrete steps and squatted down beside her. "Don't be an idiot. Fearmonger killed her. You didn't know."

Maria hiked up her slacks and crouched down beside them, her mahogany hair falling over one shoulder. "Ethan's right. The killer is solely responsible, and he's trying to manipulate you. You're just as much a victim in this as Sharon Moss. We'll find this guy."

No, she wasn't quite the victim Sharon had become. *Not yet, anyway.* "But you can't guarantee you'll catch him before he does this again."

"No, we can't." Maria grinned, looking up at Noah. "But we're the best in the department."

Maggie nodded, striving to return the detective's smile. "I know. Tell me what I can do to help. I need to do something. Anything."

Noah's hand clasped her shoulder. "We'll certainly let you know. After all, you're our only link to this guy right now. We may need to use that."

Ethan muttered a curse, rising to a standing position. Maria followed suit.

"You're not going to use her to get to him," Ethan argued with Noah. "He's a nutcase. It's my responsibility to keep her safe. Why don't you go interview the janitor some more, find out if he saw anybody driving away as he arrived or something? Do some police work rather than risk an innocent person."

The two men's glares clashed. "I'm not suggesting we put her in harm's way," Noah said, clearly offended.

"They're right, Ethan," Maggie said, wishing her legs felt steady enough to step between the men. "I might be the best chance of finding Sharon's killer. He intends to contact me again." She shuddered. "With more *lessons*." Would she have to listen to another woman's screams, unable to help?

Maria stepped into the fray, putting a hand on each man's shoulder. They seemed to calm at her touch. "We'll obviously see where the evidence leads us first. We wouldn't put Maggie in danger. Come on, Noah. Let's see how they're doing inside."

As the detectives moved away, Damian exited the building and came to stand on the steps next to Maggie. He removed his suit jacket and dropped it around her shoulders.

"It's chilly, sweetheart," Damian explained when she looked up at him, confused. "The sun's barely up."

Indeed, it was still a pink-and-orange ball on the horizon between two other campus buildings.

A sight one woman would never see again.

As she glanced away, Maggie caught the hard set of Ethan's jaw. He glared at the lapel of Damian's jacket as if the article of clothing had just personally insulted him and his mother. Maybe, despite his assurances, he was angry with her. He'd certainly made that clear at the radio station last night.

"I'm a psychiatrist, I should have known." Her chest ached with grief for Sharon and her family. And for David, who would be devastated. The young man had such an intense crush on Sharon.

Why was she always leading people into disaster? She only wanted to help, but death and destruction seemed to surround her.

She suddenly leaped up, forcing Ethan to step back to give her room. "I have to walk. I can't just sit here."

Ethan moved to follow Maggie, but Damian's hand on his arm stopped him.

"Let her go," Damian said. "Just for a minute."

The strange sensation of jealousy that had taken hold of him when Damian had called Maggie "sweetheart" intensified. Did the man have feelings for her? Was there a history between them, or something current? And why the hell did Ethan care?

He shoved a hand through his hair. He was exhausted. That was all. This was just a job, and then he'd be out of Maggie's life. He should be focusing on the crime scene.

Sandy Mitchell, one of SSAM's best criminalists, emerged from the building. Apparently SSAM team members were already standing by, watching the cops carefully to note any disturbance of evidence before they'd be allowed to process the scene themselves.

Ethan's gaze swung back to Maggie's slender form moving farther down the sidewalk. At least there were no bushes or buildings around her. Just wide-open spaces in the quad. No places for a madman to hide. But if she went much farther by herself, he'd go charging after her. After all, she was his responsibility.

"She just needs some time," Damian said, following his gaze.

Ethan's temper snapped. "For what? To adjust? Hell, you don't adjust to something like this. You and I, of all people, should know that." Catching the flash of pain on Damian's face, he backed off, immediately contrite. He shook his head, blowing out a breath that released some of the tension. "I'm sorry. I spoke out of turn."

"No. You're right. We do understand that kind of pain.

And I understand Maggie because I know her. I've known her longer than you."

Ethan's jealousy flared again. Damn it. What was it with this woman? She seemed to attract admirers—both male and female—like honey attracted bears. His jaw slid to the side as he reined in his temper. "So that's how it is, then? I thought from day one there might be something between you two. Guess I was right."

There was a long pause before Damian's wry chuckle surprised Ethan. "Yes, there's something, but not what you think. I'm almost twice her age. I'm flattered, but she deserves better." The man's eyes trailed to the sidewalk, where Maggie still walked toward the rising sun, and he kept his gaze there when he spoke next. "She knew Sam."

Ethan's breath caught. That was how Damian and Maggie knew each other. Of course. She was the right age. Sam was the common denominator. He didn't know whether to be relieved or worried, as that was a bond that would surely run deep with Damian Manchester. Straight to the man's core, his whole reason for being.

"She was my daughter's best friend. They were inseparable. Maggie became ill suddenly on the day Samantha disappeared. They were supposed to meet at the mall, and Maggie didn't show. She'd tried to call Sam before she left to meet her, to tell her she was sick and couldn't make it, but she couldn't reach her." Damian swallowed. "This was twenty years ago, before everyone on God's green earth— and their teenage daughters—had a cell phone. There was no way to get in touch. I went to the mall to find Sam but, of course, I didn't."

A mirthless smile twisted his lips. "I didn't know until a decade later that Maggie felt responsible for Sam's disappearance that day. I should have, but I never thought about it. I was too lost in my own grief. I was feeling responsible.

It never occurred to me that a thirteen-year-old girl would, too." He shook his head. "When she addressed the college at her graduation, she invited me. We'd stayed in touch over the years through letters and an occasional phone call."

Damian looked away. His voice was rough with emotion when he spoke again. "Maggie mentioned Samantha in her speech, and it was then that I realized she'd done all of this for her. She'd pursued psychology because she wanted to help others. She'd attended medical school because she felt she could do even more. And she did. And then she lost her brother because of her career path, a path meant only to help people." His eyes narrowed on Ethan's. "She doesn't know what it is to be happy, to live for herself. She deserves that. All of that and more."

Maggie had been through so much more than Ethan had even imagined. Stunned, he stood there, his mouth refusing to form the questions that weighed on his mind. But it didn't matter. Damian was already gone, his long strides carrying him toward Maggie, toward where Ethan itched to be.

Noah Crandall had seen some gruesome sights in his five years as a Chicago homicide detective, but this was one he knew would always stand out in his memory. And, on those rare occasions he reached the lucid-dreaming REM stage of sleep, it would haunt his nightmares.

"Looks like someone enjoys scaring the shit out of young women," Maria muttered.

Maria Santos, his partner of the past eight months, carefully picked her way around the crime scene. The multitude of markers denoting blood spatter patterns and other evidence made walking through what had recently been an average lecture hall, with a capacity of a hundred or so desks arranged in gently sloping stadium style, tricky at best.

But Maria was a pro.

Noah and Maria had clicked on a professional level from the start. Despite the nasty rumors they were sleeping with each other, they respected each other enough not to complicate things that way. Besides, if the pranks she'd pulled on him were any indication, Maria saw him more as a big brother than a potential lover.

Noah watched the crime-scene photographer setting up his next shot, framing the words that were scrawled across the white dry-erase board that spanned one wall. *Fear me.* If there was any doubt that Fearmonger and Maggie's caller Owen were one and the same person, this greatly diminished it. Only, this time, he'd added the words *Lesson Two.*

"It's his MO," Noah finally replied to Maria. When she tipped her head in question, he explained. "I was only a patrol officer when Fearmonger first struck, but I was aiming to make detective someday, and murders had always intrigued me, so I paid attention to the homicides that came through. Absorbed what I could through whoever would talk to me."

"He killed three women back then?"

Noah nodded. "And maybe more."

His gaze rested on the large table from which the professor lectured. And where the young woman's body had been found by the janitor, her limbs duct-taped to the table, and her face and torso sliced open in so many places it was hard to say which one had been the death of her. And yet, there had been little blood left in her body. There were spray patterns on the table and surrounding floor, and some was probably the "ink" with which *Fear me* and *Lesson Two* had been written, but most of it was simply…missing. Sandy Mitchell, SSAM's head criminologist, had pointed out a deep gash in the woman's neck that appeared to be postmortem. She hypothesized that Fearmonger had drained Sharon's blood through that wound. He'd obviously collected it, as it wasn't anywhere to be found. Where had it all gone?

Noah gingerly stepped up to the whiteboard after the photographer switched to another piece of evidence. The words the killer had scrawled there had not required much of the blood.

"God, the press will have a field day with this," Maria muttered, pushing her hair behind her ears as she rose from where she'd been squatting by the trash can, peering inside for clues. Somebody from the lab would soon be gathering that up as well.

"I'm going to talk with the president of the university," Noah said. They'd have to request cooperation on a greater level if this investigation were to proceed smoothly.

She planted her hands on her slim hips. "Which means I'm having a pleasant chat with the chief, I suppose."

He stifled a smile. "And the commissioner, probably. This'll be a high-profile case. You'll get lots of attention and get to test out those people skills you've been working on."

"Fuck you," she said good-naturedly. "You just don't want to deal with the circus."

He took a sweeping look at their surroundings. "There's enough of the circus to go around."

SIX

"MAGGIE?" DAMIAN'S face was etched with lines of worry. Maggie patted the seat next to her and the old wood creaked as he accepted her invitation.

"This bench used to be one of my favorite places on campus." She looked to her right. The medical-school building where she'd worked doing therapy and teaching classes after graduating from Columbia stood proudly, its red bricks glowing orange in the rays of the rising sun. Its quiet steadfastness gave no clue as to what had happened to her there at the hands of her previous stalker, Deborah Frame. To her left, a football-field distance away, police and SSAM agents still scurried about, processing the scene created by her current stalker. Campus was quickly filling with bad memories.

Damian seemed to know the direction of her thoughts. "Want to talk about it?"

"I'll be fine." She summoned a small smile.

Something flickered in the depths of his gaze, then hardened to flint. "I'll make sure of it." He softened his voice again. "How about your family? Do they know?"

"About this?" She waved a hand toward the police activity. She would never want her family near this mess. "Absolutely not. All they know is that someone broke into my house Monday night. I don't want them involved."

"And yet, they'd want to know if you're in danger. They love you." Something much like regret passed over his face, and he looked away. He had to be thinking about Sam.

She put her hand on his forearm. The crisp long-sleeved shirt under her fingertips reminded her that she still had his suit coat. But his arm felt warm. Solid. Sometimes she forgot Damian Manchester was human. He'd been through so much, and become so adept at hiding his emotions over the years, that she forgot the hell he'd been through. The hell he was still in.

"Will it really matter, having them know?" she wondered aloud.

"They'd want to help."

"But they can't. It's better if they're not around. I'd only worry about them, too."

Concern creased his forehead. "You won't reconsider? The more people who are watching over you, the better. If anything happens to you…"

It hit her then, and she felt like an idiot for not seeing it sooner. The successful businessman before her thought he was a failure. He'd been unable to protect Sam and had to live with a parent's guilt—ridiculous as it was—for the rest of his life.

He'd told Maggie before that she was like a daughter, and as such, she was precious to him. And if anything happened to her, he'd blame himself. It'd be like failing Sam all over again.

She slid her hand underneath his on the bench. "I'll be fine. I have you on my team, don't I?" She sighed. "I'll call my parents again if it'll make you feel better."

He gave a brief nod and squeezed her hand. "It would."

"But I don't want to worry them unless it's absolutely necessary, so I may leave some of the details out." Sensing his disapproval, she hurried on. "Besides, according to the detectives, it won't be long before they catch this guy." She paused and drew a breath. "And someday you'll find Sam's killer, too. I'm sure of it." A thought struck her as she released his hand. "You don't think this is the guy who killed Sam, do you?"

His lips tightened. "No. I almost wish…but, no. The characteristics of the crime scenes are too different. This guy has a definite fingerprint to his behavior. The scene at your house was just too similar to those three other crime scenes years ago."

"And the scene today."

"Yes, definitely."

Sharon had suffered so much. Maggie hadn't seen her classroom, but she'd seen Sharon's glassy, lifeless eyes when she'd identified her face from that photograph. And Maggie had noticed the slices on Sharon's cheeks and across her face. The bastard had even sliced off the tip of her nose.

Biting her lip to stop its trembling, Maggie straightened her spine instead. She would not turn to jelly.

I'm in control.

But she wasn't. She didn't believe her mantra anymore.

A throat cleared behind them and both Damian and Maggie turned. Ethan stood under the enormous oak tree that shaded the bench when the sun was high. His gaze skimmed over Maggie, and her chest filled with warmth at the concern she read there. It wasn't the painful pressure that signaled the onset of one of her episodes, but a pleasant feeling of… anticipation. And relief. She wasn't totally alone. Someone was watching over her and keeping her safe.

"Sorry to interrupt, but Noah's asking for you," Ethan told Damian. "You okay?" he asked Maggie.

She nodded. "Just needed some space."

"At least school's still on break until tomorrow. No classes, so no extra students and professors on campus."

She hadn't even thought of that. The psychology building was near the center of campus, away from most of the dorms. That, combined with it being a holiday break and during the summer, when fewer students lived on campus, was a little bit of good news. "That's something to be thankful for."

Ethan's frown told her there was a drawback. "It also means we have an even slimmer possibility of finding a witness who may have seen a strange car parked here in the early-morning hours."

"Or Sharon or her killer," Maggie said. "Unless security was patrolling at the time?"

Damian shook his head. "I already spoke with the head of campus security. Due to budget cutbacks, efforts have been a bit more lax with the summer term and fewer students on campus."

"But," Ethan added, "security does happen to have a camera installed in that parking lot."

Maggie sat up straight. "Then, that's good, right?"

He rubbed a hand over the back of his neck. "We'll see. There was some debate about whether the video was rolling. Budget cutbacks, again. They haven't serviced the camera in a while."

Damian shook his head. "Let's pray it gives us a lead. Noah is going to call the president of the university with an update. We'll all meet this afternoon at the Society to compare notes." He turned to Ethan. "In the meantime, stick to Maggie like superglue."

"Intended to."

Maggie felt a stab of annoyance that her life was no longer in her hands, but it was quickly replaced with gratitude. There was a madman targeting her in a very personal way. She'd learned the first time around that danger of that kind was very real, with horrifying consequences.

As Ethan guided her to his car, his warm hand at her elbow, she was once again grateful for his solid presence. She gazed out the window as he drove, trying to focus on the passing scenery, now dappled with gold and pink as the sun rose higher. There wasn't a cloud in the morning sky. It was going to be another hot day.

"Wait." She turned in her seat when she realized the direction Ethan had headed. "This isn't the way to my house. You missed the turn."

"I'm not taking you to your place." His tone brooked no argument.

Something sizzled in her blood. It took her a moment to place the foreign feeling. It wasn't alarm. Or panic. The ache she felt whenever she was around this man was much lower than her chest. There was a definite dollop of the anticipation she'd been feeling earlier. With heightened senses, she detected the same spicy, masculine scent of Ethan that she'd discovered last night. Just before he'd rejected her. The memory brought a frown to her lips.

"Where are we going then?"

"My place."

The sizzling in her blood turned into an electric storm of emotions at his firmly spoken words. She covered her zinging nerves with annoyance. "Were you even going to ask me?"

He slid her a look that told her it didn't matter what her answer would have been. "Would you like to go back to your place, where you can be constantly reminded of what happened, and of how you're in danger every second until we catch this guy, *or*—" he paused, drawing the syllable out "—would you like to go back to my place where you can catch a nap and maybe a baseball game on TV before we have to meet up with everyone at SSAM later?"

All traces of annoyance were wiped away at the relaxing picture he painted. "God, I can't remember the last time I just sat and watched a game." She grinned at him. "Can we grill some brats?"

His mouth curved. "Add a couple beers to that request and you're looking like the woman of my dreams."

The words sent her pulse racing and her breath hitched in her chest. She automatically brought her hand up to rub the expected ache at her breastbone but laid it back in her lap when she realized there was no pressure, no tightness. This wasn't a panic attack.

This was attraction. Pure physical heat. Unexpected, but not entirely unwelcome. It had been so long since she'd felt this kind of attraction to a man. And it had never happened this quickly. What they shared was on some primal level she'd never thought to experience. But then, they'd shared some emotional moments as well. The memory of Ethan pulling her into his arms after Fearmonger's early-morning call came to mind. He'd held her as she shook. Comforted her with more tenderness than she'd expected.

"You said you hadn't watched a game in a while. The other men in your life don't enjoy baseball?"

She laughed. "Is that your way of asking if I'm dating anyone?"

"Are you? I know you don't live with anyone, and that you didn't want to bother anyone you loved by asking them to come stay with you, but that doesn't mean you haven't been dating. Your file didn't say."

Her file? She had a file? She shook her head. "No."

Between throwing herself into her career for the past several years and her recent, still-sharp grief over Brad's death, she hadn't wanted to deal with the complications of a relationship. Her sister thought she just hadn't found the right man yet, but Maggie knew it was more than that. She had her own issues to confront. *Physician, heal thyself.*

Ethan shrugged, as if her pithy answer was of no importance. For some reason, the simple action irritated her. He seemed to pick up on it. "I didn't mean to pry, but I had to know. It's part of protecting you. I should have asked you yesterday, when I was at your house going over security issues, but somehow I knew the answer."

Her eyes narrowed. "You *knew* the answer? Why, because I have a cat? That's so cliché."

He chuckled, and just like that her anger was overcome by that zinging sensation again. His effect on her was annoying enough to make her angry all over again.

"No," he said, sobering. "Not because of Sigmund." Okay, so he remembered her pet's name. That earned him some points. "Because I saw your entire house, remember? It was evident that not only did you live alone, but you didn't want reminders of your relationships—*any* of your relationships. I heard you tell your mother you love her on the phone, but there were no pictures of her, or your father. No guest room for lengthy visits from family or friends. So I assume you try to isolate yourself. To keep your family separate from the rest of your life."

"You sure you're not a detective?"

"Damian was the first person you called when you were in trouble, that tells me you were protecting your family, and that you were desperate."

She sighed, the reminder of violence chasing away the last of her irritation. "I'm glad I did."

His gaze moved to the rearview mirror and he frowned. "I'm going to stop up here. I want you to stay in the car. Don't move."

"What?" She automatically swung to look out the back window, wondering what threat he saw there.

"Don't move," he said again, more sharply. "We're being followed."

"How long have you known?" Here she'd been chatting about her life, thinking of the sensations Ethan sent coursing through her body—both pleasant and annoying—and she'd totally forgotten why she'd isolated herself from others. Danger seemed to follow her everywhere.

"That white SUV has been behind us since we left the university. I thought when I made the exit off the freeway he might keep going, but he didn't. When he continued past the last couple intersections, I figured he was tailing us."

"What are we going to do?"

He pulled into a gas station, parking very close to the double doors in front. He swung to face her. "I'm going inside and I'm going to sneak out the back, around to where he just parked on the street. I'll surprise him. *You* are going to stay right here. If you hear shots, or sense any kind of danger, you move immediately through those doors and lock them behind you. Tell the clerk to call Noah or Maria. You have their numbers?"

She nodded. Noah had given her his card. "If you're not back in ten minutes—no, make that two—I'm going in there and calling the detectives anyway." She nibbled her lip.

His gaze softened, hovering about her mouth. "Worried about me?"

She sucked in a breath as a desire to kiss him struck her in the gut like a fist. She could only nod. Suddenly, one of his hands reached out and swept a stray wisp of hair off her cheek, securing it behind her ear. But he released it before she'd sensed more than a brush of his fingertips.

"Lock the door behind me," he ordered, his voice gruff as he reached for the door handle.

That command was becoming an all-too-familiar refrain. Before she could tell him to be careful, he was gone, his door closing behind him.

Maggie watched him enter the convenience store, admiring his long strides. His muscular yet lean build was emphasized by the jeans and sport jacket he'd apparently thrown on over his plain T-shirt in his rush to get to her after her frantic call that morning. His broad shoulders flexed as he reached out to pull open one of the double-doors.

Once he disappeared inside, Maggie counted to one hundred and twenty, resisting the urge to turn and look at the white SUV he said had parked on the street. She pulled her lipstick from her purse, using it as an excuse to open the visor and aim the mirror where she could see behind her.

There. There it was.

And Ethan was there, too, crouched as he rounded the tail end of the SUV and approached the driver's door. The driver's face, though shadowed by the interior of the vehicle, was obviously turned toward the convenience store. His window was open to the still-cool morning air, and Ethan reached through, grabbed the man in the driver's seat by the collar of his shirt and yanked him toward the window until they were nose to nose. Maggie caught a glimpse of a long, thin face, and even thinner graying hair.

Straining with impatience, Maggie chewed her fresh lipstick off as she watched the altercation, breathing a sigh of relief when it seemed relatively minor. In fact, Ethan let go of the man fairly quickly and was handed something by him. He shook his head in disgust and said something in return before stepping away. Ethan stood beside the SUV, hands on his hips until the man pulled away from the curb, tires screeching as the driver performed an illegal U-turn.

Maggie flipped the visor back into place as Ethan crossed the parking lot and climbed in beside her, slamming his door.

"Reporter," he growled.

She sat, stunned and dismayed. "Already? But, how?"

He pulled out his cell phone and dialed. "Someone must have tipped them off about the unusual number of police on the university campus." He held up a hand as someone picked up on the line. "Damian. We've got media attention. Channel Ten." He listened a moment. "Okay."

"Well?" Maggie asked, trying to hide her impatience as he hung up.

"He'll have someone check the guy out and handle Channel Ten, if that's really where he works." He pulled out of the parking lot and back onto the street. "We're meeting at SSAM at three. I assume he'll fill us in then. And the university president plans to call a press conference in the morning, in conjunction with the police commissioner." He grimaced. "Prepare yourself. It's all about to go public."

She sighed and sank into her seat. "It was bound to happen." It wasn't as if she hadn't been through all of this before, after Brad had died. Reporters had followed her for weeks, popping up in the most unexpected places. She rolled her neck on her tense shoulders. "Taking some time to relax before the news breaks is a good idea."

"I was hoping you'd say that."

"I'll take you up on that nap you promised me," she added, fascinated by the way his green eyes darkened.

She ripped her gaze from his. She would be napping alone. If she could sleep at all. After what Fearmonger had done, she wasn't sure she wanted to close her eyes anytime soon. But if more pleasant things would fill her dreams, such as thoughts of the way Ethan had held her... Well, she wouldn't be getting much sleep in that case, either.

As they pulled into a pleasant little complex comprised of two-story condominiums, Maggie turned her attention to the outside world. Ethan maneuvered the car so that the front faced the end of the driveway, pointing toward the road. Just in case, she supposed, they had to make a fast getaway. Thoughtful of him. But it also reminded her of their dire circumstances.

He opened her door for her and escorted her into his home with a hand at the small of her back, his eyes everywhere at once. Did he think the killer could have followed them here?

Her anxiety must have shown in her facial expression be-cause he pulled her against his side, his hand moving to her shoulder. His thumb absently stroked her collarbone at the edge of her shirt, sending delicious shivers down her spine.

"I'm just being careful," he said. "He's not out there. I'd know it."

"It's not much," he said wryly, his hands on his hips as he watched her survey the general living area of his two-bedroom condo. He'd never had to worry about what a woman would think before. Since he'd moved here from D.C., he hadn't dated much. But his mother had shaken her head when she'd seen his "bachelor pad," as she'd re-ferred to it.

Maggie spun in a slow circle, taking in the open floor plan that revealed the living room as well as the dining room and kitchen. At least it was clean. But there wasn't much in the way of decoration or personality. He'd just never cared. Since the incident in the Secret Service three years ago, he hadn't cared deeply about anything. Now, he was surprised at how much her opinion mattered.

"Stop," he muttered under his breath, angry with the di-rection his thoughts had taken. His duty was to keep her safe, not to please her. But an instant image of just how he'd like to please her took hold in his mind and he forced himself to walk past her into the kitchen. Food. It was too early for the brats and beer he'd promised her, but he could forage for some breakfast.

"Hungry?" he asked, ignoring the jolt of electricity the word sent through him. She shook her head, and he nar-rowed his eyes on her, noting the signs of fatigue. "You should be. You've been up most of the night and you haven't had breakfast."

"Neither of us has."

"Right. And I, for one, am hungry." For more than just food, he thought, disgusted with himself. The woman had been through so much in the past thirty-six hours. And it wasn't over. Not nearly.

He hadn't told Damian because Maggie had been listening to the call, but the reporter he'd cornered had recognized her, and not just from her radio show. He'd mentioned the death of her brother. If the media learned she'd acquired another stalker, *they'd* be stalking her, too. And she didn't need that kind of added frustration.

Ethan wished she weren't involved. But hell, then he wouldn't have met her. And since he'd laid eyes on her scrubbing the foul red letters from her walls and playing a wicked air guitar, he'd felt a warmth stirring within him that dispelled the chill of the past few years.

"Or maybe you'd like to rest first," he said as she stifled a yawn.

"I doubt I'd be able to sleep."

"Breakfast it is, then." Jerking the refrigerator door open, he frowned at the meager contents. "Looks like juice and toast, unless you want brats for breakfast."

"Typical bachelor, huh?" She laughed, the soft sound flowing over him like a caress.

His chest tightened. "You should do that more often."

Her eyes sparkled like honeycomb in the sun. "What? Tease my host?"

"Laugh." He turned his back on her look of surprise and slipped two slices of bread into the toaster. "Why don't you go find something on TV? I'll bring the food when it's ready."

Relieved when he heard her moving into the living room and putting distance between them, he shook his head at himself. He was flirting with a client. She should be off-limits. He didn't need the distraction while he was trying to protect her. And, other than a protector, he was no good to anybody, certainly not as a boyfriend. Women like her deserved better. Hell, all she'd had in her life the past few years, from what he'd learned, was pain. Like Damian had said, she deserved everything good from life.

Which left him out of the picture.

And yet, part of him yearned for more. Yearned for a warm, willing woman to come home to. Someone who could help him forget the mistakes of the past.

He pulled the jug of orange juice from the fridge and located two glasses and plates in the cupboard. The act of making breakfast for Maggie was strangely intimate. He found he liked the feeling.

Don't get used to it, a voice warned him.

But he could. He easily could.

SEVEN

THE FINGERPRINT IDENTIFICATION required Ethan to place his entire right hand on the pad before receiving clearance. Only then would they be granted access to the lobby of the Society for the Study of the Aberrant Mind. Maggie had known about Damian's organization for years but, as the heavy metal door swung open, she realized she'd never really understood the dangers to him or his employees.

"Just a precaution," Ethan assured her as he led her into the inner sanctum. "We've never had any lunatics show up to take us out."

"Safety first," she agreed, curious to see what, or who, the state-of-the-art security system protected. Food and a brief nap on Ethan's couch had revived her. Or maybe it had been the dream she'd been having when he gently shook her awake. In her sleep, Ethan had finally kissed her—a deep, searing kiss that had branded her soul. Whether it was the bit of rest or the shot of adrenaline that had accompanied the imaginary kiss, she was feeling restless, ready to do whatever she could to find Sharon's killer.

The SSAM offices occupied most of the top floor of a five-story building near downtown, seemingly innocuous from the outside. But then, what should a sanctuary for those who hunted serial killers look like? Certainly not a normal building with glass windows and doors.

A cave, maybe. An underground lair. After all, the FBI's

Behavioral Analysis Unit was located six stories underground.

And Damian Manchester's name was uttered with the same sense of reverence and mystique as a superhero's, like Batman's, so why not have a secret hideaway? Nobody seemed to know much about him. He was a private individual.

As they crossed a small lobby with marble floors and a comfortable seating area, a tall woman with wavy strawberry-blond hair rose from behind a counter. "You must be Dr. Levine," she said with a smile. "I'm Catherine." She scowled at Ethan. "And you—we'll talk later."

The secretary signed her in, handed her a security badge and directed them toward another heavy metal door where Ethan subjected his right palm to another security scan. The door swung shut behind them with a thud, and he led Maggie down a long hallway comprised of exquisite artwork and numerous offices—all of them locked up tight. However, this time the locks required an ordinary key to bypass. Still, she almost jogged to keep up with Ethan's long strides. She'd hate to get lost in here without Ethan's security access. She might never get out again.

"What was that about back there?" Maggie asked.

He pinched the bridge of his nose. "I'm guessing Catherine's mad about how I treated Becca. They're best friends."

"Ah. And where *is* Becca today?"

He sighed as he pulled out a key and unlocked a door on the right, gesturing for her to enter. His office was as neat and sterile as his condo had been. Not a drop of personality. But then, she wasn't one to judge. After her brother's murder, she'd rid her own house of family photographs and the little personal touches that made it a home. The reminders of how close her family had been before Brad's death had just been too much for her to face every day.

"She should be at the meeting," he said. "And I'll have to apologize."

"I think that's a fine idea."

Ethan arched a brow at her, but Maggie quickly changed the subject. How he dealt with his coworkers was his business. Still, she'd come to like spunky Becca and wanted to help her if she could.

"Was working for the Secret Service anything like this?" she asked, trailing her fingers over a top-of-the-line computer. Even she could see that the Society's employees had anything and everything they needed to get the job done. She wondered if Damian was proud of what he'd accomplished. But then, until he caught the man who'd killed his daughter and left her in a cold, shallow grave in the middle of nowhere, he wouldn't be satisfied.

Ethan's chuckle brought her back to the present. "No. Damian likes to have the latest and greatest in technology. It's the second-best perk of working here."

"What's the first?"

His grin held no amusement. "Putting the worst of the worst offenders away for good."

"Must be very satisfying."

"It is."

Maggie sensed there was more to his story. Just what made Ethan's eyes deepen with pain when he thought about serious offenders? It was more than just normal human interest. It was personal.

"Ah, good, Cathcrine told me you'd arrived." Damian Manchester entered Ethan's office, his pewter gaze drifting over her face, searching for evidence of harm. He looked tired, as if he hadn't slept in days.

"Safe and sound," she assured him. "Thanks to Ethan."

"Yes, I heard about the reporter who followed you." He

turned to Ethan. "Good work getting rid of him. I'm glad it wasn't more serious."

"Did you talk to your contact at Channel Ten?" Ethan asked.

Damian nodded. "They'll keep things quiet, provided their team gets a front-row seat at the university president's press conference tomorrow. We're definitely not going to be able to keep this quiet anymore. Now that they've seen Maggie at the crime scene, and once they connect the dots to the strange caller she's had on her show recently, they'll be swarming like gnats."

"It had to happen sooner or later," she said with a sigh.

"Did you call your parents?"

Guilt jabbed at her. "Not yet. I will, though."

"They need to know, especially if reporters are on to the story." He laid a supportive hand on her arm, squeezed gently and let it fall before turning toward the hallway. "The others are already waiting in the conference room."

This time, at least half of the dozen seats around the large conference table were occupied by SSAM team members and Noah and Maria. An unsmiling Becca sat across the room, doodling something on a sheet of paper and studiously avoiding Ethan's gaze. Damian sat at the head of the table, next to a man who had to be the president of Chicago Great Lakes University. His cut-off-your-air necktie and old suit were too careful a mix of stuffy upper management and rumpled academic to be anything else.

Maggie took the empty chair next to the man, with Lorena on her other side. She was much too far away from Ethan for his liking. Still, it gave him the opportunity to observe her from a distance. She'd tied her hair into a loose twist at the back of her head, leaving a few soft wisps springing free, catching the light and reflecting gold and fiery red. It mirrored her personality— all that restrained fire and passion.

But from several seats away, he couldn't smell her skin. He was fairly certain his house, particularly his couch after her nap there, would smell of her light, tantalizing scent. Something floral. Sunflowers? Maybe. He had no clue how he would even know what sunflowers smelled like, but they brought to mind all things golden and warm and bright. Like Maggie. Yeah, sunflowers probably smelled like Maggie Levine.

Damian cleared his throat and all attention immediately turned to him. "I'd like to introduce the president of CGLU, Mark Bellingham." Damian motioned to the man beside him. "He is, of course, as concerned as the rest of us about what's been happening to Maggie, and we need to decide on the best course of action for her and for the university following Fearmonger's actions."

Ethan knew the best course of action. His hands tightening slowly around the monster's neck.

"You might want to let up, man," Noah leaned toward Ethan to whisper. In response to his glare, Noah looked pointedly at Ethan's fist, which was clenched so tightly around his pen, his knuckles were white. "If you don't, we'll have ink everywhere. I, for one, don't want to ruin my suit."

Ethan forced himself to loosen his grip. He wasn't normally that open with his emotions. The Secret Service had taught him how to be stoic and unobtrusive. How to be nothing more than a shadow. Apparently, he was sliding even further away from his training than he'd thought.

President Bellingham took Damian's lead. "I appreciate what you all are doing to find the murderer. I'm grateful that you're taking care of Dr. Levine as well." He paused. "However, it is my job to do what's in the best interest of the university and its students. That has to be my number one priority. After discussing options with Damian, I'm planning a news conference tomorrow morning at the university."

"And what, exactly, are you planning to say?" Maria asked. "You'll have to run it by us, too. This is, technically, still our investigation."

"I just talked to the police commissioner," Damian explained. "He'll be speaking with you about it after this meeting. Dr. Bellingham's only going to give the basics—that a young woman, a student, was found murdered in a classroom over the holiday break. And that the authorities are doing everything they can to track him down."

Bellingham interrupted. "I'm hoping open honesty will help calm some of the parents' and students' fears. I don't want a panic on our hands, and if they find out this may be a serial killer at work, well, I'm afraid that's exactly what will happen."

"*Is* a serial killer," Lorena corrected. "I don't have any doubt."

"Could be a copycat," Maria pointed out. "We can't rule that out. Besides, aren't there enough differences between the murders a decade ago and Sharon Moss that it could be two different killers? The previous murder victims, for instance, still had their noses."

Ethan caught Maggie's wince.

"A trophy?" Noah asked. Becca's eyes widened at that suggestion.

"Or part of the torture," Maria suggested. "Maybe a statement about her sticking her nose in where it didn't belong?"

"They haven't found the nose," Lorena countered. "That's more consistent with keeping a memento of the kill. Are we sure he didn't keep anything from the previous victims?"

Now Maggie looked downright pale. Sharon had been a friend of hers, and these people were talking about her as if she were just some nameless victim. Just as Ethan was about to suggest the profiler and detectives adjourn to another room to discuss the fascinating subject of dismembered body parts, Damian spoke up.

"Continue to work the profile tonight," Damian told Lorena, turning back to the table at large and changing the subject, saving Maggie from the more horrific details. "In the meantime, we'll pursue this as if it is the same serial killer. Noah and Maria have agreed to keep us in the Chicago PD loop, as long as we return the favor—which, of course, we will. Open communication between the Society and the police will only help us catch this guy quicker."

"I guess that's my cue," Noah said at a nod from Damian. "Preliminary findings at the CGLU crime scene yielded no fingerprints. None. Not on the flat surfaces, not in the blood."

"What little blood there was," Maria interrupted. "There was some blood at the scene, but there's a lot of blood missing. He had to have known how to drain and collect it."

"A funeral director, maybe?" Lorena asked, her sculpted brows coming together.

"It's on our list. But he also had to be wearing gloves."

"Fibers?"

"Nothing yet, but both our criminalists and yours are still looking through the evidence collected. Fearmonger was very cautious, so they don't think they'll find much." Maria's mouth turned downward in a frown of frustration.

"Time of death?" Lorena asked.

"Time of death coincides with the time Dr. Levine received the call from the killer."

"Have they given any details about body positioning, tools used, things like that?" Damian asked. "It would be helpful in determining for certain whether we're dealing with a copycat or the original killer."

"As to that," Lorena added, looking down the table to

Noah and Maria, "if you can let us know what facts of the Fearmonger murders ten years ago were actually given or leaked to the press and public, we can see if this guy is a copycat or the real deal."

"Of course." Noah made a note on the pad of paper in front of him. "We're reviewing the Fearmonger files now. We're also investigating Sharon Moss, trying to determine how he got her to the psychology building. It's on our to-do list."

"You haven't had much time," Maggie said, sympathy in her voice.

"The first forty-eight hours after a murder are critical," Damian said, his tone unforgiving. "Many traces of evidence are lost in that time period. Be assured," he said, turning to Bellingham, "that the crime scene was processed as thoroughly and carefully as possible. I only employ the best."

"So what I want to know," Maggie said, flushing slightly as all attention turned to her, "is where has this guy, if he is Fearmonger, been for the past ten years? Why would he suddenly start killing again now? Or has he been killing all along and we didn't know it?"

Lorena nodded, her approval clear in her eyes. "Good questions, and ones I'm looking into. I'm contacting some of my old FBI colleagues to see if there are any other unsolved murders with similar attributes. The killer's fingerprint, so to speak."

Like *fear* written all over a wall in bright red blood, Ethan thought. Jesus, he couldn't let Maggie go back to her place with this psycho out there. He'd been at the scene in her psychology classroom. She hadn't. But he had no doubt she'd recognized Sharon's murder for what it was—a symbol that Fearmonger was getting closer to her. "Murdering" *her* vicariously. Trying to scare her as much as possible before he performed the final act.

"Something wrong?" his employer asked, his eyebrows arched in question.

"No, sir," Ethan replied, gritting his teeth. "Just wondering where I fit in here. I assume you still want Maggie protected."

Damian nodded. "Until this perpetrator is caught. You and Becca are still on that. In fact, I want Becca to stay at Maggie's at night. And I'll have someone from communications put a tap on her phone, in case he calls again."

Ethan's reply was a curt nod, though he wanted to object. He wouldn't put Becca through that in front of everyone, however, no matter what his doubts about her experience were. He'd just speak with her privately.

"You won't even know I'm there," Becca told Maggie with a smile, which was returned.

"Well, not quite," Damian interrupted, glancing at Bellingham. "Mark has agreed to let you go undercover as a student in Maggie's classroom."

"Sweet." Becca had apparently recovered her good humor as Damian heaped responsibility on her. "Psych 101. Always wanted to take that."

"We were going to move the class to another room," Damian continued, "but we thought perhaps the killer would return to the scene."

Ethan sat forward. "So you're going to set Maggie up as bait? Not on my watch."

"I'll never be completely safe until they catch this guy," Maggie said softly, the gentle look in her eyes calming him.

Man, she must be some therapist, if she could connect with people with just a look. And one stalker had killed her trust in mankind. Now another could kill *her*. Not to mention what she'd been through when, at such a young and impressionable age, her best friend was murdered. She could have come out so differently. She could have curled into a ball in the corner of a padded room for the rest of her life.

And yet she held it together.

But even as he thought that, one of her trembling hands moved to her breastbone and absently rubbed. His eyes narrowed. He'd seen that before. But her words drew his attention away.

"I'll agree to anything to catch this guy before someone else dies."

"And Becca will be there," Noah pointed out, "and we'll have an extra Chicago PD officer patrolling campus whenever Dr. Levine's scheduled to have class."

"Well, I feel so much better now," Ethan muttered. He blew out a breath. "Okay," he said, knowing he wouldn't win this argument, "but there's no way in hell she's going to the press conference."

Maggie's eyes widened. "Was that an option?"

"No way. In hell. Not under my supervision."

"We already decided the press conference was too risky," Damian said. "But sometimes serial killers return to the scene of the crime, or to the victim's grave. Which is why we decided to leave Maggie's class in that classroom. We have technicians working through the night to get it back in order."

"That'll piss him off," Maggie said. "Erasing his *lesson* and carrying on as if it wasn't important." Just like she'd done at her house, scrubbing her living room walls. Had she done it to piss off Fearmonger?

"Which is exactly my point," Ethan ground out. "You'll be in more danger if he becomes enraged."

"He's already escalating in his behavior," Lorena pointed out. "Dr. Levine's already in danger."

"And maybe he'll mess up." Damian's cool, steel-gray

eyes met Ethan's narrowed ones. "I won't take any unnecessary risks with Maggie's welfare."

"What about the radio station?" Becca asked, raising her hand.

Damian smiled at her naive gesture, which served to break the tension that was building. "It's an open forum, Becca, feel free to speak up whenever. And as for the radio station, you'll be following her there, too. But Marconi has canceled tonight's broadcast. They're going to replay a tape of an old show."

Lorena nodded her approval. "With this guy's increased activity of late, especially if he is Fearmonger and has had a ten-year hiatus, I'm almost positive he'll contact you again, Maggie. Soon. And if we take you off the air for a night, he'll be champing at the bit to contact you next time he has the opportunity."

"I'll be prepared." Maggie's chin tipped slightly upward in defiance.

"As will I," Becca added from across the table.

"First," Damian told Becca, "I called ahead to the state mental health center where Deborah Frame is being held. I want you to pay them a visit and see what you can find. Ethan will stay with Maggie until you get back."

"Ethan," Damian said, finally focusing on him. "Turns out a couple of parking lot cameras were working. You and Maggie will review the security tapes. See if you come across anybody she recognizes or anything out of the ordinary."

Hours of tedious work, yet somehow he was looking forward to it. He would be spending time alone with Maggie.

Looking for her stalker, a voice reminded him. How romantic.

As the group scattered to their various assignments, Maggie retraced her steps to Ethan's office in search of some privacy. Having seen him occupied with Becca in the conference room, she figured he wouldn't mind if she borrowed it for a short time. Thankfully, he'd left the door unlocked.

Fiddling with her cell phone, she flopped it from one hand to the other as she tried to dream up what she could possibly say to allay her parents' fears.

Hey, Mom. I don't want you to worry, but you know that break-in at my house? Well, it seems I've picked up another one of those pesky stalkers. Oh, and it may be on the news tomorrow morning. They're not entirely sure, though, that he's a serial killer. Well, he's killed one woman, and he may have killed several others, but there's no reason to jump to conclusions.

Yeah, like that was going to go over smooth as buttercream icing.

Before she could delay any longer, she dialed their number and chewed her bottom lip.

"It's about time you checked in," her mother's voice said upon connection. Had she already heard?

"What?"

Her mother laughed, the warm sound soothing some of the tension of the day. Oh, how Maggie had missed seeing them, and speaking to them, more regularly.

"Now don't be mad," Nancy Levine said, "but Agatha told me she saw a man at your house early this morning. I believe her description of him was 'a handsome devil.' And you still owe me an explanation of the break-in. Your dad and I are about ready to drive down to the city to check on you. We'd already talked about dropping in on July Fourth, anyway, because, well…" Her mother's voice trailed off.

The anniversary of Brad's death. And wouldn't that have been perfect? Her parents walking into her living room to find the walls covered in blood.

Or worse, they could have been at the house while Fearmonger was there. The very thought sent a chill coursing through her.

Maybe telling them all the details wouldn't be the right thing. They'd just insist on coming to stay with her. They'd want to see for themselves that she was okay, especially after last time.

"Mom, I'm fine."

"Liar." The word was whispered over her shoulder into her unoccupied ear. She spun to see that Ethan had entered the office behind her and was now dropping some papers on his desk. He turned to leave again but stopped next to her as he passed, examining her face a moment as she listened to her mom talk about what was new with them.

"Tell her," he whispered against her free ear. "She deserves to know. For her own safety." Delightful shivers cascaded down her spine, but she forced herself to listen to his words.

He was right. She was being selfish. Her parents needed to know that this freak was targeting her, and possibly people around her. Fearmonger was obsessed with teaching her about fear—which was utterly ridiculous, since she understood the emotion all too well.

She gave Ethan a nod. He turned to leave, closing the door behind him to give her privacy.

Sucking in a deep breath, she blew it out slowly before diving in headfirst. "Mom, there's a problem. It's one of the reasons I'm calling."

Her mother's monologue instantly ceased and her tone changed to one of concern. "What's wrong? Are you okay?"

Maggie could have kicked herself for causing worry, but then Ethan's words resounded in her mind. She had to warn them. "I'm safe now, but…" Better to spill it all at once. "There's something you should know."

"Hang on. This sounds serious. Let me get your dad on

the other line." Several interminable seconds passed and she heard her father pick up, probably in his office, where he'd moved his downsized accounting business upon "retirement" from a larger firm.

"Maggie, honey. It's good to hear from you."

He says that now, but...

"Hi, Daddy. I have some bad news." Her voice cracked. She almost broke down then. How much more pain would she bring to their lives?

"We're listening," he said after a pause.

"There's this man." God, did she sound like she was fourteen and crying to her parents or what? *There's this boy at school, and he's picking on me...*

She took another deep breath to steady her voice, which had suddenly frozen up along with the air in her lungs.

"What has he done?" Her mild-mannered father sounded angry. And she hadn't even told him what had happened. "Agatha told your mother there was a man at your house. Did he hurt you?"

"No, not him. There's a...a stalker."

"Deborah Frame? I thought she was locked away. Surely someone would have told us if she'd gotten out."

"She's still in the state hospital. No, it's someone else."

"A different stalker? God almighty." Her father's exclamation was muttered, but it stabbed her through the heart. He didn't deserve to deal with this in his retirement. He should be bouncing grandbabies on his knee. She made a mental note to give Julia a little push on that objective. Her sister was more likely to be successful in finding a normal, stable relationship than Maggie ever was.

"I've got Damian here," she told her parents, knowing his name would conjure thoughts of competence and security. Nancy and Walter Levine had once been friendly with Sam's parents, Priscilla and Damian Manchester, who'd lived just down the street. What the Manchesters had endured had shaken the whole community. It had shaken Damian and Priscilla so much that they'd divorced and each had moved away. "He's helping find this guy. And Ethan—he's the guy Agatha must have seen at my house—he works for Damian and used to be in the Secret Service. He's protecting me."

"That's good, at least," her mother said. "The Secret Service protects government officials, so he should know what he's doing. And Damian would understand how this stalker thinks."

As much as anyone can understand such craziness. As a psychiatrist, she knew there were reasons for such deviant behavior. But understanding on an academic level was different than being an actual target.

"We're coming down there." Her father was adamant.

"No, really—"

"Don't argue. We're your parents. We've earned the right to protect you."

"I'm a grown woman." Who sounded like a stubborn child.

"But we'll always be your parents," her mother said. "Please," she added, her voice dropping. "We need to feel like we're helping."

An image of Damian tortured by the pain of being unable to help his child came to Maggie. Would her parents feel the same if something happened to her? Undoubtedly. She'd seen how they'd clung to each other when Brad had been killed.

Her mother was still talking. "If nothing else, we need to be nearby. We can stay at Julia's."

Half an hour away. Would that be far enough to protect them? It had to be, because Maggie knew they wouldn't give up. "Okay. But you'll have to clear it with her."

"So we can't stay with you?"

"He's been to my house, despite the alarm system." There

was a heavy silence. "I won't be staying there, either," she added impulsively, hoping to smother their objections. She'd talk to Becca about finding somewhere else to stay, or stay at her place anyway and chalk up the white lie to protecting her parents.

Her mother breathed a sigh of relief. "Okay. Have you told Julia yet?"

"No."

"Want us to?"

Maggie rubbed her forehead, the beginnings of a massive headache coming on. She tried to roll her shoulders back to loosen the tight muscles of her back and neck. "Yeah, could you? Tell her I'll talk to her tomorrow."

"Better yet, let's have lunch. We'll be down there by morning."

Maggie blew out a frustrated breath. "Can't. I have classes to teach most of the day."

"Dinner, then. I'll call you with where."

"Sure. Whatever. Just let me know." It was easier to give in when she knew it was pointless to argue. But she didn't hang up. She had to tell them everything and they hadn't heard the worst yet.

"What is it, Magpie?" her dad asked.

Maggie smiled. *Magpie,* a throwback to her childhood, when she used to chatter up a storm. She'd give anything to be that carefree again.

"There's going to be a press conference from the university tomorrow. You'll hear more about this guy who's stalking me." She paused to muster her courage. They'd likely hear something before she saw them tomorrow. Or there might even be reporters hounding them. It was her duty to prepare them. "They think this stalker may be a serial killer named Fearmonger. I don't know if they'll reveal that much yet. They're trying not to cause a panic. Just in case, I thought you should hear it from me."

"Serial killer?" Her mother's question was quiet, but Maggie could hear the tears in the words. She closed her eyes and gave them the worst.

"I just want you to be prepared in any event. They think the guy who broke into my house—while I wasn't there," she hastily assured them, "killed a woman last night. She was a wonderful young woman."

"You *knew* her? And you're just telling us about all of this *now?*" her mother said, incredulous. She was nearly sobbing now. "We could have helped you through this. Don't you trust us?"

"It's not that, I just…"

"I have to go," her mother interrupted with a hiccup. "I'm too upset right now. We'll talk about this tomorrow night at dinner."

Oh, *that* would be lovely, Maggie thought, already dreading their dinner together. Her mother hung up her phone.

"Dad?" Maggie asked, her own voice thick.

"Still here, honey." Still steady as ever. She ached to wrap her arms around him. "Your mother's just worried about you."

"I know." Exactly what she didn't want. "Just, please, tell her I have a round-the-clock bodyguard." Whose focus and determination was unmatched in this world. "Two, actually," she amended as she remembered Becca. "I'll be safe."

"I'll tell her. And—" he hesitated "—tell Damian thank-you. It should be me there, but…" There was another pause. "I know he's more experienced in this kind of…thing," he finished awkwardly.

"I will," Maggie agreed. "And would you please watch out for each other?"

"Always."

She stared at the silent phone in her hand and wished she could call them back, tell them they'd found the maniac and he was dead. He could never hurt anyone ever again. But wishing would get her nowhere.

A soft knock at the door sounded before Ethan opened it enough to stick his head in. "Everything okay?" Ethan. His office. Right.

Maggie squared her shoulders and tried for a laugh, which came off more like a croak. "Define *okay*." She shook her head. "I can't believe I'm complaining about my situation when a woman lost her life last night because of me." She met Ethan's gaze. "We have to stop this guy."

He came forward and put his hands on her upper arms, rubbing them in a soothing manner. "We will. And we're going to start by looking through those security tapes, at least until Becca returns from the mental health center. Then she'll take you home and stay with you."

That still left hours with just her and Ethan. She felt ashamed, but Maggie had hoped Becca could be a shield between her and Ethan's comforting touches. Touches that sent shivers of longing over her skin.

"I…" She looked down, suddenly sheepish. "I don't want to go home tonight." His hands stilled their movement as something hot and predatory flashed in his eyes. "Do you think I could stay at Becca's?" she hastily added. "Or a motel?"

"We'll arrange something," he agreed with a curt nod. His hands dropped away and he took a step back. Whatever heat had been there a moment before was gone.

EIGHT

FEARMONGER HID A GRIN as the shed door swung open. He'd been waiting over an hour for this rendezvous. The afternoon heat was almost intolerable in the confined space, but it would all be worth it.

"Owen?" a hesitant whisper called.

"Here."

Deborah Frame's wild eyes, lit by the sunlight that poured through the shed door into the dark interior, darted toward the corner where he sat. He rocked forward so that all four legs of the wooden chair were flat on the ground.

"Hi, Deborah. I see you followed my instructions."

Her gaze scanned what she could see of the dim ten-by-ten shed he'd selected for their meeting. Seeing they were alone, her shoulders dropped and she stepped inside, pulling the rusty corrugated tin door closed behind her with a bang that made her jump.

"Sorry."

He shrugged. "No problem. You're the one on the run from the law."

"Where's Maggie? You said you'd take me to her. She's not still mad, is she?" She nibbled her bottom lip, and Fearmonger hid his disgust as she almost chewed one long, oily strand of blondish hair. Rather, it would be blond if it had been washed in a couple days. But then, she'd just broken out of a mental hospital and traveled two miles by foot in the afternoon heat.

He'd found a guard who could be bought. Nurtured a business relationship with her until she'd given him what he needed. It had been incredibly easy, actually—almost as if fate had ordained it. He'd followed the guard for weeks, learning her routine, then approached her at a bar and chatted her up. Confirmed what his surveillance had already told him, that she could use his money and wasn't overly particular about loyalty and scruples and such, especially with the economy hitting so hard. His coming from a family with money had come in handy in gaining access to Maggie's worst nightmare.

No, not her worst nightmare, he corrected with a grin. *He* was Maggie's worst nightmare. She just didn't fully realize it yet. "Are you ready for your lesson?"

Deborah's eyes darted around again. "This isn't a trap, is it? I mean, why would you help me with this?"

He chuckled. "If it is a trap, it's too late now, right?" He stood and went forward a few steps, extending his right hand and injecting a large dose of awe into his expression. "And I wouldn't do that to you. I'm a fan. Remember? I told you everything in my letters. I had to pay good money to get those letters to you. I care about Maggie as much as you do. Why else would I go to so much trouble? Together, we'll make Maggie understand."

Hesitantly, she put her hand in his, and he tried not to grimace at the sweat and grit he felt on her skin. After all, she'd made his job that much easier. She'd come to him. Yeah, he'd made it possible by cultivating their "relationship" over the past few months. And by giving her the means and directions to escape. But she'd trusted him enough to follow through. He'd reward his pupil by making this quick.

"I still don't understand." She removed her hand from his and ran it over her hair as if suddenly self-conscious. "Everyone hates me for what happened with Dr. Levine. You said in the letters that you know her?"

He nodded and tucked his hands into his jean pockets in an unthreatening way. "I do."

"Then why…?"

"Why would I show you compassion? Understanding?" God, she was eating this crap up. He could see the way her face softened as he explained. "I know what it's like to want something, or someone, so much that you do crazy things."

She scowled. "I'm not crazy. Is that what Maggie thinks? I have to explain everything to her. Make her understand. You said you'd take me to her."

"You'll see her soon enough. But you're going to have to wait just a little bit longer."

"When? Where do I get to see her? Why would she want to see me? She hasn't contacted me since…" Her throat worked.

"I'm going to send you somewhere, and you'll be free." His hand was out of his pocket within seconds, a knife glinting in the low light. He spun around behind Deborah, locking an arm at her throat as he brought the knife up with the other, holding the point to the pulsing artery exposed there.

She thrashed and bucked, but he tightened his grip until she passed out. He let her fall to the ground and stepped over her to the duffel bag under the chair. He pulled a roll of duct tape out and taped her wrists together behind her back, so tight that she moaned in her unconsciousness. Bending in front of her, he moved to strap her ankles together. Before he realized she'd regained consciousness, her other ankle swung out and kicked him in the arm.

"Moron," he muttered, slapping her so hard that her neck made a popping noise that echoed in the shed. But it was his father's voice he heard in his head.

Moron. Should have seen that coming, you idiot. Didn't

*move fast enough. Never do. Lazy piece of shit. Can't even
get through school. Always flunking out of your courses.
How could I ever leave the business to you? Over my dead
body.*

"Go to hell!" a frightened Deborah Frame yelled. For a
moment, he was confused. His father had a woman's voice?

But then the face became that of his mother—the rich
bitch, trophy wife that she was, tottering around in ridiculous
three-inch heels with drink in hand. Her nose was crinkled
in disgust—or at least as much as it could be. It had seen
the knife of more than one plastic surgeon. Her face barely
registered any emotion at all anymore. It didn't matter. Her
words dripped enough venom to convey her hate.

*You're worthless. You'll never fill your father's shoes.
Even after his stroke, he's more man than you'll ever be.*
Her voice, even in his head, was like nails on a chalkboard.

"Stop it!" he yelled, slapping his hands over his ears.

Then the only thing he heard was the rasping of Deborah's breath as she struggled to control her fear. He could
already see understanding dawning in her eyes. Pathetic,
really. Snot slid down to her upper lip as she started pleading for her life. Repulsive. And this woman had thought
she deserved a spotlight in Maggie's world. Granted, she'd
succeeded in scaring Maggie—and *that* he would have paid
good money to see.

Well, he would show Maggie who deserved her. *He* was
her teacher. Her master. Her conscience.

This was his gift to her.

He smiled and raised his knife. "Time for class."

NINE

"COULD YOU REPEAT THAT, please?" Damian rubbed his forehead. The team had dispersed hours ago, but he'd waited at the SSAM offices, hoping for good news. This call wasn't it.

"Deborah Frame escaped from the state hospital." Becca sounded distracted by the background noises. He could hear people arguing and someone shouting orders. Deborah's disappearance had obviously thrown things into an uproar.

"How could she have escaped? She must have had help." There couldn't be two separate stalkers after Maggie at the same time. That would be too much of a coincidence. Damian's gut told him Fearmonger, who seemed to get off on making power plays in Maggie's life, had a hand in this.

"My contact at the hospital won't say, exactly. They're embarrassed and are covering things up as well as they can. They're afraid what will happen when the press gets hold of this."

He'd double the protection on Maggie until her stalker was behind locked doors again. "What's being done to find her?"

"They already have."

"What?"

"The trail was pretty simple. A Cub Scout could have followed it." Becca's tone indicated disgust.

"So she's back in custody?" Damian felt his chest relax as he released the breath he'd been holding.

"Not exactly. Deborah Frame is dead. They found her

body a couple of miles from the hospital in a rusty old shed on an abandoned property."

"How'd she die?" But he already knew. In his sixty-two years, he'd learned there were no coincidences in life.

"Death by serial killer."

"Fearmonger."

Becca made a sound of agreement. "Has to be, and it was pretty brutal, though he didn't use his usual MO."

"No words in blood?"

"Actually, there were. Just not the words you'd think. He smeared *For Maggie* across the woman's abdomen."

Damian wiped a hand over his tired face. He refused to give in to fatigue. He would sleep when he was dead. In the meantime, he had monsters to catch.

"He probably thinks he's invincible about now," Becca said. "Not only getting away with murder, but also success-fully breaking a woman out of a locked, guarded facility? That takes some major planning and skill. Yeah, he's got to be feeling pretty confident."

Which was both dangerous and fortunate. He'd probably continue killing at this new accelerated rate, but maybe, just maybe, he'd get sloppy and make a mistake.

Her butt was cold. And numb. The folding metal chairs at the university's security office were unforgiving.

Maggie rubbed the back of her neck, dutifully keeping her eyes on the TV screen on the table in front of her, though she had to fight to keep her mind on the task at hand. Her thoughts kept wandering back to the call Ethan had received from Damian. Fearmonger had claimed another victim. Somehow Deborah Frame had broken out of the state hos-pital to meet up with him. Fearmonger had done his home-work, learning of Deborah's connection to her. Was nobody safe? Despite the warm night, she shivered.

"Need a break?" Ethan asked, watching his own video screen beside her.

"We're almost done, right?"

"Yeah."

It was getting late and they were both tired, but between the two of them, they'd managed to get through Tuesday night and early Wednesday morning's videos of not just the psych building's parking lot, but of a couple others nearby. Despite gritty eyes and a need to review her lesson plans for her morning classes, Maggie was determined to do her part. At least Marconi was going to replay a recording of an old show, so she and David had the night off from the radio station.

"I can hang in there."

Twenty minutes later, Ethan sat back with a sound of disgust. "Nothing. You?"

She switched off the screen in front of her. It showed the parking lot outside the psych building, with a nearly clear view of the sidewalk leading into the door nearest the classroom. "Nothing but a couple of mischievous raccoons doing some Dumpster diving."

Ethan's screen showed the other side of the building. There had been no footage of the inside.

"I don't get it." Ethan stretched his shoulders and back so that his plain white T-shirt pulled tight across his chest, hinting at the finely sculpted lines underneath. The window-unit air conditioner in the trailer that served as a security office was on the fritz, so the temp in their tiny quarters—more like a supply closet, really—was warm. Ethan had long ago discarded the dress shirt and tie he'd worn for the meeting.

He rubbed his stubbled jaw. "They both had to enter—and he had to leave—by some means. I just don't get it. There's something we're missing."

He shifted forward, leaning his forearms on the table.

His T-shirt rode up a little higher on his biceps as they bulged with the movement. The man really should wear short sleeves more often, especially in the heat of summer.

"T-shirts!" she exclaimed.

"Beg your pardon?"

"Your T-shirt—it reminded me of summer."

"Yeah?" The doubtful look he gave her was not encouraging.

She quickly explained. "It made me think of seasons. In winter, it gets bitterly cold here."

"And?" The doubt was still there, but he was going with her, willing to see where she was headed.

"And I've heard students grumbling about how they wished the tunnels between buildings on campus were still open, to avoid going outside."

Ethan sat up straight. "There are tunnels?"

"Well, maybe," she said, backpedaling. "It could all be legend, I suppose."

He lunged forward and hugged her. She was suddenly engulfed by his warm male scent, his sinewy strength pressed against her curves. He pulled away, grinning. "You're amazing."

"Well, don't get too excited yet." *Unless you'll wrap your arms around me again. If you'll do that again, by all means, get excited.* "From what I've heard, if they exist, they've been locked for years, maybe decades. I don't know if anyone has access."

Ethan was already rising from his chair. He went to the door and stuck his head out, calling to the chief security officer on duty. The short, balding man was growing a paunch but his eyes were sharp. He'd introduced himself as Officer Archie Lewis.

"Do you have video footage of the tunnels or their openings?" Ethan asked.

Officer Lewis huffed out a laugh. "No. Waste of time. Haven't used them in thirty years, except for some maintenance upgrades back in the nineties."

"But they do exist?"

"Oh yeah. The builders thought the tunnels would provide easy access for maintenance issues, as well as a way for students to get between buildings on cold, windy days." He scratched at his chin. "Unfortunately, vagrants decided to move in during the winter months, and students didn't feel safe anymore. A couple kids got stuck in one of the old supply rooms down there, too. Took a day to find them. Damn waste, if you ask me, but they shut the things down."

"Do you have maps," Maggie asked, "of where the tunnels come and go? Specifically, the ones that connect to the psychology building."

He nodded, grinning. "That, I do."

A few minutes later, Ethan and Maggie had purchased a couple sodas from a machine in the hallway. While indulging in a much-needed caffeine and sugar rush, they cleared a table in the tiny break room, where they could roll out the dusty blueprints of the tunnels beneath the school.

"Wow," Maggie breathed, aware of just how close Ethan leaned next to her. The hint of salty sweat that dampened his skin had her licking her lips. "That's quite a labyrinth."

"Most of the tunnels are blocked off at their openings." Ethan tapped a finger on one of the marked doors that had an *X* scrawled in black over it. "Locked or permanently sealed?"

"Not sure about all of them," Officer Lewis replied with a shake of his head. "But I'd guess most of them are just locked. We have a set of keys for them somewhere around here. Locked 'em for the students' safety, but a lot of the buildings' pipes run through those tunnels, so I doubt they'd permanently seal them."

"Can you find those keys?"

"Sure thing." Lewis left to search.

"Well, they sure wouldn't want students getting lost in this maze." She glanced at Ethan's profile, so intent on the labyrinth spread out on the table. "What are you thinking?"

"That our guy might just work at the university. He had to get a key to these doors somehow. And it would explain better why Fearmonger seems so attached to you. You spend most of your days and nights here." He put a finger against his lips as the chief returned. Maggie understood. He wouldn't want the man thinking they suspected someone within their ranks. Officer Lewis's accommodating attitude just might take a turn for the worse.

"Found them." Lewis held up a ring containing several keys.

"Thanks." Ethan took the keys. He didn't say anything more and the officer took the hint, leaving them.

"What do we do now?" she asked once they were alone again.

"I'm taking you to your place to check on Sigmund and get whatever you need, then to Becca's for the night. She said she'd be done at the state hospital soon and would meet us at her place."

"And you?" She suppressed a shiver at the thought he would no longer be with her. Not that she didn't trust Becca's capabilities, but just being near Ethan made her feel safer—at least physically. Emotional safety was a whole other issue, and one she didn't want to explore.

"I'll get some rest, too." But he kept surveying the maps.

"Bullshit. You're going to go down in those tunnels. By yourself. At night."

Her curse brought a ghost of a smile to his lips. "Did you just say 'bullshit'?"

She put a hand on her hip. "I did. It's something my family says. Whenever someone is, you know, *bullshitting* one of us. We don't let each other get away with it."

He grabbed her then and tugged her close, his warm lips hovering for just a second before she leaned into him, meeting his hesitant mouth with her eager one. She got the feeling he'd surprised himself by initiating their embrace, but he quickly recovered, deepening the kiss as he slanted his mouth to claim her. His passion, once unleashed, built in urgency and demanded a response, and she didn't hesitate to give him one. Her fingers gripped his shoulders, digging in and not letting him retreat.

This was what she'd wanted for the past two days, and it was worth the wait.

Delicious sensations swarmed over her as he groaned and wrapped his arms even tighter around her. She lost herself in the moment. In the heat. *Oh God, the heat.* And she'd thought the room was hot. This was downright combustible.

After a long moment, his lips left hers with obvious reluctance, but he didn't move far. His breath fanned her burning cheeks. "I shouldn't have done that."

She pulled out of his embrace. "Just what every girl loves to hear."

He grimaced. "Shit. That didn't come out right." He caught her back to him when she tried to step away. "I just meant, with everything you've been through this week, now's not the time to…"

She said the first thing that came to mind. "Combust."

His smile was back. "Yeah," he agreed softly. With a brush of his thumb over her lips, he pulled away and started collecting the maps, rolling them up again. He was clearly avoiding further discussion, but she wouldn't let him back away.

"So why did you?"

He paused in his actions, but didn't meet her gaze. "Kiss

you? Because I had to. You're so damn sweet." He heaved out a breath. "Nobody except my mother has worried about my welfare in a long time. It's…seductive."

She snorted. "You're comparing me to your *mother?* At a time like this?" Her surprise erupted into laughter and she pushed her fingers to her mouth as he scowled at her.

"I meant…" He looked so flustered that she quickly sobered.

"I know what you meant. And I'm sorry I laughed."

"I'm not very good at this."

"Kissing?" She gaped. "You're kidding, right? Because that was incredible."

He gave a lopsided grin. "Yeah, it was. But what I meant is…" He blew out a breath. He was clearly struggling to find the right words to describe his feelings. And that was the sweetest, most touching thing she'd ever seen from a man. "I'm not very good at letting my guard down."

But if he could be vulnerable with her, wasn't that the ultimate sign of trust? And that endeared him to her all the more. "You can trust me with your feelings."

"But that's just it. I don't want you to care about me."

She ached to reach out to him, to touch him, to make him turn and look at her. But he was throwing up caution signals everywhere, so she held still.

"And when this is over," she said, "if I get through this, then what?"

His jaw hardened. "There is no 'if' about this. You will be safe. That's my priority. *You're* my priority."

"Well, now that *is* what a girl likes to hear. But I don't want to hear you're going down into those tunnels alone. Fearmonger seems to be everywhere."

"If it'll get you to Becca's for some rest, I'll call in another agent to go with me. I promise to wait for them to arrive before I go in."

She could see the idea didn't please him.

"And, of course, I can call Noah and Maria to come over, if they're not too busy."

"At—" she glanced at the clock on the wall "—ten o'clock at night?"

"This case is everyone's priority."

"Man, oh, man," Noah muttered, peering into the darkness of the tunnel opening Ethan had selected as a starting point. "We need some megawatt flashlights."

That and a semiautomatic weapon *might* make Ethan feel less creepy about the black void that gaped before them. At least Maggie had agreed to let him drop her off at Becca's, so she was safely away from whatever he'd find in here. And his gut told him he would find something. Besides, whenever Maggie was around, his attention was inevitably on her.

He shouldn't have kissed her. Even now, his mind was on her sunflower scent and the softness of her lips under his as he'd taken what he'd wanted for days now. It had taken some serious refocusing to get his attention off the searing heat of that kiss.

While he'd waited, as promised, for Noah to arrive as backup, Ethan had pored over the tunnel maps again, asking Officer Lewis for recommendations on which ones went to the building where Sharon had been murdered. A tunnel that connected the basement of a dorm to the basement of the psych building was chosen as a starting point for their search. This particular dorm was mostly empty in the summer, with only a dozen or so students staying there, a couple of floors above the entrance to the tunnel. An ideal place to blend in or sneak around.

Lewis moved forward and handed Noah another flashlight. "I'll wait here for you guys. This tunnel hasn't been opened in decades. Feel free to scare away the spiders on your way through."

"Let's get to work." Ethan took a step into the tunnel. Somewhere nearby, something dripped, plopping against the cold concrete floor or one of the mossy pipes that ran down the tunnel. Cool air that could only come from underground in July whispered across his cheek like a caress.

Noah shook his head. "This is like some bad movie. Late at night, all alone, no power—why is there no power again? Oh, right, because we're stuck in some scary movie."

"No," Ethan said, "because they can't find the transformer until morning, when the university grounds manager gets here. I don't want to wait that long. The first day of the second summer-school session starts in a few hours and I'd like to figure out if Fearmonger was even down here, and whether we need to round up a crime-scene team first thing in the morning, before some student decides to try to stumble through here and ruin any…" Ethan's voice drifted off as Noah turned on his double beams of flashlights.

"Holy mother," Noah whispered, his tone reverent. "Looks like your guess was accurate."

The beams were effective, illuminating the next fifty feet or so until fading to darkness. Deep red glistened where light struck the concrete walls.

"Shit," Ethan muttered.

"Yeah." Noah moved forward so that his lights swung deeper into the tunnel. The red continued. Big. Small. Cursive. Block. The word was repeated from ceiling to floor, all the way down the tunnel, as far as they could see.

Fear.

"Definitely the work of Fearmonger." Ethan kept his voice low. He doubted the guy had stuck around, but one never knew.

Noah swung one beam toward the walls as the other lit

their way down the tunnel. But they didn't move forward. Instead, they backed out of the tunnel as Ethan dialed Damian's number. It was close to midnight but his boss answered on the first ring. Ethan suspected the man never slept.

Perhaps what he saw when he closed his eyes was just too much.

"What have you got, Ethan?"

"The killer used the tunnels."

"You know this for sure?" The excitement of the hunt colored Damian's words, infusing new life.

"The walls of the tunnel we opened are covered in blood, used to write *fear,* like at Maggie's place. Noah and I don't want to go any farther and risk destroying evidence." But gathering trace evidence in the filthy tunnel would be next to impossible, other than verifying that the blood was Sharon's, which Ethan didn't doubt. Or maybe they'd luck out and find a footprint. But this guy had been so careful, there was little chance that luck would be on their side.

"Have campus security monitor the entrance," Damian ordered. "Then go home and get some rest. I want you to have a clear head when the crime-scene team gets there in a few hours."

"Is Maggie safe?"

"Becca checked in a little while ago. They're set up at her place for the night. Sigmund's a little restless at being uprooted from his home, but everyone's safe."

The trace of humor surprised Ethan. He breathed a sigh of relief.

Damn, he wished he could be there with her. When he'd told her the news about Deborah Frame, she'd gone pale as chalk. She'd recovered quickly, but he knew she had to be thinking about it, maybe even having nightmares about it. And he wanted to be the one to comfort her. *An excuse to wrap her in his arms again?* Maybe, he conceded. He was quickly losing ground in his efforts to remain objective where she was concerned.

"Go home and get some rest."

"Yeah." He'd try, but he had a feeling Maggie's pale face would haunt him.

He hung up and joined Noah and Officer Lewis, who looked grim. "I need someone to guard this entrance until we can process the scene. And if you have the manpower—"

"I'll get it," Lewis said, his jaw set.

"Good. Have your people examine the other tunnel entrances for possible points of entry, but they can't go in. Make sure the access points are locked and secure. I don't know if this guy's used the other tunnels, and we don't want any students wandering into them. Who knows if he might be hiding out in one."

TEN

As Maggie concluded her eight o'clock class the next morning, she wiped the brand-new whiteboard clean. They'd replaced the old one. She didn't think she'd have been able to write on the same surface the killer had marked with Sharon's blood. Gone was the police tape that had sealed off the classroom. In fact, everything looked just as it should. As if a monster had never been there.

But he had. And Sharon was still dead.

She glanced at her cell phone, frowning when it noted no new calls. David, who had to be crushed by Sharon's death, still hadn't called her back. And she hadn't heard from Ethan yet. She hated to admit that she was missing his company.

Becca bounced up to her at the front of the classroom in jeans and a T-shirt proclaiming the logo of a local band as other students filed out. She'd recovered her confidence after Damian had placed Maggie in her care last night, but Maggie knew Ethan's approval would still mean the world to the young woman. "Great class."

Despite her somber mood, one side of Maggie's mouth quirked up in amusement. "You were listening?"

Becca nodded, the dangly, star-shaped earrings she wore today jingling at her ears. "Freud was a nutcase, wasn't he?"

Maggie smiled at that, a full-blown smile that lifted some of the heaviness around her heart. "Some scholars think so. However, he's certainly done a lot for the study of psychology."

"I mean, all that talk about sexuality. That's a seriously repressed man right there."

Maggie nodded a greeting to a passing student, the last of nearly a hundred to leave before she and Becca were alone. Once the lecture hall was clear, Becca straightened up. "Seriously, though, I was watching and nobody seemed suspicious."

Maggie sighed in...what? Frustration? Relief? She didn't know anymore.

"I was thinking the same thing. But then, Intro to Psych is usually full of the younger crowd. My afternoon class, Abnormal Psychology, is an upper-level course and tends to have older students." And her stalker could easily be masked among them.

"Whoa. Abnormal, huh? That's like sending an engraved invitation."

Maggie nibbled at her bottom lip. "You know, I was thinking. Maybe I should offer a special lecture about fear. Give a couple days' notice first. Maybe he'll show up."

Becca began shaking her head at the word *offer.* "Absolutely not. Ethan already reamed me for letting you try to lure this guy out before. What do you think will happen if you do that again, but out in public? Absolutely not," she added again for good measure.

"It was just a thought. I hate not doing anything. You all have your assignments, but I'm just bait."

Becca winced. "It's not like that."

"It feels like that."

Becca grabbed her book and notebook, which Maggie had actually seen her writing in during the lecture, and headed to the door. Maggie followed. "For both our sakes, let's hope not. I want to prove myself, but I'm not willing to present myself on a platter." Her voice dropped as they neared students. "I'll be behind you, but within shouting distance as you cross the quad. If you need me, holler. Once you're safe in the president's office, you'll stay there until Ethan comes to get you."

"Bait," Maggie muttered again.

"This guy is nuts." Officer Lewis's tone held a bit of awe as he stood with Noah at the entrance to the tunnel. "I hope you know how to track him. We sure as hell have never had anything like this here. And I've been here twenty years."

Noah nodded and gave the man what he wanted. An out. "We'll take it from here."

At the subtle cue, Lewis left and the CPD's crime-scene team, along with Sandy on behalf of SSAM, moved ahead into the tunnel to capture what evidence they could. One person swabbed blood samples as another snapped photographs, the light from the flash glinting off the long walls like bottled lightning.

Before Noah and Ethan could follow, however, they caught sight of Damian making his way across the empty basement. His face was taut. "Good work, finding these tunnels," he told Ethan.

"Maggie deserves the credit for that, sir."

His eyes narrowed. "She didn't…"

"*See* the tunnels? No."

Thank God for that, Noah thought. She'd had enough to deal with in her living room. This was ten times as much. The stench of dried blood, mildew and decades of dampness was nauseating even to someone who'd seen, and smelled, worse things.

And Noah had seen what she'd dealt with a year ago. Her brother, murdered in front of her. Because of some woman's obsession with her. How much could one person take?

Beside him, Ethan looked like he was ready and willing to go to battle against Fearmonger single-handedly. But not

just because it was his job. Noah had the distinct impression
Ethan would fight to the death for Maggie, if someone could
just point out who he was supposed to fight.

Damian nodded. "Good. She's been through enough."

"She's teaching?" Noah asked.

Damian checked his watch. "She should be in the president's office by now. Her first class is over, Becca reported
nothing unusual, and Bellingham and the commissioner are
about to start the press conference."

"She won't be a part of that, though." In his peripheral
vision, Noah saw Ethan gritting his teeth. The man's interest in Dr. Levine couldn't be any more obvious if he'd
worn a neon sign on his head that blinked *I've fallen for the
Voice of Reason*.

"No. She's to remain in the office until her next class.
But Becca has to leave. I want her to get back to the other
murder scene, where Deborah Frame was found."

"Part of her education, sir?" Ethan asked, clearly not excited at the prospect.

"She needs to know what she's getting into," Damian
answered. "*All* of it."

"I agree."

"Noah has things handled here. You go take care of Maggie."

Noah hid a grin as Ethan took off at a sprint down the
dorm hallway. "He could at least try to hide his enthusiasm."

Damian's gaze followed his SSAM agent's hasty retreat.
"Why bother? Life's too short."

Maggie sat in a high-backed chair in the university president's plush office, nibbling on her thumbnail as she waited
for Bellingham's face to fill the screen of the television.
The room was large enough to seat a small gathering, with
a podium just like the classrooms had, sitting in the corner,

waiting for just such an event. But an announcement of this magnitude clearly required a larger setting, and they'd set up in the quad, hoping to beat the midday heat.

Ethan sat forward in the matching chair opposite her in front of the president's desk, elbows on his knees as he waited. He had more patience than she did, apparently.

She forced her thumbnail away from her mouth in disgust. She couldn't help but worry that the conference might push Fearmonger to do something else. To kill someone else. To set off a wave of alarm that would ripple across the university.

Amidst the shining sun in the middle of campus, the university president took the podium. The police commissioner positioned himself behind him. As President Bellingham spoke, a merciful breeze lifted a lock of white hair from his forehead. The lines on his face and the set of his jaw showed the stress he'd been under for the past twenty-four hours.

"Thank you for coming," he said in a voice heavy with sincerity and exhaustion. "It is with great sadness that I confirm that a violent crime was committed on our campus this week. A young woman was murdered."

A reporter raised his hand and Bellingham acknowledged him. "Can you release her name? Was she a student? Faculty?"

"Her name is Sharon Moss and, yes, she was a third-year communications student on our campus. She will be sorely missed."

"What does that mean for university operations?" the reporter asked.

"Our numbers here on campus are greatly reduced during the summer terms and we are operating as normal. No classes have been canceled, but there will be a candlelight vigil this weekend to honor Sharon. We'll provide that information as we get it."

"Brilliant," Ethan said. "That might lure Fearmonger out. He's been so vocal that he might not be able to resist the opportunity to see the results of the chaos he's started."

"Is it true the woman was a victim of Fearmonger?" a female reporter asked. A murmur went through the crowd.

"Holy hell," Ethan muttered, standing up abruptly and swiping a hand across the back of his neck. "We didn't expect them to pick up on that tidbit so fast."

"Maybe they didn't."

Ethan swung his gaze from the screen to her. "What?"

"Maybe Fearmonger leaked it. He obviously likes attention. He's proven that by calling in to my show and provoking people on numerous occasions."

Ethan tipped his head to the side. "Makes sense. He wants the notoriety."

Maggie nodded. "Not to mention he gets some kind of power trip from making people fear him."

On the television, Bellingham was addressing the question. "We don't know *who* did this, or why. I stress that to our parents and students. We are doing everything we can, cooperating with the police to find the killer and bring him or her to justice. This campus has always prided itself on its safety record, and we will remain vigilant and watchful until the perpetrator is caught. But I stress that this is an isolated incident, and no further violence will be tolerated. I ask that students be careful, but don't let fear override common sense."

And wasn't that just a challenge thrown in the face of the killer, Maggie thought, feeling sick to her stomach.

From the shade of an old elm tree, across the quad from the media circus, Fearmonger stood among a cluster of other students and watched the show. He couldn't help grinning to himself.

"A serial killer, here on campus?" a pretty blonde to his right said to her friend. She shuddered. *Actually shuddered.* His smile widened, his eyes crinkling behind his shades. "I'm going to get an apartment off campus."

As if that would keep her safe. He almost laughed aloud.

"Can you afford it?" her friend asked.

"Are you kidding? My parents will do anything to make sure I'm safe. They'll be worried."

"Mine, too," the plain brunette said, clutching a three-ring binder to her chest.

He felt the familiar rush of power—the power that pushed him from a plain nobody into bigger-than-life Fearmonger. From someone these girls would normally overlook into someone to be reckoned with. Owen had been interesting and scholarly, but Fearmonger was so much more. Fearmonger was someone who could show these girls what fear really was. What it tasted and smelled like. How it felt.

But these girls were already afraid. The body and mind he really longed to instruct belonged to Dr. Margaret Levine. She thought she knew everything, but he had a few things to teach her. He knew Maggie was on campus. She'd taught her morning class and had another one in a couple hours. He knew her schedule better than she did, and that she had three different routes home, to avoid someone learning her routine.

He wouldn't risk approaching her. Not yet, anyway. Sometime soon, though.

What he wouldn't give to have seen her reaction. The police had found Deborah Frame's broken, carved body sooner than he'd expected. He'd cut her heart out and left it in the dirt on the floor of that abandoned shed. After all, that had been Deborah's greatest fear—that Maggie would take her heart and stomp all over it. It lacked a certain finesse he strived for, but he'd been limited by time and resources.

He ached to take credit for it. But then, he told himself,

Maggie already knew it was him. He would get credit. One day he would claim her gratitude in person.

For now, he'd be content to continue their lessons. Apparently, a murder in her classroom hadn't hit close enough to home. He'd just have to up the ante. Find something that would lure her away from her safety zone and force her to acknowledge his superiority.

Something more personal.

Sharon and Deborah hadn't hit close enough to home.

First, though, Maggie should be receiving his little gift…

Maggie let out a gasp as Ethan yanked her aside, intercepting the messenger who'd walked into her psych classroom. The room was empty of students as class wasn't due to begin for another twenty minutes. She'd asked him to let her leave the president's office early to prepare her notes. Truthfully, she'd felt stifled there.

"It's for a Dr. Maggie Levine." The young man looked like he could barely be in college himself. "I just need someone to sign for it."

When Ethan didn't move, Maggie stepped forward. "I'll—"

"Don't," Ethan ordered and she stopped in her tracks. Ethan continued to stare down the boy, who shuffled his feet. "What company do you work for?" The boy told him, pointing at the cap on his head that said the same. Ethan jerked his head toward the desk at the front of the classroom, indicating the messenger should set the bouquet of flowers down there. He took the clipboard with the paper that required a signature. "Sit."

He sat in a chair in the first row, his blue eyes wide with confusion as Ethan made a call from his cell phone. Maggie tried a tentative, calming smile, but the messenger wasn't looking. Who knew what a homicidal maniac looked like, anyway? For all she knew, the boy could be Fearmonger—which would have made him all of eight years old at the time of the initial murders. *Ridiculous.*

"Take pity on him, Ethan," she said, trying to peek at the flowers, an arrangement of white lilies, without touching them. What, did he think they would explode? He grabbed her outstretched wrist with a shake of his head and she pulled away.

"I'm calling to check on a messenger of yours," he said into the phone. "And a delivery. For Dr. Levine. Can you tell me who they're from?" His lips tightened at the response. "I know I can check the card. I'm not certain I want to open it until I know… Okay. Thanks." A moment later, his gaze met Maggie's. "Deborah. I see."

Maggie drew in a sharp breath. The flowers were from an admirer, all right. Had Deborah sent them before meeting up with Fearmonger? If so, how? Deborah's body had been found within a few miles of the mental hospital.

She reached out to check the card. Ethan took her wrist to stop her from touching it. "Any credit card receipt? Cash? Okay. Maybe a description of the person who purchased them?"

"I can help you there," the messenger said, his Adam's apple bobbing as he swallowed under Ethan's glare. Ethan ended his call and turned all of his attention on the boy.

"How can *you* help?" Ethan growled.

The boy's chin shot forward in defense. "I took the order when it came in. It came by phone. Woman's voice." He looked toward the floor. "I think."

"You think?" Ethan advanced a step.

Maggie stepped forward and knelt by the messenger. "What did she say?"

"Just asked for a traditional funeral bouquet and said the money would be delivered, along with the card to be included." The kid shrugged, suddenly looking ten years old as he hunched his shoulders. "I just did my job. But the voice sounded a little off—like when a guy impersonates a woman, you know?"

"Who delivered the money and note?"

"A kid. I remember I was surprised to see him, since he's from our neighborhood, but he just said some guy paid him to drop it off."

Maggie paled. Fearmonger was involving kids now? Why not? He'd obviously felt no compunction about preying on a mentally ill person like Deborah. The flowers weren't from her, but her name was used. Surely, that had to be part of his message. Her heart pounded against her breastbone, and she forced herself to breathe regularly.

"What's this kid's name?" Ethan growled.

Maggie smiled encouragingly to the messenger, glancing at his name tag. "Todd, we're just trying to figure out a little mystery." He returned her smile with a wobbly one of his own. "I promise the kid won't get in trouble. He didn't do anything wrong."

"Kenny," Todd blurted out. "I don't know his last name, but he's always playing basketball down the street from the flower shop."

Her smile widened and he actually seemed to perk up a little. "Thanks, Todd. You've really helped us out. You can go now." On shaky legs, the kid stood, tossed one final wary glance at Ethan, then rushed out the door.

Ethan shook his head. "If you think you're touching that bouquet, you'd better think again."

"Then what do we do?"

He pulled some nitrile gloves out of his jeans pocket and reached inside the bouquet for the card that was clipped to a plastic stick. Opening it, his mouth pressed into a firm line.

He held it up for Maggie to see. Not touching it, she moved closer so she could read over his shoulder.

"'Fear me,'" she read. It was written in bold red letters. Thankfully, it appeared to be everyday red ink. Not blood. "It *is* from Fearmonger, then."

Ethan nodded. "He's written either *Fear* or *Fear me* everywhere, like in the tunnels—"

"The tunnels?"

He looked over his shoulder at her. "Sorry. I didn't mean for you to find out this way."

"It won't help to protect me. At least not from information like that." Still, her chest was beginning to hurt. "But why pretend they're from Deborah? And who's next? If he targeted her, anyone I've ever been connected to is in danger. If he's stepping things up, what's to say he won't go after my family next?"

"I'll speak to Damian about getting added protection for your family. At least they're all aware of the danger."

"Arc they?" Maggie snapped. "They don't have a clue what could really happen. Brad was different. The woman who shot him wasn't in her right mind. This guy is cold and calculating. He truly *stalks* prey and takes great joy in torturing them." Her pulse pounded, echoing in her ears.

"From everything I've seen and heard, your family loves you. They want to help."

Maggie turned away. God, she was going to lose it. She could feel the weight crushing her chest. She was starting to feel light-headed as her breath came in shorter and shorter gasps.

"Wait, what's this?" Ethan, who seemed oblivious to her mounting anxiety, had turned the small card over. "'Rest easy, Red.' What the hell does that mean? Maggie?"

She was losing control. She lunged for the door, only to feel Ethan's steely arms come around her from behind. She tried to pry his grip loose with her fingers, but he held on tight. *God, I have to get out of here.*

"You can't go." His voice came from right next to her ear. At the sound of it, she stopped clawing at him. "We don't know if he's out there, just waiting to upset you enough to go off on your own." He turned her in his arms to face him, his brow wrinkling in concern. "What is it? What's wrong?"

"P-panic," she tried to say.

"Panic attack?" He sat her in a chair. "Don't move. I'll be right back." He raced out the door and returned a second later with a paper bag with the logo of a nearby fast-food place on it. "I snagged it from a kid in the quad." At his insistence, she breathed in and out of it. It smelled like she was breathing in oily French fries with every breath, but it slowed the hyperventilation.

"You'll be okay." Sitting down beside her, he pulled her into his lap, soothing her with long strokes along her back and crooning nonsense until her racing heart slowed and she regained control of her breathing.

She lay with her head against his chest, listening to the steady beat of his heart as her world righted itself. The recovery period had been easier, faster this time. Because of him? Probably, but that didn't stop the flush of embarrassment that spread over her neck and cheeks.

Expecting a demand for an explanation or a barrage of questions, she was surprised when he continued to rub her back in long, lazy circles as he spoke. Somewhere along the way, he'd managed to peel off his gloves, and his fingers were warm and strong through her shirt.

He kept his voice quiet and soothing. "One time, when I was guarding the vice president's family—" she realized with a jolt that he meant *the* vice president, but had little energy to do anything more than file the fact away for later "—some crazy guy with a gun and a radical political agenda cornered us as we left a meeting. It was my first experience truly guarding someone with my life."

Long and slow, the lazy circles at her back continued. As the cadence of his voice lulled her, Maggie let herself totally relax against him. Her head lay against his shoulder, and she felt the rumble of his words. His heart thumped steadily beneath the palm she laid on his chest.

"It was the first time I saw someone get shot. One of my fellow Secret Service agents. He died. After that, every time I saw a gun, I got shaky. Took a few months before they let me guard again, but I was so young, so green at the time."

His chest moved as he took a deep breath.

"I still think of that whenever I'm out on the job. About how unexpected events can impact your world and you're never the same." He pulled back to examine her face. "You have a right to lose control once in a while. You've been through so much."

He wavered before her as her eyes filled with tears. He wasn't judging her. She was a psychiatrist. She'd told herself she shouldn't be having panic attacks. She knew deep down that wasn't true, yet she held a high double standard for herself.

"Thank you," she whispered.

As he leaned forward, she met him halfway, taking solace in the tender understanding of his kiss. His hand stopped circling her back to cup her at the nape, cradling her as she accepted what he offered. For all its softness, when he pulled back they were both panting for air.

He gave a quiet, husky laugh that fanned her face. "That's the way I like to see you breathless."

She smiled, but it was brief, quickly replaced by a frown. "I've had panic attacks since Brad's death, but they've been better lately. Until now." She gripped his shirt as she remembered. "Oh God. Deborah."

It was his turn to frown. "What? She's dead now."

"The words. On the back of the card."

Ethan's eyes narrowed on her, then back to the card where he'd dropped it on the desk when she'd had her episode. The confusion in his eyes cleared as he remembered. "'Rest easy, Red'?"

Goose bumps rose on her skin. "That's what Deborah said the day before she brought a gun to our normal session. She'd begun to see herself as my protector. She told me to rest easy. And she called me Red the day she…"

Ethan's arms were like life support as he wrapped them around her. She felt like she'd start shaking and never stop— or at least not until she broke into a thousand little pieces.

Ethan didn't know everything. Oh, he knew she'd lost someone important to her that day Deborah Frame had come to her office with a gun. But he didn't know what Deborah had done to *her* afterward. If she kept on this path with him, if she got closer to him and allowed him more intimacy with her, she'd have to share the entire story. And she wasn't sure she was ready for that.

"And now Fearmonger's taken that protector role upon himself?" Ethan said, his words a rumble against her cheek.

"I think it's his way of telling me he knows more about me than I thought. He knows about my family, about my past." He knew everything.

ELEVEN

ETHAN'S CHEST TIGHTENED as Maggie spoke to her sister, making dinner arrangements for that night when it looked like she'd rather hole up in her house and shut out the world. After she hung up the phone, he put a hand on her shoulder.

"You okay?"

"Fine," she replied, but every few seconds she pressed a hand to her breastbone.

Panic attacks. He never would have thought she suffered from them. She hid it well. Her secret vulnerability made him all the more determined to protect her.

"At least I know my family is safe." She frowned. "For the moment. And thank goodness Marconi's willing to run another recorded show tonight so I don't have to face the microphone." Or the possibility Fearmonger would call in. Ethan was feeling relieved about that, too.

His phone rang and he was relieved that the caller ID indicated Noah was finally getting back to him. "Anything?"

"Just left the state hospital," the detective replied. "They found some letters Deborah had hidden away in her mattress. Looks like Miss Frame had an unusually close relationship with a male pen pal named Owen. I'm guessing the name's not a coincidence. If his letters are any indication, he was quite the motivational speaker, encouraging her to 'break out' and embrace her desires. The guy's a real charmer."

Ethan turned toward the window, away from Maggie, who was now speaking with her parents. "Can your source get us a copy of those letters? Maybe we can lift some prints or match his handwriting or something." He'd take any lead at this point.

"Working on it."

"Any ideas how Fearmonger broke Frame out?"

"Like I said, the guy's a real charmer. He apparently has connections and some serious cash. That's how he got the letters to Deborah without anyone screening them. There's a guard missing. According to her fellow employees, she's been boasting about some extra cash flow lately."

"Bribed?"

"Sounds like it. Until we find her or check her bank statements, we won't know for sure. Last night she left her post, and no one's seen her since."

"Fearmonger has to have been working on this for a long time," Ethan said. "Which means he's holding all the cards. He's in control." And that scared the shit out of him. No way was he letting Maggie out of his sight. He was instituting a twenty-four-hour-a-day lockdown, of sorts, and too bad what anyone thought of it. "But why target Maggie at all?"

"Well, there is her radio show. She's something of a local celebrity. And she's attractive."

Right. Like any man in his right or wrong mind wouldn't want Maggie in his bed. But why obsess about teaching her about fear? She'd already been through some damn scary situations. "There has to be some connection we're overlooking. There's a reason he's toying with Maggie. Let's hope Lorena has a profile ready when we get back."

As Maggie looked over the students entering the classroom and taking their seats, she wondered for the hundredth time what a serial killer looked like. If Fearmonger were so intent on being near her, wouldn't he pull just such a stunt—enrolling in one of her classes? And Abnormal Psychology would probably be right up his alley.

Most of the students were in their early twenties, but some were older. With a medical school on campus and an outreach program designed to bring more "seasoned" adults back to college, she frequently got older students mixed into the crowd.

Her eyes found an older man, probably around forty, smiling at her. She smiled back but knew the welcome didn't quite reach her eyes.

Fearmonger would likely be around that age. By Maggie's count—and she'd done some in-depth studies of violent offenders after Deborah's attack—he would be at least in his early thirties, but could be in his forties. Probably a white male, since serial killers often stayed within their own race and ethnicity.

This man fit the rough profile she'd created.

The class was settling, looking expectantly at her. Becca was in the crowd, blending in with her jeans and T-shirt, but near the front, where she could defend Maggie if need be.

Maggie began her lecture and soon lost herself in the material. An hour and a half later, the class was filing out. There had been no incident. No need to defend herself. And Maggie was beginning to feel ridiculous. Was she on a witch hunt? But then the man who'd smiled at her earlier approached, and she felt her heart drop into her stomach.

"I'm looking forward to the class, Dr. Levine," he said, smiling as his light blue eyes surveyed her. Was he mocking her? Was he the killer? Little lines formed around his eyes as he squinted. "Is something wrong?"

Concern. The man was concerned. Surely a sociopath wouldn't—couldn't—express concern. At least not in a way she, as a trained professional, couldn't see right through. *Right?* Becca, sensing her distress, stepped forward, neatly inserting her smaller body protectively between Maggie and the student.

"I'm Becky," she said, reaching out to shake the man's hand. "Looks like we'll be in class together. And you are?"

His smile appeared genuine as he shook her hand. "Robert. It's been a while since I've been in school. Got married young. Had kids. You know how it goes." He laughed. "Well, maybe you don't. What are you, nineteen?"

"Twenty." Becca gave a disarming smile. Only Maggie knew that Becca was really several years older. "And I could use some help with all the notes I'm sure Dr. Levine will be giving us. Let me know if you hear of any study groups, will ya?"

"Sure thing. See you next class, Dr. Levine." And then he was gone. Maggie supposed she'd made the appropriate goodbye response, as he hadn't seemed concerned anymore.

"Thanks," she whispered to Becca.

"Just doin' my job, ma'am," she said, tipping her imaginary hat to Maggie. "Seriously though, I've got your back. You did fine."

"Thanks," she said again.

She wanted nothing more than to return home and sink into a bubble bath. Relaxation. She needed it desperately. She wasn't going to get it, she reminded herself. She had a dinner date with the family, and "home" was currently Becca's apartment.

At three o'clock, Damian began another SSAM meeting. Everyone appeared more fatigued. Their previous meeting had been only twenty-four hours ago, and there was one more dead body. One more person connected to Maggie had been brutally murdered.

"Deborah Frame is dead," Damian began without preamble, "and the authorities are almost certain Fearmonger is responsible, though he didn't leave his signature message behind this time." Damian's long fingers steepled under his chin as he leaned back, surveying the group before him. "He only wrote *For Maggie* this time. Nothing about fear."

"But we're certain it's Fearmonger," Ethan added. "According to the delivery Maggie received, he's basically admitted he had been in contact with her previous stalker."

"Stalking her stalker," Maria mused. "Adds a whole new dimension to the sport, doesn't it?" She grimaced with distaste.

It chilled Ethan to think that Maggie was in the middle of all of this. It had touched something deep inside him when she'd fallen apart in his arms earlier in her classroom. It had felt good to hold her. Never before had he wanted, needed, to help someone so badly. And when he'd leaned in for a kiss, hesitating as he rethought his decision, his heart had melted when she'd moved forward to claim him.

She'd tasted of sweetness. Goodness. And he wanted to taste her again.

She sat ramrod straight, quiet as midnight, next to the university president, Bellingham. What was she thinking about, with her lips pursed like that?

"Do we have a profile yet?" Damian asked Lorena.

"I do." She passed around a stack of thin folders. "I've conferred with Noah and Maria, as well as with a couple other mindhunters here at SSAM, and this is what we came up with."

Maggie opened the material with long, slender fingers. Shaky fingers. She was hiding her anxiety well from the others, and he imagined she'd had a lot of practice in the past year.

"I believe he's a white male, between the ages of thirty and forty," Lorena said, highlighting the pertinent details from her report. "Probably drives a nondescript, well-maintained car or van. A model with a big trunk or plenty of room in the back, away from windows. When we reviewed the case files for Fearmonger's victims of ten years ago, they were each transported from one location where he abducted them, to the place where he tortured and killed them.

"He'll appear normal," she added. "He might even have a girlfriend or wife. He's proven he can charm women into places and situations they wouldn't normally enter. He likes being in control. He enjoys being in power, and, of course, taking the teacher role. He may even be a teacher, but in a field where he doesn't feel they appreciate his full potential. Or, he may have been rejected for a teaching job, which explains why he's obsessed with instructing others. Perhaps to prove himself. If you saw his house, it would be neat and tidy, perhaps obsessively so. His appearance is probably neat and tidy, too. He'll hold a steady job, or at the least be responsible in his work ethic."

Maggie spoke up. "So, he's an organized serial killer."

Lorena nodded, looking surprised that she knew the term. "He's highly intelligent and has shown an ability to plan, and carry out those plans over a long period of time. Very methodical. He's probably already selected, if not taken, his next victim, judging by the accelerated rate of recent behavior. Something, some kind of stress, triggered this recent period of killings."

"So why is he targeting me?"

"He has an avid interest in psychology—as evident in his rants on your show and his constant need to challenge you openly. And he's familiar with the university grounds. He may know you from some activity here on campus. Something made him latch on to you, Maggie, and it might not make sense to us. But I guarantee it makes sense to him. There are deep personal issues at play here. Perhaps family or job stressors. Something that messed with his sense of control. Something that happened about a year ago that made him focus on you and Deborah Frame."

"That was all over the news," Maggie said, looking deflated. "Everybody in this town knew what happened."

"If you think of anything that stands out from that time, let us know. It could be crucial to identifying this guy."

"What about his connection to the state hospital?" Ethan asked. "Any leads there?"

"He's a master manipulator. And he has access to money. Those are the two things we can conclude from his ability to bribe the guard for months, as well as his skill in luring Deborah Frame where he wanted her to go."

Bellingham leaned forward, his eyes narrowed. "And you got all of this stuff in the profile from what? How do we know it's accurate?"

"I'm well trained," Lorena said, her back suddenly stiff with defensiveness.

Damian claimed the president's attention. "I have the best mindhunters outside of the FBI's Behavioral Analysis Unit."

"Each crime scene is like a fingerprint," Lorena explained. "The perpetrator leaves behind clues to his behavior. From his behavior, we develop a picture of his personality. I've reviewed the files from ten years ago, and the details of the current crime scenes. Add all of that together and you get a pretty substantial pattern of behavior.

"But there's more," the mindhunter said, her midnight eyes glittering black. She met Damian's gaze. "I just heard back from my contact at the FBI this morning. There were two unsolved murders that fit Fearmonger's fingerprint during the ten years he was quiet in the Chicago area."

Damian leaned forward eagerly. "Where was he?"

"If this is the same guy, he was in Cleveland."

"What makes you think the murders are linked?" Ethan asked.

"The murders in Cleveland four years ago were definitely linked to each other. The victims were sisters, found dead together. As for linking them with the crimes here in Chicago, not only was *Fear me* written on the walls in the victims' blood, but they were drained the same way Sharon was, so that he could use the blood as, well, ink." She passed around a couple photographs.

"He wanted to prove his point about fear." Maggie was a deathly shade of white as she spoke, her eyes wide.

Ethan fought the urge to go to her. He knew she'd fall apart in his arms if he did. And she'd never forgive herself—or him—for doing it in front of the group. She had her pride. He tried to catch her eye, but she was looking at the photographs on the table in front of her. He could almost see her counting to ten, concentrating deeply on breathing in and out.

That's it. You can do it. Fight the panic. He breathed a sigh of relief as she slid the photographs toward Becca, who was next in line around the table.

"He strapped the two sisters to opposite walls and made them face each other as he tortured and killed them," Lorena explained.

"They were twins?" Maggie asked. "He's recreating his victims' worst fears."

Lorena confirmed her theory with a humorless smile. "That's the conclusion I came to, too. They had just finished a semester of school at the local community college, were renting an apartment together, and all reports say they were still, and always had been, inseparable."

"So he separated them." Maggie blew out a breath. "I should have known. He's been insisting on teaching me about fear all along, I should have known he was doing it with others."

"You, however," Lorena pointed out, "are being stalked. That's new for him. He's targeting people associated with you."

"Great, so he's adapting," Maria muttered.

"He did this fear thing with the other victims, too?" Maggie asked. "It seems like it would take time, that he'd really have to get to know his victims before he knew what they were afraid of."

Was this guy someone Maggie already knew? Ethan wondered. But then, her life had been exposed to the general public in the past year, thanks to the news media.

Lorena flipped through a large file marked *Chicago PD* and withdrew more photographs. "These are the other three crime scenes, from ten years ago, here in Chicago," she said, sliding more photographs toward Maggie. "They took place within a year of each other, each at a separate crime scene within a fifty-mile radius."

"Fifty miles is pretty big," Noah added. "So this guy is definitely able to get around."

"As you can see, the murderer wrote *Fear me* on the walls at each of these scenes. He's shortened it to *Fear* at the more recent crime scenes, but we think he was still finding his way back then. The crime scenes were a little more chaotic and—" she paused to clear her throat "—and gruesome."

"It's as if he couldn't decide how he wanted to kill them, so he did everything," Maria added.

Lorena nodded. "I think he was still discovering what gave him the biggest rush of power. That, or he didn't know his victims as well, and he tried things until he got the effect he wanted."

"What can you tell us about these victims?" Damian asked.

"All three were young women between the ages of twenty and twenty-three. All were living at home with their parents while they attended college. They were intelligent and popular with their classmates. The murder scenes were abandoned warehouses or buildings around town." Lorena looked up to survey the table. "They were places where he could make them scream without worrying about interruption or discovery."

"All of these women were linked to a university or college setting," Maggie pointed out.

"Yes," Lorena confirmed. "I assume that ties into his teacher-student fantasies."

"I appreciate your hard work," Damian told her as the room fell into silence, digesting her information. "Let us know if you come up with anything more." His gaze shifted to the detectives. "Do you have anything you'd like to add?"

Noah fielded the question. "After reviewing the old case files of the first three victims, many of the details were withheld from the press. They were told that *Fear me* was written on the walls where the victims were found—but not that it was repeated or that it was in blood. That's how the press adopted the name Fearmonger."

"It seems he liked the attention." Damian looked grim. "He kept the name. He even flaunts it."

"There also wasn't much information released about the murder weapon," Maria added. "He prefers a knife, but what's more, he uses a bowie knife. He's very particular, and the three victims were all killed with it. As was Sharon," she added. "The criminalists can confirm that now. They're still working on Deborah Frame's autopsy, but I'm guessing we'll find the same weapon was used in all five murders—seven, if you add the Cleveland murders Lorena mentioned."

"So unless our perp has an intimate knowledge of these case files—" Noah began.

"—this is no copycat," Lorena finished.

"Okay," Damian said as the table fell into silence, "let's get back out there and find this guy. Noah and Maria are investigating Sharon's murder, and now Deborah's. Lorena will continue to profile and consult with the FBI about these murders, as well as looking for other murders that may match our killer's pattern. Becca, you get your hands on these 'pen pal' letters Owen sent Deborah Frame and get them to Lorena. Maybe she'll catch something else in them. Everyone, keep your eyes open. This guy may pop up at any time. He seems more and more desperate to gain Maggie's attention." He turned his attention to Ethan. "I won't tell you how to do your job. I think you know what you need to do."

"Yes, sir." Stick to Maggie. He wouldn't let her out of his sight.

The moment everyone began to rise, Maggie headed out the door. Ethan followed, grabbing her gently by the arm and guiding her into his office, away from the ladies' room where he suspected she'd been headed.

"Let go," she bit out between gritted teeth as she tried to pull away. He only tugged harder, and she gave in, sinking into a chair in his office as he shut the door and squatted down beside her. "You must think I'm such a wimp."

He thought nothing of the sort. "I think you're brave." He took her hand, stopping her from absently rubbing her chest. "I think you're smart." He kissed the hand he held and set it gently in her lap. "And I think you're strong."

Leaning forward, he kissed her lips lightly, trying to convey comfort and confidence. With a moan, she leaned forward and opened her mouth to his, letting him in.

Her soft surrender unhinged him, and something shifted deep inside, pushing against his breastbone. Unable to keep things tender as the blood pounded through his body, he slanted his mouth against hers and took what he wanted. She seemed to need his power, his fierceness, because she responded in kind. Her tongue danced with his as her arms wrapped around his neck. She pulled him closer, deepening their contact as her breasts pressed against his chest.

His breath hitched. It was like kissing a lightning bolt—suddenly all heat and passion and electricity. He wondered if he'd ever be the same.

She moaned again, her fingers sliding into the hair at his nape and making him shiver. "More," she said against his lips, bucking her hips against him where he knelt in front of her. He sensed her need for sanity, her desire for alternate feelings to conquer the fear swarming in her head. He obliged her, stroking his hands up and down her sides, brushing his thumbs against the sides of her breasts and making her arch into him.

The urge to pull her from her chair and to the floor where he could cover her body with his and take what he wanted was nearly overpowering, but he resisted. It was too much too fast.

And there were about a dozen people on the other side of his office door, just down the hall. He clung to that thought, reining in the needs that pounded through him. Still, he continued to kiss Maggie, wanting her to be the one to end it.

When Maggie finally pulled away with a shaky smile, her lips looked deliciously plump and red. He wished they were at his place, where he could continue their passionate play. But wishing was futile.

"I don't think I've ever done that," she said in breathless wonder. She touched his face. "Lost myself. *Let* myself lose control." He saw her eyes dim at that thought and spoke quickly to cover her anxiety.

"You didn't lose control. You found it again."

Her mouth twisted wryly. "I suppose that's one way to look at it. Do you have a degree in reverse psychology?"

"Graduate level," he responded with a grin.

A knock at the door had him standing, giving her some distance as she ran a hand over her hair. He wished she'd always keep the sexy, rumpled, just-kissed look. He wanted to make it his personal mission in life.

"Sorry to interrupt," Becca said as Ethan pulled open the door. She met him with an overly bright smile that didn't match her piercing gaze, as if she knew just what had happened here.

"I don't think you're sorry at all," he muttered. No, she probably enjoyed catching him doing something he shouldn't, something he'd lectured her on.

Don't get personally involved with your job.

And after he'd given her hell for how she'd done her job, *he* was the one caught with his pants down, so to speak.

Becca summoned a smile of innocence. "I'm here to protect and serve." She looked pointedly at Maggie. "It's my job to protect against *any* threats. And I take my job very seriously."

Suddenly her smile didn't seem so sunny anymore. Ethan shifted uncomfortably from one foot to the other, like some schoolboy caught planting stink bombs in the girls' room toilets.

"Maggie, did you want to go home and change before dinner with your family?" Becca asked.

Still looking wonderfully rumpled and slightly bemused, Maggie nodded. She turned to Ethan. "You are coming tonight, right?"

"Wouldn't miss it. Becca will escort you to the restaurant. I plan to go there early to check things out." As Maggie walked past him, he touched her arm to stop her. Becca waited in the hallway, just out of earshot. He leaned forward, catching the soft sunshine scent of her hair as he staked his claim. "You're coming home with me tonight, so pack your things at Becca's."

Her gaze locked with his. He could almost see the unspoken questions winging through her head, but there was heat there, too. Ethan held his breath, waiting. Then she smiled. Maybe she'd seen the determination in his eyes, and that he would not be persuaded otherwise. But then, maybe her intelligence and psychiatric training had helped her see just how much he needed to protect her.

Needed her, period.

"Go with Becca." He nudged her toward the door. "Get some rest."

"You're going to get some rest, too, right?"

He shook his head. "I'm going to track down the florist who delivered that bouquet first. See if I can find that kid, Kenny, and get a description of our guy."

She dug in her heels. "I'm coming with you."

He started to object but saw argument would be futile. At least she'd be by his side, where he could keep a watchful eye on her. "Fine. Let's go. I'll drop you off at Becca's after."

Noah soaked up his surroundings. It was the typical college student dorm room, with the typical feminine touches of a typical young woman. Sharon Moss had apparently had a busy life and a generous heart. Textbooks from her speech and communications classes lined the desk on her side of the room. Her roommate, Mindy, sat on one of the twin-size beds, sadness in her eyes as she watched Noah and Maria sort through Sharon's things.

"What do you think you'll find?" Mindy had agreed to stick around in case they had questions.

Noah turned from the book he'd been flipping through to face the young woman. She sat cross-legged on her bed, which was identical to and directly across the room from Sharon's, hugging her pillow.

"Did you know Sharon long?" he asked.

"We have been—*had* been—" she corrected with a gulp,

"—rooming together for over a year now, since we met in sophomore year."

He tried a gentle smile and sat on the other end of Mindy's bed. "Sounds like you two were close."

She nodded, her ponytail bobbing with the movement. Her eyes were red from crying, as was the tip of her nose. "Even went to her parents' house for the holidays last December when I couldn't afford to go home." She sniffed, a ghost of a smile playing about her lips as she apparently remembered a happy time. "She was a really good friend. Her boyfriend's going to be devastated when he finds out."

"Boyfriend?" Noah caught Maria's glance from where she looked through desk drawers. They'd been wondering how Sharon had been lured or taken by Fearmonger without a trace, so late on a Tuesday night. David, another devastated friend of Sharon's, told them he'd walked her to her dorm after they got off work at a little after midnight. But sometime between one and three early Wednesday morning, Sharon had left her dorm room again. Her roommate had stayed at a friend's that night, so she couldn't provide a time frame. But they knew, because of the phone call Fearmonger had placed to Maggie, that Sharon had been killed right around four that same morning.

"She'd been seeing someone new. She was really excited about him, but I was gone the first summer-school session. Just got here last week and so I haven't met him yet.

"Does this guy have a name?"

"Christopher. That's all I know. Except that he's really built, and a little older than Sharon. I guess he worked in some job that used his muscles or something. Sharon talked about how sexy his chest was. She said he was ripped."

Maria turned on Sharon's desktop computer and waited for it to start up. "I don't suppose she has any pictures of this guy?" She examined the corkboard, to which several pictures, club brochures, and campus flyers were tacked.

"No." Mindy's brow crinkled. "You know, I thought that was a little strange, except that she'd only been dating him a few weeks."

"And he hasn't been back since her death? Hasn't tried to call or anything?"

She shook her head. "No. I thought that was a little weird, too, but maybe he's just upset. I mean, her death was on the news, so he probably heard."

Noah handed her a business card. "If you think of anything else that might be helpful, please call us." He went to look over Maria's shoulder at the computer screen. "Anything?"

She shook her head, dropping her voice so Mindy couldn't hear. "Nothing. The guy didn't send her any emails. No messages on her cell phone, either, according to the SSAM communications guy who took a look. But if her boyfriend is Fearmonger, which is a big 'if,' he'd be very careful about leaving any traces. When he called Maggie's house the night he broke in and vandalized her place, he used a pay phone across from campus."

"Still, we'll get her phone records. See if anything jumps out at us." He put his hands on his hips. "The campus seems to be a central theme here."

Maria nodded. "It certainly does, but that's probably because Maggie is a central theme and spends so much of her time on campus. Although the other victims were all college girls. Is he meeting them at college?"

"Maybe. I'll see about getting a list of registered students, professors and employees at the various schools these girls attended. See if any names coincide, or if anyone named Owen or Christopher stands out as a red flag." He glanced up at the corkboard again. A business card was nearly covered with a picture of Sharon with her friends. He carefully removed the picture to look at the card. "I think I know why he cut off her nose," he muttered to Maria. He turned back to Mindy. "Was Sharon considering plastic surgery?"

The roommate looked up in surprise. "Yes, a few months ago. She'd thought about it, but she was still comparing the pros and cons. She thought her nose was lopsided or something. I kept telling her she looked fine, but she seemed obsessed. Until she found a story about a botched job that made a woman look like a freak." She shook her head. "She didn't mention it much after that, but she was always worried about her appearance."

Noah nodded, satisfied one mystery was explained, and turned to tack the card back to the board. "So that was something she feared. Botched plastic surgery, or simply imperfection. I'll let Lorena know." He paused in the process of pushing in the tack, spying a key ring with one key and a small black square device attached hanging from another tack.

Maria followed the direction of his gaze. "Is that what I think it is?"

Noah took the key ring and turned it over in his hand. "I don't think Sharon would have much use for one of these, living here in the dorm. I think we may have just solved another little mystery."

Ethan pulled his car to the curb in front of the flower shop. Along the wall on the sidewalk were several large white buckets full of colorful bouquets. Maggie could smell their sweet scent as she got out of the car.

"Let me handle this," he said. "I didn't want you to come along in the first place."

"That makes me all warm and fuzzy inside," she said,

trailing behind him. A small bell jangled overhead as he pushed open the door.

"Can I help you?" An elderly man stepped out from behind the counter, an apron covering his jeans and polo shirt.

"I'm Ethan Townsend. I phoned earlier about a delivery for Dr. Levine."

"Didn't Todd get that to you?" The man muttered something about "new kids" under his breath.

"I got it just fine," Maggie said, stepping around Ethan with a smile. Ethan groaned, but she refused to look at him. Her mother always told her you could catch more flies with honey than vinegar. Ethan was definitely exuding more sour than sweetness lately. But then, the poor man hadn't had much sleep, either. "The arrangement was beautiful, Mr...."

"Maurice," he said, his attitude doing an abrupt about-face. He extended his hand. "Just Maurice is fine. It's a pleasure to meet you, Dr. Levine. My wife listens to your show all the time." He leaned forward as if sharing a secret. "She has bouts of insomnia."

"Thank you. Tell her I really appreciate that. My friend and I are looking for the person who sent the bouquet."

The man's furry, caterpillar-like brows slammed together. "I thought that was on the card."

She looked to Ethan, but he gave the "go-ahead" gesture with his hands that meant he would be no help. She was on her own. Well, she'd defied his orders. She'd have to deal with his grumpiness.

She faked a sheepish smile. "It seems I have a secret admirer. And I'd really like to figure out who it is."

The man chuckled. "Now that's a different story." He grinned at Ethan. "Jealous boyfriend, huh?" He moved back behind the counter, speaking again before Ethan could correct him. "Now I understand. Let me see if I have any receipts. But," he said, arching a thick brow at Ethan, "I wouldn't want to get this person in trouble. I'm sure he didn't mean any harm."

"Oh, if this person is innocent, I'm sure my, um, boyfriend will restrain himself," she said, grabbing Ethan's hand and squeezing. He squeezed back, but grumbled something under his breath.

"Here's the receipt." Maurice pulled a slip from the shoebox he'd lifted from under the counter. "But it just says 'Deborah' and she paid in cash." He scratched his chin. "I remember now. That was Kenny that came in. Kid from the neighborhood, always playing basketball on the court across the street."

"Yes, that's the name Todd mentioned. Kenny." Maggie's heart pounded, and she felt Ethan's hand squeeze hers again. She'd forgotten she was holding it. Was it possible they'd find someone who could provide a description of Fearmonger? Or had Kenny met the same fate as so many other people in this mess?

"Unusual, but if you have a secret admirer, I suppose the secrecy was to be expected." Maurice eyed Ethan. "Especially if you have a boyfriend who's built like a fighter." He chuckled again as he replaced the box under the table. "Although…a woman admirer. And a funeral bouquet. That's odd, isn't it?"

She kept her smile frozen in place. "All part of the mystery I'm trying to solve. Thank you for your help, Maurice."

"Anytime."

"And I'll say hello to your wife on my next show."

His face lit up. "That would be great. Her name's Regina."

The bell jingled again as they left the shop. Ethan pointed to the courts across the street and a little farther down. "Over there. There are some kids there now." Still holding her hand, he tugged her along behind him. The summer heat warmed her feet through her sandals as they moved across the pavement.

"Do you think Kenny's still alive?" she asked, relieved when he slowed his steps so she could walk beside him. "If he's seen Fearmonger…" She bit her lip to keep from voicing her fear.

"So far the killer's targeted females, but he's also escalated in his killing. Then again, he's not being as cautious as he once was, so maybe he let Kenny go. Or maybe he used a disguise."

Maggie hadn't thought of that. The man had disguised his voice when he called the florist's shop. Barely. For the sake of the investigation, she hoped Fearmonger hadn't thought to use a disguise, even as she hoped, for Kenny's sake, that he had.

About a dozen kids populated the basketball court that had been fashioned out of a concrete slab wedged between two buildings. The boys, who ranged from preteen to adolescence, looked up as Ethan and Maggie stepped onto the court. Suspicion had their open expressions instantly closing down.

"I'm looking for a kid named Kenny," Ethan said.

Maggie winced at the hardness in his voice. A couple of the boys looked to the side, where another boy, about twelve years old, shifted from foot to foot. She was about to step forward, presenting herself as a shield between Ethan and him when Ethan beamed a smile and walked over.

"Hey, Kenny," he said. "Saw your jump shot. Pretty good."

Some of the suspicion in Kenny's gaze lifted. "Yeah? You play?"

Ethan chuckled. "Not in a while, but I used to. Used to play with Jared Knight."

His eyes widened. "From the Bulls? No way." His voice

held a significant amount of awe as his friends gathered closer.

Ethan shrugged as if it were no big deal. "We went to the same high school. We'd play almost every afternoon, kind of like you guys do." The group clearly thought that was extraordinary—that Jared Knight had once spent his afternoons just like they did.

"Kenny, do you think I could ask you a question?"

"Sure." He wiped his sweaty forehead on his sleeve. "What about?"

"Did a man approach you recently about buying some flowers?"

His nose crinkled. "Yeah. Yesterday afternoon. Told me to go into the flower place this morning. And I did. I delivered the money like he said. I didn't do nothin' wrong."

"I didn't say you did," Ethan said, "but we need to find that man. What did he look like?"

Kenny shrugged. "About your height. White."

"Did you recognize him from your neighborhood?"

He shook his head. "No."

"He wasn't from around here," another kid said.

Ethan turned his gaze to him, squinting against the sun. "What makes you say that?"

"He had a White Sox cap on," Kenny explained, then puffed out his chest with pride. "This is Cubs territory."

Maggie laughed. Wrigley Field was just a few blocks from here. "Very clever of you guys to notice what he was wearing."

Kenny shrugged. "Around here, White Sox stuff stands out."

"Did any of you happen to notice anything else?" Ethan asked. "Hair color? Eye color?"

"Nope. He had that ball cap pulled down tight. Dark sunglasses. I couldn't see much. Just handed me the envelope and said he wanted to surprise his girlfriend. Paid me twenty bucks to help."

Ethan clapped Kenny on the back. "Thanks for your help. If the guy comes back, do me a favor and don't talk to him. Go home immediately and call this number." He handed Kenny a SSAM business card.

"Sure." He cocked his head. "Did you really know Jared Knight?"

Ethan winked. "I'll get you an autographed picture."

"You really know him?" Maggie asked in a hushed voice as they left Kenny, surrounded by a group of excited boys, on the court.

"Played ball with him almost every day of our sophomore year in high school, before he became a star." His eyes sparked with humor as they found hers. "Mom still has him over for dinner on occasion, now that he's back in town. He's just one of the boys to her."

"What if Fearmonger comes after Kenny?" she asked when they were headed back down the sidewalk and out of hearing range.

"Then we'll catch him. I'm going to have an unmarked car watching the kid's house."

"You amaze me," she said, shaking her head. "You've already thought of everything, haven't you?"

"Well, don't get too excited. I have a hunch Fearmonger's not coming back to this one. He's just trying to taunt us. He's getting too cocky to care that some kid can provide a vague physical description. He disguised himself enough that we have little to go on."

Maggie tried not to be disappointed. "At least now I know you can be nice when you want to be," she teased instead. "I was afraid you were going to shove Maurice up against the wall earlier, but with these kids…" She shook her head. "You were a different person."

As they approached his car, he aimed a thumb over his shoulder. "That, back there? That was just getting information." He opened her side of the car.

"Bullshit," she accused as he swung her door closed.

His chuckle trailed behind him as he made his way around the car.

TWELVE

"LEAVE HER ALONE," Becca murmured to Ethan as Maggie entered the restaurant ahead of them. She'd made up a reason to pull him aside, and Ethan, tired of her uncharacteristic glares, was actually relieved she'd finally decided to confront whatever was wrong between them head-on. Becca hadn't said a word while Maggie had packed what few things she had at Becca's, but something was ready to boil over.

"I beg your pardon?" Ethan unlocked his car and retrieved the lightweight sweater she'd used as an excuse to get him alone. He crossed his arms expectantly until she shrugged into the thing, obviously not needing it in the ninety-degree summer heat.

At his incredulous look, she pulled a face, looking much more like her playful self. "I get cold in restaurants."

"We haven't even gone inside yet," he ungraciously pointed out. "If you have something to say, then out with it."

Her glare returned. "I know Dr. Levine likes you."

He raised a brow at that, a ridiculously pleasant heaviness filling his stomach. "She does?"

Becca mimicked his stance. "She does."

"How do you know?"

"We were passing notes in class." She rolled her eyes. "It's the way she looks at you. She obviously finds you attractive."

More ridiculous heaviness, but this time it was in his chest. He frowned in annoyance. "So?"

"So *leave her alone,*" she repeated. "I like her. I don't want you to hurt her."

His scowl deepened. "What makes you think I'd hurt her?"

She gave him a look of disbelief. "Do you feel like you've got your act together? After shoving anyone within arm's length of you away, tell me you suddenly feel ready for a relationship. Convince me you've put your past behind you."

She'd hit him in his weak point. No, he did not feel like he had his *act* together. But recently, he'd felt like he could maybe get it together. To think only three nights ago, he'd been trying to forget his past in a dingy bar. Now, he was actually thinking about living his life. He was thinking about a future for the first time in years.

All because of Maggie?

He didn't know, but after three years in a tunnel of darkness, he'd like the opportunity to explore that bright point of light up ahead.

"It's none of your business." He turned on his heel to leave.

Becca hurried after him. "She's been through a lot, Ethan. Leave her be."

And what if he could actually be good for her? Why was that so hard for Becca to grasp?

Because maybe I wouldn't be good for her. The thought had him walking faster. Suddenly, his starched collar itched. He resisted the urge to reach up and scratch his neck.

"I won't hurt her." He said it as much for his benefit as for Becca's.

Becca shook her head, unconvinced. "I guess I'll have to take your word for it, since she's staying at your place tonight."

He stopped and held the door to the restaurant open for her. As she sailed past, she added one more thing, just to shove

the bamboo shards a little deeper under his nails. "And I'll
be staying with the two of you." She smiled sweetly. "Can
you say *pajama party?*"

Inside the dark interior of the steakhouse, Ethan waited
for his eyes to adjust. Maggie was embraced by a smaller
woman with the same rich red hair and profile. She had to
be Nancy Levine, Maggie's mother. Beside them was a smiling woman with darker hair, more brown than red, whose
features more closely resembled the man who watched from
beside Maggie. Her sister and father, he guessed, Julia and
Walter.

Becca started forward, having located the table. "See,
it's like a freezer in here."

Ethan chuckled as he followed. "You can drop the pre-
tense. Your cheeks are flushed. Just take the damn sweater
off. It's done its job. I received your message loud and clear
and I'll tread carefully. Are we okay now?"

She glanced back over her shoulder with a grin. "Yeah.
I forgive you for being a hard-ass. You can't help it." She
timed her comment to end as they arrived at the table, leaving him without an opportunity to respond. With a chuckle
of appreciation, he shook his head.

Smiling at them as they approached, Maggie introduced
them to her family. As expected, he was thoroughly assessed, both covertly and openly depending on the assessor.
Walter was less obvious than his wife, Nancy. And Julia—
well, he was surprised she didn't point a finger at the floor
and twirl it, commanding him to spin so she could inspect
the whole package.

Catching his frown, Julia grinned. "Maggie's never
brought a man to meet the family before."

"Or a bodyguard," Maggie muttered, her creamy skin
blushing beautifully as she snatched up a menu from the

table. "Make that two bodyguards," she said, adding a smile for Becca.

As dinner progressed, Ethan enjoyed watching Maggie with her family. And Becca seemed to fit right in like a third sister. The family was comfortable with Ethan, joking with him and asking about his parents and three brothers. He entertained them with a story or two of sibling rivalry. The night was relaxed, but there was ground that needed to be covered, and the arrival of coffee and dessert reminded them the evening was almost over.

"Come home," her mother said after Maggie had laughed at some story her father had just finished telling. And just like that, the mood changed.

Maggie's smile froze, then slipped. The light in her eyes dimmed. "I can't."

"We miss you."

"I miss you, too, but I can't do anything until this is over."

Nancy set down her spoon. Suddenly, nobody had the stomach to finish off the slice of cheesecake they'd opted to share. She crossed her hands in front of her like a schoolteacher about to reprimand a student. "We need each other. Now, more than ever."

"Mom." Maggie's voice broke on the word.

"You're just hurting *yourself*," Julia tossed out, her gaze boring into Maggie.

Ethan shifted in his seat. His unease at getting caught in the midst of a family squabble warred with the familiar need to protect. He wanted nothing more than to take Maggie away from here, back to his place. Where she'd be his for the evening.

Except that Becca seemed determined to tag along. She looked as uncomfortable as he felt, sitting in on a personal and private family conversation.

"No." Julia tossed her napkin onto the table in disgust.

"I take that back. You're hurting all of us. You're hurting the family." She shook off the hand her mother laid on her arm. "She needs to hear this. We've let her go off and sulk for a year now, but this family is broken. She needs to get over what's been done and move on. With us. We need each other."

"Get over it?" Maggie's temper flared. "Get over what that woman—someone I tried to *help*—did to me and Brad?"

"She's dead now."

"Yeah. But what she did stays with me. With all of us. Always."

"Because you let it. We all miss Brad, but he wouldn't want us to hold on to bitterness. I think about him every day, but I choose to focus on the good times. You only seem to remember the last instant of his life. That's not who he was."

"And what about Fearmonger? He's still out there."

"And you've got protection." Julia jerked her head toward Ethan and Becca. "You'd think, after what you've been through, you'd want to live life to the fullest. Instead, you hide away at the university and at your house, making excuses not to see us. I, for one, refuse to hide."

"That's enough," their mother intervened. "Stop it, Julia. Maggie will come back to us soon. I know it." Her gaze found Maggie's. "And when she's ready, we'll be waiting." Nancy looked up as a shadow fell across the table. "Damian. What are you doing here?"

Walter rose to shake the man's hand. "Good to see you again. Can't thank you enough for all you're doing for Maggie."

Nancy's eyes filled with tears. "No, we can't. Please," she said, waving a hand, "join us. We were just having coffee and dessert."

"Thank you," Damian said, his smile warm but not quite reaching his eyes. Something was wrong. "I think I will have a cup. But first, I need to speak to my team members." His gaze went to Ethan and Becca.

"Can't you tell us all? Please, we don't like being left in the dark."

After a moment, Damian nodded. Ethan moved over so Damian could squeeze a chair in at the table. After the waiter had brought him a cup of coffee, he got to the point.

"I don't mean to intrude on your evening." His face was drawn. "Detective Crandall called. They think Fearmonger had been targeting Sharon for weeks. He may even have been dating her."

Maggie gasped. "Poor Sharon."

Damian's tired gaze met Ethan's. "It's looking more and more like our guy's been targeting Maggie for a while now. Months. Carefully and methodically planning to hurt those around her. And we still haven't located the guard who helped Deborah escape." He turned to the rest of the group. "I think Nancy, Walter and Julia should come stay at my place for a few days. I have excellent security."

"That's a generous offer," Walter said. His wife nodded. "We'll take you up on it, especially if it makes Maggie feel better."

"It does," Maggie replied. "Thank you, Damian."

"What about you?" Julia asked.

"I can't. I don't want to bring this guy any closer to you all."

Julia clearly wasn't happy with her response, but she didn't argue. She turned to Ethan. "You won't let anything happen to my sister. Do you hear?"

"I hear. And I promise," he replied, intent on doing everything he could to protect his client. Maggie looked exhausted.

"I think I'd like to go now," Maggie said. "Even though I don't have a radio show tonight, I have class tomorrow."

Becca and Ethan rose with her as they said their goodbyes. Maggie hugged her family and whispered words of caution, urging them to be safe. Julia scowled, but returned her sister's hug.

"I'll see that they get settled in," Damian promised.

On the way to the car, Becca took the lead, leaving Ethan to walk with Maggie. Perhaps she sensed that Maggie could use an encouraging word from him. Otherwise, he had no doubt his protégé would be watching his every move.

He took Maggie's hand and squeezed. "You have a nice family."

"I know." She sighed. "I haven't appreciated them lately, I guess."

"They were a bit hard on you about separating yourself from them."

"They were honest."

"Because they love you."

She nodded. "Because they love me."

Maggie entered Ethan's home as if it were her own, feeling an immediate sense of familiarity and…comfort? Yes, she was feeling comfortable.

Well, I should. After all, I took a nap on the man's couch.

Despite the weariness that weighed on her, she smiled at the memory of waking up to find his gaze on her. Though she'd just been having an incredible dream about him and wasn't fully awake at the time, she didn't think she'd imagined the flash of heat she'd seen in his eyes before he'd quickly masked his feelings.

Becca nudged her. "You look like the cat that swallowed the canary. Want to share?"

Grinning like a loon, Maggie shook her head. "Nope."

"Well, there go my fantasies of a pajama party and sharing stories of our first kisses." Becca shrugged. "But I'll still braid your hair if you want me to."

They both laughed. Ethan came in behind them, frowning as he set down their overnight bags at their feet. "Tell me again why I'm doing all the work. And what about Sigmund? Who's taking care of him?"

"Sigmund has food and water and a clean litter box. He'll be fine for one night, and we are your guests," Becca said pertly, then linked arms with Maggie and pulled her toward the kitchen. "Let's see if the man has cookie dough in his fridge."

A moment later, Becca shot a disgusted look at Ethan as he entered the kitchen. "No cookie dough? What kind of bachelor are you?"

He reached past Becca into the open fridge and snagged a beer. "The kind that works too many long hours to bother with a grocery store."

Maggie laughed, feeling relaxed and safe with these two. She'd sensed some tension between them when they'd entered the restaurant earlier, but that seemed to have cleared. She suspected part of their friendly banter was for her benefit—to put her at ease after the stress of the day.

"How about movies?" Becca grabbed Ethan's beer and ignored his frown as she sauntered into the living room.

He reached into the fridge and grabbed a couple more, handing a bottle to Maggie.

She arched a brow. "She seems to have forgiven you."

He scoffed. "Forgiven me? For what, doing my job and making her the best she can be?"

"And for being overprotective."

"It's my job to protect you, Maggie."

"I meant *her*. You're worried about her becoming a full-fledged SSAM agent and she knows it. She's trying not to let it hurt her feelings that you don't trust her ability to do her job. After all, her job is *security.* If you don't trust her to know her job, how can you trust her to keep others safe?"

Ethan looked away. "Maybe I have been hard on her. She called me a hard-ass."

Maggie laughed but quickly sobered. "When Becca and I were talking the other night, she mentioned your past. She thought the way you acted had something to do with it, though she wouldn't say what *it* was."

He picked at the label on his bottle, avoiding her gaze. "Then she's more perceptive than I gave her credit for."

"Is it about that agent you saw die?"

"No, it's something else. Something…more."

She cocked her head. "Want to talk about it?"

He took a gulp of cold beer before replying. "No."

Maggie couldn't hide her disappointment, so she turned away. It was his right to keep his past to himself. Still, she'd felt so close to him these few days they'd had together. Something in her thirsted for more of that closeness. Somehow he'd gotten past her walls, and now she wanted to scale his.

She felt the warm, gentle pressure of his hand on her arm, turning her to face him. "When I'm ready to talk, you're the person I want to talk to, okay?"

"Okay." He'd said *when* he was ready, not *if.* She smiled. "Let's go see what Becca's into."

Becca stood in the living room, hands on her hips, surveying Ethan's meager DVD collection. "Just as I suspected. All action flicks. Don't you get enough intensity at work?"

Ethan snagged the video she'd been looking at. "Gee, guess not. Or maybe my soft and cuddly movies are in the other room, along with my assortment of teddy bears."

As Becca perused the titles, Maggie settled on the couch next to Ethan. The warm, spicy male scent of him filled her nostrils, mixed with the faint, tangy smell of beer. Tempted to lean closer, she crossed her legs under her and leaned away instead.

"Do you really have chick flicks in your bedroom?" she teased.

He arched a brow. "Wanna see?"

"No, she does not," Becca said firmly, settling on the couch between them like a good chaperone. "We're going to watch *Die Hard*."

But as the opening credits disappeared, a happy tune intruded. "Shoot. That's me," Becca muttered, shifting her hips upward so she could dig in her jeans pocket for her ringing phone. She moved to the sliding glass door as she answered, then out onto the porch to talk in privacy. Ethan paused the movie, then rose and flicked a switch to turn the porch light on for Becca.

When he came back, he sat in the middle of the couch, closer to Maggie. She reached out and took his hand, interlacing her fingers with his and effectively bringing his attention from the frozen image of Bruce Willis on the screen to her. "Thank you for being there tonight, with my family. It...helped."

His smile brought crinkles to the corners of his eyes, reminding her just how much of life this man, only a few years older than her, had seen. And endured. There were secrets behind those deep green eyes. "I liked them. And I'm glad it helped."

She thought he might have leaned in to kiss her if the back door hadn't slid open at that moment. Becca, who had apparently taken it upon herself to protect Maggie not only from serial killers and stalkers but also from big, bad Agent Ethan Townsend, would probably not like to see them cuddled together, hands entwined, on the couch.

But instead of the expected reprimand, Becca looked like a woman on a mission as she marched over to her purse.

Alarmed, Maggie asked, "What happened? What is it?" *Or, who is it? Please don't let it be another dead body.*

"Ethan, I have to go handle something. Can you manage without me?"

"What is it, Becca?" Ethan came to stand beside her, taking her arm. "You don't have a car. It's still at your place. I drove you tonight, remember?"

"Another SSAM agent is picking me up here. He'll be here any minute."

"Is that who called?" Maggie tried again. "Is it about this investigation? Please, I need to know."

Becca's distraught gaze met hers. "Yes. It's about David. I didn't want to tell you, but…" She met Ethan's gaze and something unspoken passed between them.

"Damn it, what?" Maggie's imagination was starting to run wild. "Is David dead?"

"No," Becca answered, startled. Then she sighed. "But I didn't want you running off to help him. The message our SSAM communications guy intercepted was off of your voice mail. David said he wanted to talk to you."

Confused, Maggie rubbed at the ache that was starting in the middle of her forehead. "Why wouldn't I help David? He's a friend. And I had no idea SSAM was monitoring my messages," she added as an afterthought.

Ethan took Maggie's hand and squeezed to get her attention. "What Becca's not telling you is that we don't want you running off to meet with David because he's on our suspect list."

Maggie's jaw dropped. "David? A suspect?"

"We didn't want to tell you until we were sure," Becca said. "Fearmonger would want to be near you, is familiar with campus, and it's looking more and more as if Sharon knew her killer. David fits the profile."

David? *Her* David? He'd always been so sweet and attentive. "But what about Owen? David was around when he called in. He couldn't have called in as Owen."

"He could have had an accomplice," Becca pointed out. "And he's a sound expert. He would know how to disguise voices, maybe even record them ahead of time."

Maggie shook her head, not wanting to consider the possibility. David wouldn't do such a thing. "He'd have been thirteen at the time of the other murders."

"Rare," Ethan admitted, "but not impossible. We're not saying David *is* Fearmonger. We just have to be careful until we check him out. And he's resurfacing after we lost track of him for twenty-four hours, during which two murders took place. That looks more than a little suspicious." He turned to Becca. "You'll take backup with you?"

She nodded. "Of course. I'll call David and suggest he meet me and Maggie at my apartment. Only, of course, Maggie won't be there when he arrives. I'll have backup within shouting distance just in case."

"You're not going to do anything to David, are you?" Maggie pleaded. "He's been through so much. I'm sure he's just been really upset about Sharon."

"I plan to have a nice little chat with him, to find out what's going on in his head."

"We're just keeping an eye on him," Ethan said. "And that's why I think Becca is perfect for this. He's met her and they got along. She doesn't come across as threatening. Maybe she can get him to open up." He looked to Becca, who seemed to grow taller under Ethan's words of confidence. "But don't do anything without backup."

Becca's pressed her lips into a firm line. "I know how to do my job."

"I know. I wouldn't have chosen you if I didn't think that. It's just that if he happens to be our guy, he'll do anything to lure Maggie out, including use you."

"I'll be ready for Fearmonger, whether it's David or someone else," Becca said, the tone of her voice more eager than afraid.

After Becca left with a fellow SSAM agent, Ethan checked the locks on all the doors and windows and settled next to Maggie on the couch again. "Want to watch the movie?"

She shook her head. "Somehow, I'm not in the mood to watch villains wreak havoc on helpless people."

"At least the villain is destroyed in the end, by a guy who chose not to be helpless."

"Too bad it's only the movies."

"Maggie, I've caught my fair share of bad guys. Believe it or not, the odds are against him." He rubbed a thumb across her wrist. "And if it makes you feel any better, I don't really think David is Fearmonger. We're just covering all the bases. I want you to be safe."

She gave a small smile, appreciating more than he knew the way he tried to comfort her. She laid a hand on his cheek, coarse with the beginnings of stubble. "I believe it. With you, here, I feel safe."

His jaw hardened and he pulled away. "You shouldn't get too comfortable. I'm not as safe as I seem."

Startled, she longed for him to look at her, but he seemed intent on avoiding her gaze. "What do you mean? You'd never hurt me."

A muscle in his jaw pulsed and she stared at it, mesmerized. "I'm not sure about that. I'm not sure I'm good for anybody right now. Haven't been for years."

"Why?"

He didn't respond right away, and she began to wonder if he'd answer her.

"My dad was a cop. The only thing he valued in his life was the reputation he'd earned on the job—until a bullet put him on disability. He was never the same." He'd never spoken to her of his father, she realized, but his bitter laugh told her volumes.

"I thought he'd notice me, be proud of me, if I had a career like his, in law enforcement. So that's what I pursued. But I had to be the best, the one who guarded the most important people in the country. So I went into the Secret Service."

But something had happened there. Something more than watching a colleague get gunned down.

"And my father? He never knew. He died while I was in college, just before I graduated and moved on to train for the Secret Service."

She took his hand between both of hers. "I'm so sorry."

"Yeah, well, it happens." Though he shrugged, she could see the little boy in him was still suffering. He would never see pride shining in his father's eyes.

"I was good at what I did."

She didn't comment on his choice of the word *was*.

"I protected the vice president and his family. But one time, I messed up." And once was all it took to dent this man's self-image. Because of his father, he thought he *was* his work. He was only as good as his success on the job.

"What happened?" she urged, knowing he had to be out with the bad feelings. Best to cut it out with a knife than to let the wound fester any longer.

As if he couldn't look at her, he pulled away and stood. He began to pace the living room. "Three years ago, I was guarding the vice president's daughter Mallory."

A clear picture of the girl came to Maggie's mind. The press loved her, the darling of America, and reported on her as if all of the country was watching her grow up. Now fourteen, the young lady was about to enter high school. But what had happened to her three years ago that made Ethan beat himself up daily?

"She was going to a friend's party. A birthday party. A group of eleven-year-olds having cake and soda and fun." He continued pacing, unable to meet her gaze. Was he afraid he'd find judgment there? It was difficult, but she forced herself to remain seated, not wanting to interrupt his story. "You wouldn't expect someone to pull a gun on a young girl, especially as she left a kid's birthday party…" He paused, his throat working.

Finally, unable to keep from touching him any longer, Maggie rose and went to him. "But that's exactly what happened," she murmured, running a hand down his arm.

She remembered the story now. It had been all over the news, but the vice president's daughter hadn't been hurt, and the story had been replaced by bigger news within a couple days. How could Ethan see his performance as a failure?

His tortured gaze finally sought hers, and he accepted her arms around his waist. His voice was hoarse when he spoke. "There are all kinds of pain in this world. And all kinds of monsters." Absently, his hand fisted in her hair, then loosened and he ran his fingertips through it. "That experience, and this job with Damian, has taught me that."

She ignored the shivers his touch evoked and focused on him. "I know. Mallory was okay, though, wasn't she?"

He nodded. "I tackled her when I saw the glint of the gun across the street, from the window of a passing car, but she was okay. Just a few scrapes and bruises. It was her friend, the birthday girl, who'd rushed out of the house because Mallory had forgotten her bag of party favors." He paused and she felt the column of his throat move against her cheek as he swallowed. "She ran right into the spray of the bullets."

"God." Tears sprang to her eyes. If he couldn't cry, she'd cry for him. "That must have been absolute hell for you."

"I had to make a choice. I could have leaped up to grab

the other girl—her name was Bethany—but that would have left Mallory exposed."

"And you chose Mallory."

He nodded, his throat working. He couldn't seem to speak.

"You chose duty, Ethan, as you were trained to do."

He pulled away, looking surprised that he'd shared all of that and survived. She kissed him then. One minute, he was looking into her tear-filled eyes. The next, she was pulling him down to meet her lips, coaxing a response that was already there, just waiting to be tapped. She gave him all that she had, opening to him in her eagerness to comfort him. And to seek her own comfort.

He breathed her name, pulling away enough to look into her face, then leaning his forehead against hers. "I feel like I'm taking advantage."

Julia's words at dinner had haunted her all evening. She'd said Maggie didn't know how to live anymore since Brad's death. And maybe she didn't. But she wanted to. Right now, she wanted it more than anything she'd ever wanted before. She wanted Ethan.

"I think you've got that backward. You're the one who just gave me a part of you. I think *I'm* taking advantage." Her hands came up to frame his face. "So let me. I need this as much as you do."

Her eyes searched his for several long seconds, seeing the war waged within. He was trying to be strong and resist, to live by his own code of honor while on the job. But she wouldn't let him be noble. She wanted—no, as she'd told him, she *needed*—him to let her help.

When he released a breath and leaned toward her, she knew she'd won. Pulling his face to hers, she claimed another kiss. Vaguely, she was aware of long limbs bumping as they moved. He was walking her backward to the short hallway that led to his bedroom.

A thrill of anticipation coiled and struck through her belly. Her fingers moved from his face to his shirt, gripping the cotton fabric at his waist as she tugged the shirttails from his pants. Frantic fingertips fumbled with the buttons and he released a husky laugh into her mouth. As the backs of her knees met the edge of his mattress, his own fingers found the edges of her shirt and pulled it loose, his thumbs brushing against the skin of her abdomen underneath.

It was then that Maggie froze.

THIRTEEN

SENSING A CHANGE in atmosphere, Ethan pulled away. "What? What is it?" Her eyes were still luminescent from the tears she had yet to shed for him, her cheeks flushed with emotion and from their shared passion. Her breasts rose and fell as she caught her breath.

God, he'd never wanted a woman so much. He was shaking from holding back. But something was obviously wrong.

"Tell me, honey," he encouraged, sitting her down on the bed. He knelt in front of her, taking her shaking hands in his.

"I didn't know it would be this difficult."

"What? Talk to me." He turned her chin until she met his gaze. "I opened up to you. You listened. Allow me to do the same for you."

She sucked in a breath and blew it out slowly, averting her eyes despite his grasp on her chin. "I have...scars." Her hands fluttered around her abdomen.

"Scars?" he repeated, confused. Following the vague motion of her hands, he swallowed the curse that rose to his lips. "Deborah Frame physically hurt you? I thought it was Brad who got hurt."

"It was. She killed Brad." Liquid honey eyes finally met his gaze. "I'd been treating her for months, primarily for schizophrenia. Her symptoms were getting worse, and she was behaving more strangely toward me, bringing gifts that I had to refuse. But I never thought she was harmful.

"Finally, after a lot of discussion, she was going to change from outpatient therapy to inpatient care at a state facility. I'd talked her into doing it so they could monitor her medication for a while and find something that worked better. She agreed to be admitted, as long as it was under her terms. One of those terms was she wanted one more session with me 'on the outside,' as she called it. She told me to rest easy, because she was ready for this change, especially if I would be there for her."

Rest easy. Like the card had said today. No wonder it brought back bad memories.

"Except something changed her mind," Maggie continued. "The next week, when she appeared for her session, she saw Brad as he was leaving. He'd stopped by to tell me about his engagement."

Her lips trembled as she tried to smile. "We were laughing. He kissed my cheek, and I guess she thought, in her skewed thinking, that I was betraying her." She looked at Ethan then, and his heart broke at the pain and betrayal sparkling in her eyes. "I found out later she'd decided she was in love with me. When she saw me with Brad, she thought my attempts to send her to the state hospital were a way of getting rid of her to be with him. She shot Brad."

"She shot Brad," she said again, her tone one of bewilderment. "One second he was standing beside me, deliriously happy. In the next..." She paused to take in a breath and pressed a hand to her breastbone, where her panic was no doubt beginning to build.

Ethan wanted to stop her and pull her into his arms, to tell her it was okay and she didn't have to relive it. But after he'd told her his story earlier, he understood how important it was to get the words out of your head. Like debriding a wound. Excise the bad tissue and clean it all out so it can heal.

"She brought a gun with her that day?"

Maggie nodded but her mind was clearly in another time.

Another place. "She said later that she'd been carrying it around with her for weeks. For protection, she said. She'd been hearing voices on occasion, and sometimes thought it was actually another person. She'd never indicated to me that she was dangerous in any way. But she was.

"Poor Brad. One moment he was so happy. In the next moment, he was lying on the floor and she was coming after me, tackling me to the ground. She'd dropped her gun somewhere, but then she had a knife in one hand." She squeezed her eyes shut.

"I didn't feel the pain right away. I was too worried about Brad, even though I could see the blood pooling under him. He was dead, but I had to get to him. But I couldn't. By then, she was on top of me, the knife slashing. She called me 'Red' and laughed, thinking it was a joke. That the blood was the reason for the nickname."

Ethan squeezed her hands in his. "She *cut* you? With a knife?" She nodded and he swallowed another curse. Anger wouldn't help her now. Hell if he knew what would, though.

"But I was lucky." *Lucky?* "Help arrived before she could kill me."

"Do you think she would have?"

"Without a doubt, in the state she was in that day. Every day, I see or feel those scars and remember."

Moving from his kneeling position to sit on the bed next to her, he pulled her against him. His heart tore in two for her. He didn't give a damn about physical scars, but she obviously did. Or maybe they were just constant reminders of her emotional scars. In that moment, he thanked Fearmonger for ridding the earth of such threats as Deborah Frame.

But Fearmonger was next. Ethan would make sure of it.

"We all have scars, honey," he whispered against her hair. "I just showed you mine." She was quiet, but Ethan could sense she was listening. He prayed for the right words.

"There are all kinds of scars—physical, emotional. And mine didn't repulse you. You're beautiful." His hands moved to her waist, and she didn't push him away as they lifted the edge of her shirt again. He shifted so he could see her eyes. A tear spilled over and ran down her cheek, splashing against his hand. "Let me see you, Maggie. Let me love you."

She stopped his hands. "Promise…" She swallowed, and started again. "Promise to be honest. After you see them, if you don't want to…" Her breath hitched. "If you don't want to continue, tell me." Her eyes pinned him as she waited for his vow.

No way in hell would he ever let her push him away. But he had to convince her of that first. He nodded, then resumed removing her shirt as she waited, frozen.

He lifted the shirt up and over her head and arms. Her lacy white bra had him sucking in his breath before he looked further, his gaze moving to her abdomen. She stared at the wall behind him, probably thinking she'd see the revulsion clear in his eyes. But he wasn't repulsed.

He was fucking *angry*.

Vicious pink ridges of scars rose up where the monster had carved an *X* across Maggie's abdomen, marring the otherwise creamy white skin. Not deep enough to kill her, thank God, but enough to make her suffer—while she'd already been in shock from Brad's death.

Becca's warning flashed in his head. *Maggie's been hurt before.* Yeah, she didn't know the half of it.

He gritted his teeth against his anger, managing to bring it under control before he leaned forward and placed a gentle kiss on her belly. Followed by another, and another. When he pulled back, she looked down at him, hope shimmering in her eyes. He took her hands and kissed her fingertips.

Sorry, Becca, he silently apologized, not really sorry at all. He didn't want to hurt Maggie. God, that was the last thing in the world he wanted. But if he moved away now—if he stopped—she would see it as the ultimate rejection. And that would hurt her more. He had to show her how special, how unique she was. How much he wanted her, despite her scars—or maybe because of them. After all, they were a part of her.

And she was something special.

"You're beautiful," he told her with all the sincerity and honesty of an eternal vow. "I know you've been hurt in the past, but I'm your present." *And your future.* The thought came at him like a lightning bolt, and it wasn't at all unpleasant. It filled him with energy and hope. "I'm your here and now."

On a sob, Maggie leaned forward to kiss him, pulling him against her as she wrapped her arms around him. He nudged her back on the bed, a palm spread over the obscene markings on her otherwise perfect body. It was still perfect to him.

It was Maggie.

His hand moved up to her heart, feeling it pound beneath his palm. He traced the flow of blood up to the pulse in her throat, then moved to place kisses there. His fingers brushed her breast, and she arched up to meet him, showing him what she wanted. Their mouths met in natural alignment, their tongues learning each other eagerly. But as his hand dipped lower again, over her belly, she stiffened.

He quickly moved his hand up to her face again, stroking her cheek. "It's okay. I'm not pressuring you too much, am I?"

"No, it's not you. It's me. I thought I was ready." She bit her bottom lip, stopping its trembling. "I want to be ready."

She turned over on her side, her back to Ethan. He curved his body around hers and draped an arm over her waist, pulling her snugly against him. With one hand, he lifted the hair off her neck and nuzzled her, inhaling deeply of the scent that had become so familiar to him.

"It's okay," he whispered. "We're both exhausted, emotionally and physically."

She was silent for several moments as they watched the darkness outside his bedroom window, lost in their own thoughts.

"I want to," she said in a hushed voice. "So much."

"I know." His breath tickled the nape of her neck and she shivered in his arms. He leaned up on an elbow and looked down at her profile on the pillow. "I'll wait, Maggie. You're worth it."

She turned enough to meet his gaze. "I hope so."

"You hope I'll wait, or you hope you're worth it?"

"Both," she murmured, turning away from him again.

"You don't have to prove anything," he said. "We don't have to *do* anything."

Maggie felt a rush of feeling and struggled to identify it.

Anger? Maybe a bit. She was tired of Deborah's actions having such power over her.

Frustration? Yes, definitely a healthy dose of that. After all, she had the ideal man snuggled against her, desiring her, and she was too scared to let him make love to her.

She was tired of feeling incapable of taking what she wanted. And now her fears had changed the tone between them. He was being noble again. She didn't want noble. She wanted to heal. She wanted to live—fully, no-holds-barred.

She rolled over in his arms, her chest tingling as it brushed his through the lace of her bra and the open V of his unbuttoned shirt.

"You're wrong." She held his gaze. It was important that he knew she'd made a decision she wouldn't regret. "Not only do I have to do this, I *want* to." She stretched her body against the long, hard length of his like a cat waking from a nap. Still, he kept his hands at his sides. "I want you." She nipped his bottom lip between her teeth.

"You're sure?" The huskiness of his voice indicated he wasn't the unaffected male he was trying to project. His green eyes were intent on her, watching for any sign of hesitance or doubt.

Slowly, her smile widened. "Very," she said against his lips. "Touch me. You can't break me."

On a groan, his arms came around her and crushed her to him. His lips, tasting faintly of the beer he'd had earlier, teased her own and she opened to him, reveling in the pleasure he could arouse with just his mouth.

His hands skimmed the sides of her breasts as they stroked across her ribs. Unwilling—or unable—to relinquish the kiss for even a few moments, they explored each other with hot mouths and frantic hands. She shoved his shirt from his shoulders and he shrugged out of it, the movement rubbing his bare chest against her hardened nipples and making her gasp. She weaved her fingers through the thick dark hair at the nape of his neck, glorying in the silky feel of it as it slid through them. But her greedy hands weren't content to stay in one place. Once given permission to touch, they ran over the sculpted planes of his chest, the flat hardness of his abdomen. His breath hissed against her lips as he laughed.

"It's been a while," he said on a groan, moving one of his hands to keep hers against him, guiding it back up his chest before he nipped at her fingertips.

"Good. That makes two of us." She reached for his mouth. But he dodged her and pulled away, examining her face for traces of uncertainty. She met his gaze levelly. "I mean it, Ethan. I want this. I want this with *you*. Now." Seeing the movement of his Adam's apple as he swallowed, she leaned forward to place a kiss there.

"Okay. Okay. But we take it slow. If you want to stop—"

He swallowed again, and she knew he was holding on to his restraint. She loved him for it. "If you want to stop, tell me. Promise me you'll tell me."

"Yes. I will." She tried to pull his head down to hers but he ducked away again, this time with a grin that made her heart skip a beat.

"I said we'll take it *slowly*." He scooted downward, his lips trailing down her neck to the place where the edge of her bra met skin. His wicked tongue trailed into the valley that led between her breasts. She twisted to the side, wanting the same contact on her nipples. On her stomach. God help her, she wanted to hold his head against her and never let go.

He chuckled, the huff of breath tickling the damp spot where he'd kissed her and heightening her arousal. "Anticipation never killed anyone. I think," he added.

"There's a first time for everything." Her words ended on a gasp as he finally kissed her nipple through the lace at her breast. Pleasure shot through her to her core as she arched, her body begging him for more.

It had been a long time since her last sexual encounter. In fact, her boyfriend from med school had become a distant memory. And the man she'd been dating when Deborah attacked had run for the hills without a look back. She'd never felt like this with either of them. Their fumbling getting-to-know-each-other times had never filled her with such a sense of rightness. Of womanly power.

"You're so warm and sweet," he breathed as he unclasped her bra with one hand and nuzzled against the exposed skin of one breast. "So responsive."

Part of her recognized his words as his attempt to build her confidence, and she loved him for it. She shut the analytical part of her brain away and simply luxuriated in how he made her feel.

As he distracted her with the attention he laved upon her

breasts, a hand slipped lower, until it was pressed against her belly, under her slacks. The tips of his fingers slipped under the waistband of her lace-trimmed panties, and she sucked in a breath at the warm pleasure.

He lifted his face to see hers, silently questioning if she was okay to continue, and she nodded. She hadn't even thought about his hand brushing the scars Deborah had left behind. She was Ethan's now. Entirely his, heart and soul and body, scars and all.

She sifted a hand through his hair in gentle encouragement and felt his smile against her breast. His head dipped lower, to her abdomen, and he kissed her there. She stiffened a moment, then relaxed into the pleasant sensation, focusing on the tension coiling inside her, making her toes curl into the mattress.

She thought she heard him murmur something. *Mine?* A flutter in her belly responded to the possessiveness.

His. Yes, it felt right. And he was hers. And he would always be the man who set things right for her. She felt so safe. Protected. Cherished.

She lost all coherent thought as his fingers found the most sensitive part of her, toying with her until she moaned his name. Wriggling away from the exquisite torture, she tugged at his shirt until he lifted enough to let her remove the article. Sensing her sudden urgency, her need to feel his skin against hers, he sat up and slid her pants off, following the brush of fabric with his lips. Her underwear came next. When she was naked, he pulled back to look down at her. His breath seemed to hitch, and she felt the warm rush of a different kind of pleasure.

She felt beautiful. Proud of her body instead of ashamed.

She held her arms open to him, but he shook his head with a smile and rose from the bed. He unbuttoned his pants and kicked off his shoes. She heard two thumps as they were forgotten in some dark corner of the room.

When he came back down on the bed beside her, he rolled to his back, bringing her with him. Her eyes widened in surprise as her hips cradled his arousal. "I want you to be in charge. Do whatever you feel comfortable with. And stop if you need to." His voice was husky, but the demand that she be true to herself was clear. Emotion tickled the back of her throat and pricked at her eyes.

Stroking the side of his face, she smiled. "You are something, Agent Townsend."

"But I'm no saint, either," he growled, pulling her down for a kiss that stoked their ardor again. She poured her heart into the kiss, taking possession of his mouth. She felt his arousal pulsing against her, and he pulled away enough to mutter, "Protection. Side drawer."

With a grin, she leaned over him, intentionally rubbing her breasts against him until he groaned. She reached into the tableside drawer and found a condom. He teased her nipples to hardness, her body preparing itself for him as she lifted herself and slid down his legs.

He reached for the condom she'd ripped open but, grinning, she shook her head, slipping the protection over him and exploring his hard length. He hissed out a breath between clenched teeth. She slid back up to claim his mouth again.

He clenched his fists in the sheets, and she realized he was trying not to touch her, trying not to push her toward something she might not want. But she was beyond her fears now. She wanted him—all of him—now. Taking his hands from the sheets, she placed them on her hips as she shifted to join them together fully. Slowly, she sank down on him, enjoying the heat of hunger and passion in his eyes. The flash of animal that wasn't frightening. It was arousing.

She was in control. She had the power over this strong, loving man.

He arched into her as she shifted her hips, picking up the rhythm that seemed made just for the two of them. His hands gripped her hips as if she would float away. And she just might have, if he hadn't been anchoring her to the earth. Her head felt light and her belly heavy.

She increased the tempo. His hands slid up to her breasts, gently stroking until she felt herself shatter inside, shooting sparks of pleasure from her core outward. He cried out a moment later as he found his own release.

Their bodies sated, she collapsed on top of him. His arms wrapped around her and held her close. Safe. Protected.

She laughed as gratitude filled her. Ethan had helped her overcome her demons. And in the process, he'd opened a whole new world of pleasure and love to her. She turned her cheek enough to place a kiss on his shoulder. His arms tightened around her and she felt his warm lips at her forehead.

"You okay?"

"Never better," she replied with another laugh. "I believe *giddy* sums it up. You?" she asked into his neck.

"An ex-government agent is never 'giddy.'" He chuckled. "But I think I'm about as close as a man can get." He placed another kiss on the top of her head.

Leaning up on an elbow, she looked down into his face. "Thank you." Her smile widened at his look of surprise.

"Thank *me*? For what?"

"This is the first time I've felt alive in years." She frowned. "Is that wrong, with everything that's going on?"

He ran a hand over her hair, smoothing it back from her face. "We'll find Fearmonger. We'll stop him from hurting you, or anyone else."

"I know." She sighed and lay back down on his shoulder.

She knew he would do everything he could to protect her. She only hoped it would be enough.

She was pretty. Not exactly like his Maggie, but close enough. He knew no other way to get through to his stubborn pupil. Maggie was hiding, abandoning her radio show rather than face him on air, refusing to acknowledge that she was wrong and he was right.

Framed by a window in her ground-floor apartment, the woman's silhouette moved away as she hung up her phone, then moved toward what Fearmonger knew from previous scouting expeditions was the bedroom. Soon, she'd be getting ready for bed. Most of the rest of the apartment complex was already dark and quiet. This one would be a bit more of a challenge, with so many people so close by, but that would only heighten the excitement. When she was asleep, he'd break in and steal her away.

And wouldn't dear Maggie be in for a surprise then. She'd be so scared at how close he'd gotten to her that she'd taste it.

Fearmonger knew what fear tasted like. Like the fresh, warm blood of a lip, bitten to stifle a scream.

He scowled. His parents had made sure he knew the taste and feel of fear, in their misguided attempts to make him appreciate their false superiority.

His lips curved. Now they appreciated *him*. Appreciated the strong, powerful man he'd become. And someday soon, the whole world would recognize it, too. Maggie would be the catalyst.

But first, he had a lesson to prepare.

FOURTEEN

IT WAS LIKE A HIGH SCHOOL crush. Ethan walked Maggie to her class, his hard, warm body not touching hers, but so near she couldn't stop thinking about how she'd woken up with him that morning. A tangled mass of warm limbs pressed against each other.

The memory had her cheeks burning. She'd been afraid to get close to men for a year, going so far as to push some away, uncertain how she'd react to any man who got close enough to touch her scars. Perhaps she'd only had to find the right man to unlock her pain.

Once at the classroom, Ethan stepped away and allowed her to mentally prepare for her lecture. She looked up from her lecture notes to find him scowling at the class as it filed in.

She moved to where he stood by the wall. "What's wrong?"

"No sign of Becca. I'm not leaving until she's here."

A shiver crossed her skin. "It's still early." But she heard the doubt in her voice. People around her just weren't safe.

"Sure." He sounded doubtful, too.

A student approached the table where Maggie stood at the front of the class and handed her a manila envelope. "I found this in my seat. It has your name on it, Dr. Levine." Before Maggie could reach for it, Ethan's hand snaked out and grabbed it by the corner with two fingers. He scowled at the surprised student, who backed away.

"We have a few minutes before class starts," he told Maggie. "Come with me." They found an empty classroom adjacent to hers, where Ethan removed gloves from his pocket and handled the envelope with caution. Slitting it open with a pocketknife, he slid a single, heavy-weight linen paper from within. They tensed as they both recognized it.

"A menu. From the steakhouse last night." Her heart pounded.

"There aren't any markings on it," Ethan muttered, turning it over carefully.

"There doesn't have to be. He's just letting us know he's got Becca."

"Somebody say my name?" Becca came in, closing the door behind her. "Just got here. The natives are restless next door. What's going on?"

Ethan couldn't hide his surprise. "You're okay."

"Yeah. I'm sorry I'm late, but I sat up with David last night. He's pretty upset about Sharon, but I got him to talk to me and his alibi for the night of Sharon's murder checks out. The guy's a big softy. He says he went to his parents' house after work Tuesday night, and that he didn't hear about Sharon until Thursday morning when he returned to campus. He was too upset to work or go to his classes. He spent last night on my couch with Sigmund." A wrinkle formed just above the bridge of her nose as she looked from Ethan to Maggie to the paper in his gloved hands. "You look like you've seen a ghost. What's up?"

Ethan held the menu up between two fingers. "We just got another message from Fearmonger."

Becca looked it over without touching it. "I don't get it."

Maggie sank down into a chair, fumbling for the cell phone in her pocket. "I think I do." Heart pounding in her ears, she dialed. It took her three times to get it right.

"Hello?"

Relief flooded her. "Oh, thank God." Her eyes met Ethan's as she spoke to her mother. "Are you at Damian's? Are you all okay?"

"Yes, honey. Of course. Dad and I are here…"

"And Julia?" But she already knew. Fearmonger didn't send a message until he was confident of success.

"She left last night. Insisted on sleeping in her own bed since she had an early meeting at work. She wouldn't take no for an answer, so Damian talked to Noah, who arranged for a police escort. The officer parked outside her place all night."

"Julia had a police escort?" Maggie looked to Ethan for confirmation, but his jaw was tight as he took his own phone from his pocket, probably calling someone at SSAM to verify. "Have you talked to her since, Mom?"

"Yes, she called when she got home." Maggie nodded so Becca and Ethan knew what the answer had been.

"How about this morning?"

"Well, no, but I didn't expect to see her until lunch today. I… Oh no, what's wrong?" Maggie heard a whisper of her father's voice through the phone. He was asking her mother the same question. What could she tell them? That she'd endangered another sibling?

Ethan hung up his phone. Maggie didn't like the look on his face. "Catherine says the patrol unit Noah sent over to Julia's hasn't checked in this morning. But don't panic yet, okay? She could still be at her place."

He took the phone from her and handed her his. "Call your sister," he mouthed, as he took over explaining the situation to her parents.

She prayed as she dialed. She made an effort to focus on her breathing as the ring repeated four times, then went to voice mail. A recording of her sister's voice greeted her. Maggie left a message, but her body knew. As she struggled to sound normal, just in case Julia was okay and did receive the message, her body rebelled, her stomach roiling and blood pumping with the truth.

Dear God. The monster had her sister.

Ethan's hand touched her arm as he hung up with her parents. His touch steadied her, kept her from giving in to full-blown panic. "Cancel class, Maggie."

Her spine stiffened. "And let him win?"

Ethan shook his head. "You won't be any good today. Not until we hear back from Noah. He's heading over to Julia's place right now to check things out."

Becca stepped forward. "He's right. And Damian will want to meet right away to regroup."

"Becca, can you call him and fill him in? He'll need to contact everyone and move up today's meeting." As Becca moved away to make her call, Ethan tried to draw Maggie into his arms. She resisted a moment before allowing herself the comfort of his strength and warmth.

"I'll walk in with you," he said when he pulled away.

She nodded and made her way to the classroom podium, her hands gripping the smooth wooden sides as if it were a life preserver. A hush immediately fell over the students as they looked at her expectantly. "I'm sorry, class, but I've received some bad news." The words clogged in her throat as images of her sister in the hands of Fearmonger filled her head, overlaid with images of Sharon and the other victims. What kind of maniac had Julia?

Ethan stepped forward when she couldn't continue. "Dr. Levine has a family emergency to attend to." He rattled off an order to check their syllabus for their homework assignment and told them she would return for next week's classes. But Maggie didn't think she'd ever feel normal enough to do anything so mundane as breathing, let alone working or teaching.

How many victims had the killer claimed now? And how

many didn't they know about yet? Was Julia already one of them? She felt sick to her stomach. Her throat was constricting, and she felt the blood leave her head.

The scuffling noise of the students gathering their belongings retreated into white noise as her vision wavered. With a supportive hand at her elbow, Ethan hustled her back to the nearly empty classroom where Becca held a phone to her ear and paced in short strides.

Ignoring her, Ethan maneuvered Maggie into a chair and pushed her head down, between her knees. "You look like you're about to pass out," he explained, holding her head down when she would have looked up.

"We're moving the meeting to an hour from now." Becca began punching more numbers into her phone. "I'm calling half of the gang while Catherine calls the other half."

"I can't believe this is happening," Maggie said, her voice muffled by her slacks. She tried her mantra. *I am in control. I am in control.*

What a joke. Fearmonger was in control. He had been from the start.

The blood was returning to her head, pumping at a normal rate. At least she almost had this attack under control. She would not panic. She *would not*. She wouldn't be any use to Julia if she fell apart.

And she thought perhaps Julia *was* still alive. Wouldn't Fearmonger keep her around a bit to screw with Maggie's head? Yes, she thought he might. After all, his primary goal was to frighten Maggie. To teach her about fear. The man definitely knew her weaknesses. Her family.

"My parents?" she asked Ethan as he sank into a chair beside her, his face near hers as she looked up. He examined her with a critical eye.

"Better," he pronounced, then returned to her question. "They're still safe. Understandably upset, but safe. They wanted to rush right over here, to see you, but Damian's keeping them at his place."

Maggie felt some measure of relief. "Good." She sat up, waving off Ethan's offer of assistance. "I'm okay now. Really."

"Yeah, well, maybe I'm not."

Her eyes widened. "What?"

He rubbed a hand across the back of his neck before muttering, "Hell."

In a move that appeared to surprise both him and Maggie, he reached out and cupped her chin, moving in to claim a quick, hard kiss before she could say anything else. His lips were fiercely possessive on hers, but only for a moment. Still, it served its purpose, reassuring both of them.

"I was worried," he admitted in a low, rough voice.

"About me? It's Julia who's in trouble."

His jaw tightened. "It could have been you."

Becca stormed over to them, snapping the phone shut. Jabbing Ethan in the shoulder with one pointed finger so hard that he had to lean back to get away from her, she focused an angry glare on her colleague. "I told you to stay away."

Maggie watched in wonder as Ethan stood toe-to-toe with the younger and much smaller Becca, who wouldn't back down. Indeed, with her temper flaring, she was an equal match for Ethan or any man.

"I made an executive decision," Ethan said, through gritted teeth. Maggie just sat there, confused.

Becca bristled like a cat rubbed the wrong way. "And now I'm going to have to kick your—"

"What is this about?" Maggie interrupted, inserting herself between the two of them and facing Becca.

The air crackled with tension. At her back, she could feel

the ripples of annoyance coming from Ethan. She felt his breath against her neck as he pushed the air from his lungs.

"You." Ethan's hands came down on her shoulders from behind. "She's worried about you."

"Did he hurt you?" Becca said, her anger making her bite the words off one at a time.

"Ethan?" Maggie couldn't hide her astonishment. "Of course not."

"If he does, you call me immediately." Becca turned on her heel and stormed out.

"What's going on?" she asked, still watching Becca as the door closed behind her petite form.

"You have a protector." Ethan's breath tickled her ear. And then his hands were gone. "And maybe she's right. She warned me not to hurt you."

Maggie turned to gape. "But you would never…"

"Not physically. She's talking emotionally. And she was right. Because of me, you opened up. You're haunted by the past again."

Did everyone think her so meek and vulnerable? Anger flared, quickly followed by embarrassment. Perhaps they were all right. Perhaps they saw her clearer than she saw herself.

She folded her arms. "My emotions are my concern. No one else's."

"I thought you and I had gotten past this last night. As for Becca, she idolizes you."

"And you? What's your excuse for treating me with kid gloves? You and I both know Julia could be dead right now, but you're acting like there's hope."

He reached out and ran his hands up and down her arms, but she refused to unfold them. "There is hope. As for treating you gently, I thought that's what you needed. I thought maybe, after all that we shared, things need time to settle. We got intimate pretty fast last night."

"Maybe too fast," she muttered under her breath, hugging herself.

Ethan's hands dropped. "What should I have done? You gave every indication that you wanted to make love last night." Passion smoldered in his gaze, stirring her own response. "Should I have pushed you away?"

"Maybe." Because she was a mess, her life in chaos. She didn't want to become Ethan's mess. And she certainly didn't want to put him in danger simply be being involved with him.

She heard Ethan suck in a breath, but she stepped away, toward the door. Whatever she had, or didn't have, with Ethan, there were other priorities at hand. She wanted to get to the meeting at SSAM and find her sister. Only then could she focus on figuring out her own life.

The conference room was once again full of concerned team members, with a few new guests. Walter Levine stood in the corner of the room, too agitated to sit still. Both he and Nancy looked to have aged five years overnight.

Maggie didn't look any better. Ethan wanted to take her home and make everything okay. Her last word to him before they'd left to find Becca and head to the meeting rang in his ears.

Maybe.

Was she saying he should have rejected her advances last night? He didn't think he'd have had the strength to do that. More important, he'd done what he thought was best—for both of them. Maggie was throwing up defenses again, and he'd be damned if he could figure out why. But he *would* figure it out. Now that he had her, he wouldn't let her run away. If she let him in, he'd do what he could to help her get over her fears. Of men. Of living. Of the future. He'd show her what kind of future they could have if she could trust him with her heart.

"It looks like we're all here," Damian began, claiming their attention. "Mr. and Mrs. Levine have joined us today." The couple nodded in acknowledgment of the introduction. "Let's begin with updates." He nodded to Noah, whose head had been close to Maria's as the two partners discussed something quietly between themselves. "You said you had news. What have you found?"

Noah sat forward, dangling a keychain from his fingers. "Maggie, does this look familiar?"

She clasped a hand over her mouth. "Yes, it does. I totally forgot. You found that at Sharon's, didn't you?"

"Yes. And assuming Sharon's mystery boyfriend is Fearmonger, I think we just figured out how he got into your house."

"That's your key?" Ethan asked.

Maggie nodded. "And the device on the keychain disarms my security system. Kind of like automatic door locks for cars. I changed the code on my keypad, but with that, he would have been able to get past it."

"Why did Sharon have it?" Maria asked.

"She took care of my house and cat while I was away at a conference a few months ago. I just never got around to asking for it back. I never use the device, anyway. I just punch in the code when I walk in or out."

"And Fearmonger, if he'd been watching you closely by that time, would have seen Sharon coming and going."

"So he began to date her because he'd seen she had access to my house," Maggie theorized.

Maria nodded. "That's our current assumption. That, and she worked with you at the station. Sharon's roommate said the boyfriend's name is Christopher, but didn't know anything else. Does that name stand out for any reason, Maggie?"

Maggie shook her head. "I don't remember anyone named Christopher."

"Of course, it could be another alias."

"Fearmonger sure has a way with the women," Becca said into the silence that followed. She placed a small stack of papers on the table. "Fascinating reading."

Noah looked a page over. "These are the letters between Fearmonger—going by the name Owen—and Deborah Frame?"

"Yep. Copies, anyway."

"That probably explains why Fearmonger knows personal details of your relationship with Deborah," Ethan said to Maggie.

Her eyes widened as she silently implored him not to share those intimate details—the scars that a madwoman had left behind. He gave her a slight nod to indicate he understood her wishes and would respect them. The fact that she so had so quickly forgotten their newfound bond of trust irritated him.

"And did they find the guard who helped Frame escape?" Damian asked.

Becca shook her head. "Not yet. It's like she just disappeared."

"Convenient."

"For Fearmonger, yes. She could be one of his victims, for all we know, and we just haven't found her yet."

Damian grunted in agreement. "Either way, it leaves us without a physical description of our killer. What else do we have?"

With a nod toward the Levine family, Noah spoke. "Julia Levine is missing, but she didn't go willingly. In her apartment, there are smears of blood in the hallway that connects her bedroom to the living area. Her car is parked under the carport. We have officers canvassing the neighborhood, asking anyone if they saw or heard anything."

"So are we proceeding as if this was an abduction, not a murder?" Lorena inserted. She shot an apologetic glance to the Levines. "Sorry. I had to ask."

"We understand," Mr. Levine said, his voice weary but strong. "We just want her found—alive if possible, of course. We know you have to consider all the possibilities."

"There's no sign she was murdered. Yet," Noah qualified. "The amount of blood was minimal and the smears of palm prints on the walls indicated she was conscious and struggled with her captor."

"And the police officer who was supposedly watching over her?" Walter asked.

Noah shook his head. "The department had an emergency call nobody else could handle. A report of shots fired a few miles away. Someone made a decision and pulled him off the stakeout."

"How long of a window of opportunity did Fearmonger have?" Becca asked.

"It was about half an hour before the officer could get back to Julia's place. The apartment was dark, and he assumed she'd gone to sleep."

"Still, it's a very populated area, even if people were asleep," Maria pointed out. "Fearmonger risked someone hearing her scream."

"He subdued her," Maggie suggested.

"He must have," Maria agreed. "But she put up a hell of a fight." Admiration rang clear in her voice. "In the bloody handprint she left behind, we found a couple of what appears to be the attacker's hairs that she'd pulled out."

"DNA?" Damian asked, leaning forward. The room held its collective breath.

Maria nodded, her eyes glittering with excitement. "It appears so."

"If you can give it to my lab," he said, "I'll have Sandy put a rush on it."

"I'm working on getting it cleared through our facility to get a sample over to you."

"Good work." Damian said, turning his attention to Lorena. "Are we sure Fearmonger has her?"

Lorena nodded, her look grim. "It has to be. It's just too coincidental that Miss Levine would have been taken by someone else at the same time Fearmonger is intent on harming Dr. Levine by targeting people in her life."

At this, Ethan glanced at Maggie and saw her wince. He knew she was blaming herself for a killer's actions. He'd set her straight as soon as he could get her alone.

"There wasn't the usual bloody message of fear," Lorena added, "but he might not have had time, especially if Julia struggled. He didn't exhibit much of his usual behavior at the scene of Frame's murder, either, but claimed responsibility the next day with that bouquet. The menu left in Dr. Levine's classroom this morning was the same kind of message."

"He seems to enjoy leaving me little presents," Maggie muttered.

"Yes, he does, doesn't he?" Lorena tapped her pencil against the table.

"What are you thinking?" Damian asked.

"This man can't seem to keep from approaching her, whether by messenger or on his own. And as he escalates…"

Noah spoke up, completing her thought. "He won't be able to resist approaching her himself. You've always been the key, Maggie, but we don't want to put you at risk."

Maggie's laugh was harsh. "I'm already at risk. And if he hurts my sister, he'd better be wearing full body armor before he approaches me. Use me. Use me as bait, *please.* Anything to draw him out before he hurts Julia."

He'd had something much different in mind. Something like wrapping her in bubble wrap and locking her in a padded room at the top of a very tall tower. Anything to keep her safe.

The table was silent, obviously considering her plea.

"No," he said, his voice hard as granite.

Maggie's stubborn glare collided with his, flashing all the fire of a sunset at him. "It's the only way."

"No," Nancy said. "How can we risk losing you, too?"

"Maggie may be right," Damian said, putting a hand up to subdue Ethan's objection. "But so is her mother. However, we might be able to do this without putting her in danger. We'll put her back on the air. It worked last time."

Putting her on the air would be just as bad, Ethan wanted to say, knowing Maggie was prone to anxiety attacks. However, he wouldn't give her secret away.

"I can talk to Steve," Maggie said, more animated now that she had a purpose. "He could advertise a special edition of my show. After two nights of playing reruns of old shows, he'd love this idea. I can talk about victims, and families who have lost loved ones to violent crime, as well as sharing my personal experiences with Brad and…Sam." Her gaze collided with Damian's, but after an uncomfortable moment, the man just nodded. "He won't be able to resist calling me. Tap the phone, trace the call, do whatever you need to do."

Noah and Maria exchanged a look. "It could work," Noah agreed.

Damian nodded. "Okay, Maggie, set it up with your station manager."

Ethan had a sinking feeling his job of protecting Maggie from Fearmonger just got a hell of a lot more difficult.

FIFTEEN

As THE MEETING CONCLUDED, Maggie realized her mother's hand was still on hers, providing gentle support. "Honey, come back to Damian's place with us."

She met her mother's pleading brown eyes. "I can't. Not yet. I have things to do."

Her mother's lips pressed into a tight line but, with a sigh, they suddenly relaxed. "I know you blame yourself for this, but we don't hold you responsible. We never did."

Maggie felt her chest tighten. Her father came to stand behind her as the room emptied of other occupants. He laid his warm hands on her shoulders.

"Listen to your mother. We don't want to lose you, too."

Maggie stood suddenly. "Julia's not dead. They'll find her. Don't talk like she's gone forever."

"I didn't mean that, Magpie," her dad insisted. "I just meant, we can't watch you pull away again. Julia wouldn't have wanted that. Neither would Brad."

Maggie felt the childish urge to slap her palms over her ears and shake her head until they stopped talking. Instead, she folded her hands into fists at her sides. "You're talking like she's dead again."

Her father paled. "I didn't mean to. Your mother and I have hope."

"You know what happened to Sam," she threw at them, wanting for some strange reason to lash out. Probably to get it through to them that this was why she'd kept them at a distance this past year. This was what she'd been hoping to avoid.

Pain. But you couldn't avoid pain. It was everywhere.

Her mother stood and wrapped her arms around Maggie's waist, pulling her into an embrace that had the tears tumbling free. "We do have hope, honey. And faith. And yes, we know what happened to Sam. Probably more than you do. You were only thirteen at the time. And we were Damian's friends, his neighbors."

Her mother pulled away but laid a smooth, warm palm against Maggie's cheek. "And I refuse to believe the same thing will happen to Julia. As a parent, I can't afford to think about that. We'll focus on the hope. But we could use your help."

Maggie nodded. "You have it. But I have to do what I can. I want to prepare a broadcast on just such a topic—the pain of families who have fallen victim to these psychopaths."

"Interview us."

"I don't know if I can. It's too close to us. I don't know if I can let myself be that vulnerable." Not without having a panic attack. But she had to admit, letting her parents speak on the radio was a good idea. It would definitely earn Fearmonger's attention, making it that much more tempting to call in. "I'll get back to you, okay?"

Sensing a presence behind her, she knew who it was without turning. Was it possible to know someone by the heat he gave off? And in such a short time span?

Ethan said something reassuring to her parents before her father led her mother from the room. A police officer waited outside to escort them to Damian's house.

"You okay?" He came to her and placed a hand against her cheek. She resisted the urge to lean into it. If other people saw her as emotionally crippled, it was time to stand on her own two feet.

She nodded, trying not to feel regret as his hand fell away. "I will be."

"I don't like the idea of you luring Fearmonger out with your radio show. I don't think it's a good idea."

No, last time it had cost Sharon her life. But maybe that was only because Sharon would have been able to identify Fearmonger if she became suspicious. Maybe Julia still had time. "It's our only chance at the moment."

"You're not to leave my side."

"Except just this once." There was something she had to do.

"What do you mean?"

"I have to talk to Damian. And I think it's best if I do it in private." She'd seen the way his jaw had clenched when she'd mentioned Sam. He'd left immediately after the meeting, without speaking to anyone.

Ethan nodded. "I'll be in my office when you're done."

Damian greeted the knock on his office door with a curt response. He didn't even raise his head from his notes when he called, "Enter."

"I'm sorry if I'm intruding." Maggie stood in the doorway, looking tentative.

He stifled a sigh. She'd obviously seen the pain he'd tried so hard to hide. Knowing her as he did, she couldn't turn her back on it. Caring and perceptive, she was an extraordinary woman. When she'd mentioned Sam in the meeting, and how she wanted to discuss the circumstances and impact of Sam's death on her show, it had taken him off guard.

"Come on in. How can I help?"

She huffed out a mirthless laugh. "I think you're doing all you can already." Seating herself across the desk from him, she eyed him with concern. "I'm worried about you. You look tired." He tried to stifle his annoyance, wanting everyone to just leave him alone. If she finished what she had to say, he could go back to thinking about Sam. "Everyone could use a break. Killing yourself isn't going to find Julia any faster."

But did anyone know that for sure? If he'd tried harder with Sam, if he'd made sure Maggie planned to be at the mall that day before she'd left the house, would she still be alive?

"How do you know? How does anyone know what will help?" Maybe, once upon a time, he'd wanted to die. And still, on occasion, he had flashes of hopelessness and intense, almost crippling grief, but a sense of purpose changed all of that. At least on most days. One side of his mouth lifted. "I promise you I'm not trying to kill myself, but I can't promise I won't work to exhaustion. I will continue to do everything humanly possible to find Fearmonger."

"And some things inhuman." She leaned forward, reaching across the desk to still his hand, forcing him to set his pen down. "It won't bring her back."

Frustration and anger surged within, but he contained them with the skill he'd developed with years of practice. Had Sam lived, would she have become as bold and caring as Maggie? He smiled as he recalled his daughter's stubborn streak. It rivaled that of the redhead sitting in front of him. Undoubtedly, Sam would have forced him to take care of himself, too.

When he spoke again, his voice was hoarse with tenderness. "I know, Maggie. You don't have to play psychiatrist with me." Hurt flashed in her eyes and he cursed himself. "I know nothing will bring my daughter back. But I have to help those I can."

"But not at the expense of losing yourself," she persisted. "There are people who care about you. Deeply. Me. My parents. Your employees. They won't tell you how worried they are, but I will. We have ties that will never be severed, no

matter what I say. At least, I hope that's true. Please take
care of yourself. That's all I ask."

He nodded. "I will. But taking another murderer off the
street is what my heart and soul needs right now."

"And I can't wait to help you. Deborah and Fearmonger have thrown my life so far off track, sometimes I don't
know who I am anymore. And look what I've done to my
parents and sister." Her voice caught as she undoubtedly
pictured her sister in the clutches of evil. Damian could
well imagine, probably even more so than Maggie, what
Julia was enduring.

"You're so young. Too young to be going through this."

"You were only about ten years older than I am now when
Sam disappeared. You did the same thing."

He scowled. "And I wouldn't recommend it," he snapped,
then wiped a hand over his face. "Priscilla and I… Our marriage fell apart because of pain neither of us could endure. I
wouldn't let myself lean on her. And I couldn't be there for
her. I couldn't even be there for myself. I was a failure as a
father and a husband."

He blew out a breath. "I've never told anyone that before. Pride wouldn't let me admit it, I suppose. But I want
you to understand, so that you'll keep the same thing from
happening to you. Don't shut your parents out." He raised a
hand against her objection. "After this is over—and it will
be over soon, I promise—make sure you make amends.
Don't wait until it's too late."

"I will. It's recently come to my attention how much of
life I've shut out."

He chuckled. "I suspect Ethan has something to do with
that. Am I right?"

She blushed and his grin widened. "Yes."

"Then grab at it. At life. Hold on to the people who love
you. If Ethan's the person who can help you live again, don't

let him go." He knew all too well what his inability to see past his pain had cost him. "Besides, he could use your help with a thing or two in his own life."

"I don't feel like I can be any help to anyone, the way things are right now."

"I can tell you, he feels the same. You two are perfect for each other."

"And you?" she asked. "When will you open up, let the pain out?"

His smile turned grim. "Guess I haven't found the right woman." And if he never put any effort into it, he never would. But he doubted there was such a person out there for him, anyway. Priscilla had been a good wife and wonderful mother, but she hadn't understood the need for justice that had consumed everything in his life, including his marriage.

"It would help if you would make yourself available. Not work so hard."

"It might. But then, everything has its right time and place. You just have to recognize it and seize hold when it comes along."

"Bitch!" Fearmonger screamed as he clasped his bloody wrist to his chest with his good hand. She'd bitten him, breaking the skin. He wouldn't allow her to make that mistake twice.

He smacked her across the face hard enough to make her head snap back. Maggie's sister had more fire in her than he'd expected. He'd miscalculated, assuming he could break into her apartment once she was asleep and drug her. Instead, she'd heard him and put up a fight. He should have known that after what Deborah had put Maggie through, the women in her family would take self-defense courses.

Stupid. The voice in his head was his father's.

"I'm not stupid!" he screamed at the walls.

You thought you had everything under control again. Idiot. And you thought you could handle the factory after my stroke, too. Look how that's working out. You never were worth shit. And now you've miscalculated with this little bitch. You're going to pay. His father's mirthless laugh echoed in his head.

Julia hadn't been sleeping when he walked into her apartment, not deeply anyway. But he hadn't been able to wait any longer. The cop who'd been parked outside her place had been due to return anytime. That was the chance he'd been waiting for.

She'd kicked and elbowed, clawed and spit until he'd subdued her in the hallway with his special syringe. For emergencies. He'd never had to use it before, and it gave him a little thrill to see how well his cocktail had worked. Really, you could find anything on the internet these days. He had another little cocktail just for Maggie. But that was a different, special brew just for her.

He'd been in a good mood. Until he'd checked just now to see if Julia was awake and she'd bitten his wrist hard enough to draw blood.

Bitch, he thought again. But it was a minor wound. She could have her petty attempts at escape. In the end, it wouldn't matter.

A grin spread across his face. He'd enjoy the challenge. His last victims had been way too easy. Of course, Sharon and Deborah had trusted him. He'd taken the time to cultivate relationships with them. And after his employees had dared to question him today about how he was running things in his father's absence, he could use a little stress relief. People were starting to notice that his dear mother and father hadn't been around in a couple weeks. He wouldn't have long to enact the rest of his plan.

Thinking of his plan, in great detail, was enough to cheer him.

"Ther-a-py," he said, enjoying the way Julia's eyes sparked with anger and confusion. He'd finally gagged her, but he could see the question in her eyes, so he continued. Because he felt like it. Because there was no longer anyone on earth who could make him do anything he didn't want to do. "Therapy. You're my therapy today, babe. And Maggie will be next. Sweet Maggie.

"If only Fearmonger had emerged earlier, if only my mother and father had seen this side of me, they never would have dared to touch me. But then, Fearmonger would never have been created." He chuckled. "What a puzzle. And another example of how fear is the most powerful emotion in the world. It's like a drug. Why else would people jump out of planes and ride roller coasters? For the thrill that comes with fear."

His laughter died and he scowled. "And my parents will never know I was smarter than both of them, even without a fucking graduate degree. That I had the follow-through to succeed despite Maggie and her committee rejecting my med-school application. Righteous hypocrites." Julia's chin quivered in his hand as he refocused his thoughts. "My parents didn't recognize my intelligence. But *you* will. Maggie will."

He ran the back of his hand down her creamy cheek, smeared with dried blood from the cut she'd earned when she struggled. When she pulled his hair, he'd slapped her so hard she'd fallen into a table, cutting her head.

Yeah, she had spunk. It was going to be fun to teach her a lesson.

Julia flinched and jerked her face away from his touch. He smacked her again. The sound rang against the cold concrete walls along with her moan. Then his cold laugh replaced all sound.

Julia's tears made him feel a little better. Just a little.

He'd kept her longer than the others. Because she was just the bait.

Maggie was the prize.

But it was harder and harder to keep from just ending Julia's life. The desire to see her blood flow free was growing by the hour.

No, he told himself. Patience. Maggie had to be there for that part, or everything would be ruined.

As the splintered rays of sunset pushed their way through the grimy barred window, he turned on the radio in the corner of the room. It was always tuned to the appropriate channel.

He smiled. They'd been advertising all afternoon. Dr. Margaret Levine was going to feature a special segment of her talk show this evening, beginning in a couple hours. And he'd be one of her many eager listeners. And the only one who mattered to her.

Soon now, he would be her whole world.

SIXTEEN

THE RESEARCH AND PREPARATION had filled her afternoon, but with this topic, Maggie's thoughts inevitably turned to Julia. And Sam. And the other victims of Fearmonger.

She shook away memories for the hundredth time as David came into her sound booth. He set down a glass of water with a twist of lime, just how she liked it.

She looked up and smiled. "Thank you."

"Anything I can do to help." He dropped his voice, looking away. "And I think this will help a lot of people."

She was going to address victimization on a wide scale. Not just murder, but other violent crimes. And still it would just be the tip of the iceberg. "Thanks," she said again.

"I'm sorry I flaked out on you the past couple days."

"It was your right. You cared deeply about Sharon."

David swiped the back of his hand across his nose, hiding evidence of his emotions. "I didn't even know she had a boyfriend."

"Me, either. She kept it to herself."

"If maybe I'd gotten up the courage to ask her out…"

He was blaming *himself* for this? Maggie closed the distance between them and hugged him tight. "You couldn't have known and neither could I." He sniffled as she stepped away. "But we'll do the best we can to put on a good show and help others. And maybe give Sharon justice."

He gave her a wobbly smile. "Your parents are in the break room when you're ready."

"Thanks. You can tell them we're about to start. It's almost eleven."

He nodded and joined Becca and Ethan where they waited in the production booth. It reminded her of the last time she'd been on the radio. The same crowd was gathered—minus Sharon. *This is for you, and victims like you, Sharon.*

As her parents took their seats beside her, in front of another microphone, her mother reached over to squeeze her hand and her father gave her a reassuring pat on the shoulder.

The intro music for her show began, and she refocused as David cued her to talk. Blowing out a breath, she switched on her microphone.

"Welcome to a special edition of *Live with Levine*. I'm Dr. Margaret Levine. In light of what's been occurring in our community, and in my own life, we're doing a broadcast on a topic that is close to my heart.

"You may have heard about the murder that took place on the university campus. What happened to Sharon Moss shook up a lot of people, including me, but most especially her parents and siblings. This show is dedicated to victims of violent crime and their loved ones. It's not about fear. It's about awareness, and empathy. It's meant to be a place to share with the community what they've experienced—and still endure—as a result of someone's violent behavior. It is my hope that this will, at the very least, make you aware of the dangers that lurk out there, so that we can prevent horrors like this from happening to others."

She paused to take a drink of water, grimacing when her hand shook. She felt shaky on the inside, too, but if she was to ask her loyal listeners to participate in this exercise, she had to set the example. She met her mother's gaze, saw her smile of encouragement and felt that familiar ache in her chest ease.

"What some of you might not know is that I was the

victim of a stalker. About a year ago, a woman, a former patient, became obsessed. It evolved into something dangerous, something in which she hurt me both physically and emotionally. She killed my brother, an innocent bystander, while I watched helplessly. My family and I still deal with the ramifications of that one person's actions."

Her gaze sought Ethan at the window and he gave a nod. She knew he was also thinking of last night, when her body had frozen under his gentle caresses. Yes, Deborah's actions had resulted in all kinds of scars.

Her voice hardened with conviction. "But I am determined to overcome my fears. One of our listeners, a man who calls himself Owen, called in earlier this week to profess his beliefs about fear. To taunt us with his theory that fear is the basis of everything. He believes that the only true emotion is fear. Well, I want to prove him wrong. Letting go of those fears, facing the pain, embracing love and hope, will free us."

She broke eye contact with Ethan as David flagged down her attention. He grinned as he pointed to the board of glowing lights in front of her.

"It looks like we have several callers, but first, I'd like to introduce my special guests, my parents, Nancy and Walter Levine." She gestured to them to say something into the microphone.

"We're pleased to be here," her father said, "though the topic is, of course, a difficult one."

"Our family has been through so much," Nancy added. "But if we can help others in similar circumstances, I'm happy to help. When Brad died—" Her voice broke but she quickly cleared her throat. Maggie saw her father's hand clasp her mother's and knew they had gotten each other through that tough time. They had wanted to share their strength with her, and yet she had pushed them away. "That was an extremely difficult time. We questioned our faith, our future. We questioned everything."

"But we had the love and support of those around us," Walter added. "And we knew that it was nobody's fault but the killer's."

Maggie swallowed the lump in her throat. Her parents were obviously speaking to her as well as to the listeners. She hoped Damian Manchester was listening, too. He'd spent decades hunting monsters, and going it alone. Maggie had almost followed in his footsteps. But Ethan, her parents and her sister were persistent enough to stick with her when she tried to push them away.

"And what would you say to the people left behind, the victims' families?" she asked.

"Be open to the healing process. What I want people to understand is that nobody can ever be totally safe." Her mother took her hand where it lay on the table and squeezed. "And what kind of life would it be if we lived in giant bubbles, never able to touch each other or share ourselves for fear of hurt and rejection? There are enough good people in the world to make reaching out to others and living an open life well worth the risk."

"Everyone is touched by tragedy at some point in their lives," her father added. "But the beauty of the human condition is survival, the desire to overcome the pain and live again."

Her mother's gaze held her own. "And if you're lucky, you have people around you who are willing to help. That's why we're so proud of you, and what you've become. You help so many people."

Maggie smiled. "Thank you both for sharing that." She sincerely needed to hear it. She'd spent too much time lately focusing on the ones she hadn't helped—like Deborah. She'd forgotten the good in the world, and that she'd been a positive influence on many other people. "And we'd love to hear from some of our listeners out there who have similar tales of grief and survival."

The time flew by quickly, and Maggie was amazed by the number of phone calls—some with tragic stories and others just wanting to contribute words of support—that she received.

So many people out there were in pain. And so many people had found so much to live for. They had found strength in their families and loved ones and comfort in everyday pleasures. Or, like Damian Manchester, they'd found solace in doing valuable work.

It made her all the more certain in her decision to live again. To let go of her past, or to deal with it. With Ethan's help, she believed she could.

But after an hour of fielding calls, there was still no call from Fearmonger. Nothing about Julia. And despite the hope she felt listening to others, despair made her heart heavy again as she closed the show. It was as if she was closing off her opportunity to reach her sister.

"Thank you to everyone who called in tonight. I truly appreciate you sharing your stories. I hope that people see them for the inspirations they are, and you—the ones who trudge on in the face of adversity—as the everyday heroes you are. And thank you to my parents," she added. "You are my own personal heroes. In the meantime, everyone, please treat yourselves gently."

She sat, begging another light to blink, another call to come in. Hoping, for once, that Owen—Fearmonger—wouldn't be able to resist. And her heart ached in desperation for Julia and the fear she must be feeling. If she was even alive.

Strong, familiar arms wrapped around her shoulders and

she leaned back in her chair, into Ethan, closing her eyes against the pain. "He didn't call."

His arms tightened. "It doesn't mean anything. He might not have even known about the show's topic. It was such short notice."

"He knew." Fearmonger was following her every move so closely, he probably knew Ethan had his arms around her at this very moment. "He wants me to suffer. He wants to make me sweat it out. He'll call, but he'll wait until he can have me to himself. And until he can hurt Julia the most."

The sound of Sharon's cries resounded in her ears. He'd made her listen to the young woman's final moments. She'd barely survived that. She didn't think she could bear hearing Julia's useless cries for help.

She shivered.

"You okay?" He squatted down beside her and spun her in her chair until she faced him.

"I am now." She smiled. So caring. So gentle. This man would never hurt her. He'd chosen to guard people as his career, but it was also in his nature to protect. She touched a hand to his cheek. "Take me home."

Passion and need flared in his eyes. "Yours or mine?"

"Yours. I feel safe there."

With a nod, he rose and pulled her out of the chair with him. Suddenly realizing they were alone, Maggie turned to him. "Where's everyone? My parents?"

"Noah was waiting to take your parents to Damian's house. I assured them I wouldn't let you out of my sight. Becca escorted David home." He laughed. "He put up a stink about it—a man being protected by a woman—but she batted her eyelashes and twisted it so it seemed *he* was protecting *her*." He chuckled again and it warmed Maggie's heart. "I admit I haven't given her enough credit."

"You should tell her, not me."

He looked at her thoughtfully. "I suppose I should."

"Definitely. Your opinion matters to her."

"And you? Does it... Do *I* matter to you?"

"Yes," she said, her voice husky under his heated gaze. "You definitely do."

"What happens after we find Fearmonger?"

Was he worried about what she'd demand from him when the chaos of her life settled? Though they'd opened to each other like two flowers surviving a long, hard frost, she didn't kid herself that their relationship was more than based on the needs of the moment. Ethan had needed someone to unburden himself with, and she had needed the same. "I promise, no strings."

"And if I want them?" Ethan asked.

Her eyes widened. Could he really be thinking long-term? "It's not the time to be making these kind of decisions."

"Bullshit."

Her jaw dropped as he called her bluff.

"You're avoiding the question," he said, gently. It was too much too soon. He wrapped his arm around her, pulling her close. "Forget I asked."

"No. I won't forget." She pulled away and touched her hand to his cheek. "After we find Julia, after she's safe, we'll talk about it."

"I haven't told you how proud I am of you. Fearmonger didn't take your bait, but you tried."

She'd laid her heart on a platter and served it up to Chicago on the air. But it all seemed for nothing now. "He wants me to stew about it. To spend every hour—awake or asleep—wondering what he's doing to my sister."

Ethan's bent to place a soft kiss on her lips. "We'll find her. I promise."

Yeah, but in what shape?

SEVENTEEN

"SAWDUST?" MAGGIE repeated, looking around the SSAM meeting room in confusion. She'd slept fitfully the night before, settling only when Ethan wrapped his arms around her and held her tight. Still, she'd heard screams in her sleep, followed by Fearmonger's horrible taunts. Damian's call this morning, requesting that they come in for yet another meeting because of some new evidence, had been the only thing that had her hanging on.

And now they were talking about sawdust. It was surreal.

Ethan leaned forward. "Maybe you can explain further, Sandy, because I'm not getting it."

"Of course." Sandy Mitchell's mocha skin glowed with enthusiasm for the subject. Whatever SSAM's lead criminalist had found, the woman thought it was important. "We were going over the bloody smear in Miss Levine's apartment and the few hairs that were stuck in it. Apparently, when she made that handprint on the wall she left behind some pretty amazing evidence. Evidence other than the hairs, I mean."

"Sawdust," Ethan repeated.

Sandy nodded vigorously, her springy dark ringlets bouncing around her round face. "The DNA in the hair didn't match anybody in the system, but the sawdust should lead us to the killer."

"How?" Ethan asked.

"There was no other trace of sawdust in Miss Levine's

house, which leads us to conclude it came in with the suspect. As it was in his hair—not simply on his shoes like some kind of mulch byproduct—I believe Fearmonger works with wood." Sandy sat back and let the room digest her information.

Maria shrugged. "So the guy is doing some renovations on his house. That only narrows it down to the suburbs or one of those lofts they're renovating downtown. Or maybe he works at a lumberyard or do-it-yourself home store."

"Or maybe he just likes to whittle when he's not kidnapping and murdering," Ethan added, his jaw set tight with frustration. Maggie understood the emotion well. They'd been counting on this breakthrough to lead to something concrete.

"Or he could be an artist," Lorena pointed out. "He does like to make a statement on the walls where he kills his victims, but it's more crude than artistic, I would say. Then again, art *is* subjective." She shot Maggie an apologetic look, but Maggie was too intent on finding out why Sandy's smug smile was still in place.

The criminalist leaned forward, regaining everyone's attention. "But do any of those places, with the possible exception of an artist's studio, have ready access to African mahogany?" Sandy, who may have been an actress in a previous life, paused for dramatic effect. "I have a friend who owed me a favor. This friend just happens to be a specialist who knows how to identify woods. The sawdust is from African mahogany, a rare wood. Only specialty furniture factories—or artists," she qualified with a nod of acknowledgement to Lorena, "would use it. It's very expensive and hard to come by. And distinctive in its pattern. And because it was in the suspect's hair, he had to have been around it. The most likely guess is that he works with it."

Ethan spoke up next. "So we're looking for someone who works in, what, an artist's studio or a fine furniture factory?"

"That would be my guess."

"Great," Maria said, grimacing. "We've narrowed it down to all the furniture businesses and their employees and—oh, yeah—all the artists within the great state of Illinois."

Sandy scowled. "Not at all. Fearmonger is obviously within listening range of Dr. Levine's show, and all his recent activity has been within thirty miles."

"But he could just be on vacation or something. It *was* a holiday. We don't know he lives or works in this area. In fact, he could attend the college as a commuter and only be in the area on certain days."

"But we can start in the area and spiral outward, targeting only the furniture factories where they build custom furniture," Ethan said.

Damian cleared his throat. "At least we have a new direction to pursue. I'll have Catherine pull together a list of furniture factories and artist studios. Noah and Maria will be doing some of the footwork." He turned to Becca and Ethan. "I thought you two might be added resources today and check out some of them. Maggie can stay here with me."

"No," Ethan said.

"No way," Maggie blurted at the same time. "Damian," she continued, "it's Saturday. I have nothing to do anyway, no classes to teach. I really want to be out there, looking for Julia."

"And if Fearmonger sees you?" Damian asked. "You've just blown our chances of catching him."

She felt the blood drain from her face but was determined. "I can wait in the car and observe. Maybe I'll notice something or recognize someone. Please, I have to do something, or at least feel like I am. Besides, if you think you've found him, I can recognize his voice."

"And he knows that, Maggie. He's obviously disguised it before, if Sharon didn't recognize him as Owen."

"I won't be any safer here than I would be out there. He doesn't seem to have any problem getting to me, or people I care about."

Ethan touched her arm in a supportive gesture, then spoke to Damian. "Sir, it's my job to protect her. With all due respect, I can't leave her here and go out with Becca. On the other hand, I don't want to put her in more danger by taking her with me."

"Quite a dilemma."

"I insist on going with Ethan," Maggie said. "Besides, I think I might be more of an asset than a hindrance. The way Fearmonger's behaved, I don't think he'd run if he saw me. On the contrary, maybe he'd even approach me." Ethan's hand stiffened on her arm and she reached out to lay her other hand on his. "But I promise to be careful."

"Lorena? Your thoughts?" Damian invited his mindhunter to share.

"I think she has a valid point," Lorena conceded. "And I can pair up with Becca. We can cover more ground if there are three teams looking." A spark lit Lorena's eyes. Maggie got a glimpse of the FBI agent she must have been. Tough. Formidable. Intelligent. Of course, that went without saying. Damian only hired the best.

"You two can look into the artists who work with wood. I'll have Catherine compile a listing, and get the list of furniture factories to Noah and Ethan."

"You stick with me," Ethan said in Maggie's ear as chairs were pushed back and each pair left to see to their assignment. "You do what I say, when I say it. No arguments. No questions."

She nodded, sensing the urgency in his voice. Was it fear? For her? The thought warmed her blood. She already knew the stakes. "I will. I promise." She wasn't looking to lose her life just after she'd seized hold of it again.

Damian approached and embraced her. "Be careful." His voice dropped so that only she could hear. "And I'm glad to see you took my advice."

Maggie felt her cheeks heat. Was it so obvious that she and Ethan had grown close? Damian's rusty chuckle warmed her and had several heads turning to stare in surprise. The man obviously didn't laugh much. When all this was over, she'd have to talk with him about that.

"Can I come in this time?" Maggie pleaded, aware this was their last stop, and Ethan had had no luck going into the last four furniture factories on his own.

He gave her a no-arguments look. "No." Firm and immovable. Then he reached out to touch her face, turning in the front seat of the car to face her. "It's my job to—"

"Keep me safe. I know." Maggie sighed. "I just have this cramp in my leg. It would be nice to stretch. And I'm starving. Maybe they have a vending machine or something."

"We'll stop for dinner after this. It's the last one on our list." His look was so full of compassion that Maggie had to turn away.

"Okay. Be safe." It was the same thing she'd told him before each of the other stops. She hoped to heaven that Noah and Maria or Becca and Lorena had experienced better luck narrowing the field. The pleasant smell of freshly hewn wood filled her senses as Ethan opened his door and climbed out, dipping his head back into the open doorway to say the same thing he'd told her at each of the stops. "Lock the doors."

Nodding, she did as he asked as his retreating form disappeared through the building's front door. It was another hot day, and he'd left the air-conditioning running for her.

She pulled her shirt away from her skin to let the air circulate against it until she shivered.

This factory exuded more charm than the others had. Two stories of solid brick located near an old industrial section of Chicago, the building was a character in itself. Obviously constructed many decades ago, it stood proud and square among newer, less interesting buildings.

A knock on her window startled her. A man stood on the other side, and she hesitated until he smiled. His dark hair was in need of a trim, and his skin was tanned as if he'd spent some time out of doors. She rolled her window down a crack. If this handsome, boy-next-door type of guy was Fearmonger, she'd know it by his voice. And his eyes. The eyes always told.

"Hi," he said, not indicating that he might find it odd that he was speaking to her through a one-inch gap. In today's world, and in this part of town, people were probably considered smart to be on guard. For Maggie, it was a way of life now.

She felt some relief that the man's accent was Southern. It didn't have the smooth, cultured polish of Owen's voice. It wasn't even close.

"You lost?" he asked.

"No. Just waiting for my friend. He'll be back any moment." She hoped that was true. The man seemed friendly enough, but you never knew. She'd let the man chew on her response and decide what to say next.

The man jerked his head toward the building, a lock of hair falling in his eyes. "Place is about to close up for the night. We hate working Saturdays, so we try to get out quick."

Maggie forced a pleasant smile. "Then my friend will be back even sooner."

His eyes studied her a moment before he shrugged and nodded. "Okay. Just trying to help." He turned to walk away.

She didn't care if she'd offended him. It was a small price to pay for one's life.

"That your friend?" he asked, once again jerking his head toward the building.

Maggie, startled the man was still by her window when she'd seen him turn and take a few steps away, looked toward the entrance where, sure enough, Ethan strode in long, purposeful strides toward the car.

"Who are you?" Ethan's look was black enough to make her new friend back away, his hands raised to his chest, palms out.

"Hey," he drawled, "I was just keeping your lady company. Making sure she was okay."

"And you are?"

"J. P. Randall. I work here."

"Then you're on your way home." It was a statement intended to push him along his way.

J. P. just grinned. "After a drink at Sullivan's, down the street. Just thought I'd look for company."

"I hear bars are great for that—finding company."

J. P. laughed, then rapped his knuckles against the roof. Maggie, who'd been watching Ethan through the window where he stood in front of the car, jumped at the noise.

"That they are," J. P. said. "Goodbye, ma'am." He tipped an imaginary hat to her—a cowboy hat, no doubt. With his Southern accent, he only needed a piece of hay sticking out of his mouth to complete the picture of smooth Southern boy. "Hope to see you again sometime soon." He turned and sauntered toward a truck parked across the lot, with the employees' cars.

Ethan climbed in and glared at her. "Put your window up. Are you crazy?"

She complied. "It was only a little bit."

"Enough to stick a gun barrel through."

"If it were a gun, he wouldn't need me to roll down the window in order to hurt me. Besides, Fearmonger prefers a knife," she pointed out, but that only made him scowl all the more. "What did you find out in there?"

Ethan's jaw tensed. "Nothing. The boss had already left for the day. There was just a worker or two cleaning up. One didn't speak English and the other hadn't seen anything unusual. Couldn't think of anyone we'd be looking for." He ran a hand over his face. "Sorry. Looks like we'll have to continue the hunt tomorrow."

Maggie slumped against her seat, emotionally drained. *Oh, Julia, I hope you're hanging in there.* Her sister was tough. Maggie just hoped she was tough enough to withstand Fearmonger's so-called lessons. Of course, he'd always said Maggie was his pupil. What he wanted was her. He wanted to teach her about fear. And, God help her, if it meant saving her sister, she would offer herself to him, wrapped in a big red bow.

Of course, with Ethan determined to keep her safe, that self-sacrifice would be difficult to achieve. And it wouldn't be smart, anyway. Fearmonger wouldn't let her sister go, no matter what Maggie did.

"I'm sorry," Ethan continued when Maggie didn't respond. "I know you had your hopes up. Maybe the other teams found something." But they left the reality unspoken. If anyone had found Julia or Fearmonger, Ethan would have received a call immediately. "I'll check in with Damian and see if anybody else had some luck." Damian must have picked up right away, because Ethan was suddenly talking to someone on his cell. "We're done for the day. Have the other teams checked in?…Where are they?…That's not too far from here. We'll meet them at—" He pulled the phone away from his mouth to talk to Maggie. "What was that bar that guy mentioned—the one nearby?"

"Sullivan's. Just down the block."

He nodded. "Tell them to meet us at Sullivan's."

When he hung up, Maggie pinned him with a look. "Why there? I thought J. P. was kind of creepy."

"Me, too." He shrugged. "Wouldn't hurt to check him out a little more. He's probably just an average Joe. Or Joe Bob," he drawled, mimicking J. P.'s accent.

"That would make him a J. B. not a J. P.," she pointed out.

"Noah and Maria are only a few miles from here, and it'll give us a chance to compare notes. Damian's calling them for us now."

He drove the short distance to Sullivan's, which, judging by the number of beat-up trucks in the parking lot, was already doing a decent amount of business on a Saturday evening.

He climbed out and Maggie followed suit. The heat of the Chicago summer day rebounded off the parking lot, radiating through her thin-soled sandals. A sidewalk sign in front of the corrugated-tin-roofed bar proclaimed Saturday's special featured half-price wings, fries and draft beer. Her mouth watered. She felt the warmth of Ethan's hand at her back as he guided her down the sidewalk, the touch at once protective and proprietary. Maggie didn't mind.

Sullivan's was dimly lit but the air-conditioning was heavenly. It was large enough to accommodate a dozen or so people at the bar, another dozen booths around the perimeter, and a smattering of beat-up wooden tables in the middle. The overall appearance fit the industrial atmosphere of the neighborhood, with tin and neon accents on the walls and a painted concrete floor.

Ethan's hand returned to Maggie's back, directing her to a table in the corner big enough for the six of them when the others arrived. He promptly claimed the seat that faced the door. From there, he could also keep an eye on the group that had gathered at a table in the opposite corner of the room. J. P. was among the after-work crowd of men gathered there. Judging by the level of noise, most of them were clearly not on their first half-price beer. The few other patrons were relatively sedate.

Maggie waited patiently for Ethan to finish scanning the room and return his attention to her. When he did, his eyes softened almost imperceptibly, but his jaw remained rigid.

A waitress stopped at their table, jutting her hip out in half annoyance, half innate come-on. She flipped open her notepad and dug in her apron for a pen, then stopped in midmotion and smiled when her eyes finally focused on Ethan. Estrogen responded to testosterone.

"Hiya." It was clearly a welcome meant only for him. Her gaze eagerly slid down what she could see of Ethan's torso. "You're new here." She turned reluctantly to Maggie. "What can I get you two?"

With a smile, Ethan arched a brow at Maggie. "What do you want, sis?"

Sis? She recovered from her surprise quickly. "Whatever's on tap." Something to help her relax. If they weren't going to get anywhere today, a beer might do the trick.

"Basket of fries and a Coke," he added.

The waitress gave him a look of disbelief. "What, are you working the twelve steps or something?"

Ethan's sexy smile had Maggie gaping. Was he flirting? "Or something. Hey, do you know who those guys are over there? My sister thought she may have recognized one of them."

The waitress turned her head, snapping her gum between her teeth. "Locals. At least, they work around here. Come in here on Saturdays to wind down from the long workweek.

Real fond of our half-price menu. Not very good tippers, either, but at least they keep the business going, you know?" Her curious gaze turned back to Ethan. "You work around here, too? You look like you got the biceps for it, but you're not dressed right."

"You're very perceptive," he said, scanning her name tag and hinting at appreciation for her breasts, "Denise."

Her smile grew sly. "I'm a woman of many talents."

Ethan's deep chuckle heated Maggie's blood. She could only imagine what Denise was feeling as he aimed the full force of his charm directly at her. "And one of those many talents is bringing a man what he wants?"

Of course, he was only trying to get information, but it still made Maggie's heart lurch to watch him work another woman over.

"You bet, sugar." Finally, Denise left to fetch them their drinks.

Maggie watched Ethan survey the men in the corner, his body deceptively relaxed as one arm draped along the back of the chair next to him. The tension in his jaw told her he was ready to pounce at one wrong move. J. P. was over there, cracking jokes and making the group laugh. The man actually looked over and winked at her before moving to the bar to talk to Denise. From the corner of her eye, Ethan's jaw hardened. She reached out and laid a hand on his forearm, where it rested, muscles clenched, on the table.

"They're just blowing off steam," she said quietly. "Not everyone's a suspect."

"They are until I figure out who Fearmonger really is."

The ruckus across the bar built in tempo, and some catcalls were thrown in when Maria and Noah arrived. Maria's reply was something mumbled in Spanish as she slid into a chair.

"You couldn't have picked a more civilized dive?" Maria asked Ethan.

"I think it was meant as a compliment," Noah said, jerking the knot of his tie loose as he sat next to Maggie.

Maria rolled her eyes. "Or maybe the whistles were meant for you, partner." She leaned over the table toward Maggie. "Wouldn't be the first time. I heard a story about one of his undercover operations where he had to—"

Noah cleared his throat and gave his partner a warning look. "Another time, maybe?"

Becca and Lorena entered soon after and joined them as Denise returned with their drinks and appetizers, her predatory gaze now sizing up Noah. He took it like a professional. Of course, with his rugged, sandy-blond good looks, he probably got that kind of female attention all the time.

Maggie smiled behind her glass as Noah met Denise's advances with good grace, politely rejecting them. She took a drink, feeling the cool crispness of the beer soothe her.

After Denise moved away again, Ethan leaned in. "So, did you find anything? Anything we can build on?"

Becca looked grim. "Talked to eight or nine artists, who all agreed to let us look around. Only a few fit the profile Lorena drew up. None are working with African mahogany right now."

Maggie sighed. "Dead end." She paled immediately, realizing her word choice. She took another gulp of her drink.

Noah spoke into the heavy silence. "Maria and I went to six furniture factories, all on the outskirts, or in suburbs, and had the same experience. There were two employees we didn't speak to who may have fit the profile, and one was on vacation, one home sick—from different companies. We've sent officers to question them, if they are indeed in town and at home. If not, they'll question their neighbors. Someone will have seen something. But none of the businesses admitted to working with African mahogany at this time. We just need to be ready when something breaks open."

"And it will break open," Maria said, her eyes full of compassion.

Maggie nodded, but she felt sick to her stomach. Her chest was feeling tight, too. In fact, it seemed to be constricting with every second that passed. "Excuse me," she mumbled as she stood. "I need to visit the restroom."

"Go with her," Ethan told Maria, but Maggie managed a smile and a shake of her head.

"I just need a minute. Please." The plea was for Ethan, who assessed her carefully. The squeeze in her chest tightened still more.

"One minute. If you're not back, I'm coming in after you."

Nodding, she grabbed her purse and headed toward the back of the bar to the hallway that led to the restrooms. She rounded the corner and leaned her head back against the wall where a pay phone hung. But it wasn't enough. Dizziness was coming in waves now, and she was fairly sure vomiting was in the near future. It wasn't quite like her other panic episodes, but she still felt as if she was losing control.

She pushed open the bathroom door, thankful the place was empty and fairly clean. She emptied the meager contents of her stomach in the toilet and flushed. Though she wished for nothing more than to sink down next to the cool wall and rest, she forced herself to stumble to the sink. If Ethan was going to check on her any second, she didn't want him to know how sick she was. He'd make her go home, effectively ending her part in the search for Julia. And he'd probably insist on going with her, which would be two less people looking for her sister. That was unacceptable.

She swished water in her mouth and pressed a cold, wet paper towel to her closed eyelids. The ladies' room door opened on her right, but she didn't remove the soothing towel.

"I said I'd be okay," she said as the sound of heavy male footsteps came closer.

"Then you still have a lot to learn."

The hairs on Maggie's neck rose. She dropped the towel into the sink, her eyes flying open. Owen's voice. No, Fearmonger's. She looked up at his smiling face in the mirror.

"We meet at last," the image of J. P. said. He'd lost his Southern accent, and all his Southern charm with it.

She began to shake, the pain behind her breastbone building to match the throbbing behind her eyes. She pressed a hand to her chest and he laughed.

"Looks like drugging your drink worked. Did you think you were having a panic attack, Maggie?" He stepped closer.

Maggie had nowhere to go. She spun to face him head on, a wave of dizziness washing over her as she groped in her purse for pepper spray or hairspray. Anything to fight off her worst nightmare in the flesh. She fought to control her breathing as her hand wrapped around a slim bottle. *In. Out.* "How did you know about my attacks?" she managed to push out between gasps.

He laughed again. "I know everything about you. Including how much you care about your sister. Julia's been waiting for you to join our little party."

Maggie's vision wavered, and the image of evil split into two mirror images. She brought her hand up and aimed for the middle of the two, spraying the small bottle of hairspray, just as Ethan had mentioned. *If the perp corners you in the bathroom...* But it wasn't enough. The drug was too powerful, and she'd missed Fearmonger's eyes. With a curse, he ripped the bottle from her hands.

"Surprisingly pathetic, Maggie. But resourceful. I'll give you that."

She was going to vomit again, which might be good if it got this drug out of her system.

"I know your MO," Fearmonger said. "I knew you'd run for the bathroom at the first sign of panic. And that you'd want to be alone. It pays to know things. Like I told you before, I'm a student of human behavior. More specifically, fear. And you made it so easy, coming to find me."

Keep talking. Ethan will be here soon.

"It took some of the challenge out of the game," he continued, "but also some of the risk. I guess I can live with that." Chuckling, he glanced at his watch and Maggie knew then that Ethan wouldn't get there in time. Fearmonger was much too careful at planning these things. As the monster pulled a needle from somewhere, there was a knock on the bathroom door.

"Maggie? Ethan wanted me to check on you."

Becca. She'd had training, but could she take on Fearmonger? As Maggie looked into the eyes of evil, glinting with amusement, she realized he'd already laid his plans. He was confident in them. As Maggie opened her mouth to scream, he struck her. Hard.

She saw blackness as the world tilted and the floor rose up to meet her.

EIGHTEEN

"JUST GO CHECK ON THEM," Noah urged Ethan. "You've checked your watch every few seconds for the last two minutes."

And he checked it again. "Becca should have been back by now."

"Want me to go?" Maria popped a French fry into her mouth.

"No." Ethan rose. "Apparently, that ladies' room is like a black hole. I'm through waiting. She could be having a panic attack in there." He winced.

Noah raised his eyebrows at the revelation. "She covers it well. But after what she's been through…"

It bothered Ethan that Noah had shared Maggie's experience, had seen her cut and bleeding and vulnerable, and had been there for her after Deborah Frame's attack and Brad's death. But he was also grateful that she'd had someone like Noah there to help. He felt the weight of something pressing on him. Something was very wrong.

"I'll come with." Noah wiped greasy fingers on a napkin and followed Ethan to the ladies' room.

Ethan pressed his ear to the door. Hearing nothing, he knocked, hoping they could hear it over the pounding of his heart. "Maggie? Becca? Everything okay?"

When nobody answered, he and Noah simultaneously pulled their guns from their holsters and stood to either side of the door. Ethan turned the knob and nudged the solid wood door open with his foot. Watching Noah, who had a clearer view through the crack that Ethan had created when he opened the door, for some kind of cue, he saw the other man's eyes widen. Noah used his free hand to push the door open farther, and the sight that greeted them had Ethan's stomach lurching.

Becca lay motionless on the floor of one of the two open stalls, bleeding from a cut on one temple. An empty syringe, the plunger in all the way, lay nearby.

"Jesus." Holstering his weapon as a visual sweep of the small restroom showed nobody else was present, Ethan bent down to feel for a pulse. His fingers shook as he pressed them to her neck. "She's alive." He turned her head gently from side to side. "I don't see any punctures."

Noah took a closer look at the restroom, careful not to touch anything. "Maybe the syringe was for Maggie." He used a paper towel to carefully collect the evidence and put it into a baggie he'd had on him. Taking out his phone, he called for medical assistance.

Ethan took off for the rear exit, at the end of the hall past the restrooms. He searched the empty alley that ran behind the building, then ran to the front and through the parking lot, but found nothing. No sign of Maggie.

Had it been less than a week ago he'd sat at just such a bar, nursing a drink that he'd hoped would cure him of the ghosts from his past? When he'd first seen Becca lying there, bleeding, Bethany's face had come to mind. Another girl who'd been in the wrong place at the wrong time. But this time, he hadn't been haunted by the old feelings of inadequacy. Opening up to Maggie had helped him shed those ghosts, but now there were other things haunting him.

There were all kinds of monsters in the world. And one of them had Maggie. Sweet Maggie, who only wanted to help people.

Trying not to let despair suck the breath from his lungs, he returned to the bar.

Back at the ladies' room, Maria and Lorena had set up a human barrier to the hallway, keeping customers in the main bar area while they waited for help to arrive. Noah bent over Becca, speaking words to her as if he could rouse her.

"She hasn't come to yet?" Ethan asked, striving for patience. He hoped to hell Becca had some information that would lead him to Fearmonger.

Noah shook his head. "Not yet."

At the bathroom sink, Ethan noted the discarded wet paper towel as well as several small red spots.

"Blood?" Noah asked, seeing the direction of his gaze.

He nodded. And he would guess it wasn't Becca's. She didn't look as if she'd gotten very far into the room before she'd been knocked unconscious. Which meant Maggie was hurt, too.

Noah apparently saw the desperation in Ethan's eyes. "Maria called Maggie's description in. There are cruisers out there looking already. Fearmonger can't have gone far. We'll find her."

Striving for calm when his heart was slamming against his chest, Ethan moved aside and surveyed the scene from the hallway as the paramedics arrived. A spot of blood on the edge of the door caught his attention. Had someone slammed the door into Becca's temple—or vice versa—as she entered to check on Maggie? It seemed plausible. If Fearmonger had succeeded in knocking Becca out, he'd probably used the syringe on Maggie. And what exactly had been in it?

"Get that syringe to Sandy," Ethan told Noah.

The detective nodded. "The SSAM team will have the quickest way to process it. Better yet, I'll have Sandy meet us at the hospital. They have the equipment there to analyze it, and we'll know what we're dealing with."

Ethan ran a hand through his hair. *Please, God,* he prayed, *keep Becca alive and protect Maggie and Julia from this madman.*

Noah worked with Maria to round up the crowd and move them back toward the bar where they could start questioning possible witnesses. Ethan's heart squeezed as he prayed somebody had seen something. Becca was lifted onto a stretcher in the hallway, dislodging him from the protective stance he'd taken nearby.

Ethan moved into the bar area, intent on heading out the front to get his car and drive around the neighborhood, looking for Maggie. Several of the rowdier locals still laughed and caroused in the corner, apparently unaware or disinterested in the sirens and the medical personnel that hustled about.

"Where's Christopher?" one of the gang called out. "He's supposed to buy the next round."

"Probably trying his ridiculous accent out on Denise in the restroom," someone said. Someone else snickered.

"He's gonna round himself up a cowgirl," one of them said in a ridiculous attempt at a Texan accent.

Christopher. Tensing, Ethan redirected his steps toward the group. The men quieted as he approached, eyeing him with distrust. Of course, he probably looked like he wanted to kill someone. Because he did.

"Who's Christopher?" he demanded. "What does he look like?"

When they didn't respond, he grabbed the nearest one by the shirt and hauled him up, getting in his face. "Who. The hell. Is Christopher?" he bit out.

"Hey, relax," the man tried, making a plea for sanity. Ethan was fresh out. The man's eyes darted toward the back hallway, then widened as the paramedics wheeled Becca's unconscious body by their table. "He'll be back any minute. Probably just went to take a leak."

Like hell. They would have seen anyone anywhere near the restrooms in the last five minutes.

"Describe him."

Noah suddenly showed up at his elbow, loosening Ethan's grip. "Let's try this the proper way," he said, giving Ethan a don't-fuck-with-my-case look.

Playing good cop, Noah inserted himself between Ethan and the group. "My friend here wants to know about Christopher." He glanced back at Ethan. "And in a bad way. I'm guessing this is important to the case we're working on." He flashed his badge, and several of the men began shuffling their feet. "So it's important to me, too. Now who here is going to cooperate?"

There was a lot of grumbling among the group, but one man looked Noah in the eye. "Christopher Armstrong. He's the boss's son, over at the furniture place where we work. He offered to buy us a round of drinks tonight."

"And he faked an accent tonight?" Ethan asked, ignoring Noah's sharp look. But as the question sunk in, Noah's look turned more curious. "A Southern one," Ethan added for his benefit.

A man snorted. "Yeah. He's always pulling pranks like that. Guy seems a little off sometimes, if you know what I mean."

Ethan had a bad feeling he knew exactly what the man meant. He grabbed Noah and pulled him aside. "This guy approached Maggie in the parking lot of the furniture factory just up the street. She didn't recognize his voice, but he was calling himself J. P."

"Because he recognized her and disguised it," Noah finished for him.

"And he's the boss's son. Sounds like he's been filling in lately. So he has access to all areas of the facility."

Noah's eyes narrowed. "What are you getting at?"

"The property we were on, it extended back a ways. There are other buildings they wouldn't let me look at until Monday, when they opened again."

"A base of operations for a killer?"

Ethan jerked a nod. "It's worth checking out."

"Let's go."

Maggie stirred as she felt herself falling. But not onto the cold tile floor she'd imagined in her dream, where she'd been in the radio station's bathroom fighting off another panic attack. This was a hard, damp concrete floor under her cheek. Willing herself to open her eyes, even as her head pounded, she saw the world sideways. And heard Owen's laughter.

"Not so confident now, are you, Maggie? Don't worry, I only gave you a little bit. Just enough to get you out of there without a fight. The drug will wear off soon."

As it all came back to her, she pushed herself up from the floor, pausing halfway as the world swayed. He held a knife pointed at her, only feet away.

She was groggy from the drugs, but her head, why did it ache so badly? She put a hand to her temple, touching it gingerly. Oh yeah. He'd slammed her head into the porcelain edge of the bathroom sink. Knocked her out.

Just like he'd done to Becca. As she remembered hearing the woman's voice, her gaze flew around the room. She pushed the dizziness aside, gulping in air as she waited for her pulse to steady. A woman's form lay in the corner, unconscious, her dark red-brown hair fanned out around her. Heart lodged firmly in her throat, Maggie turned to crawl toward the woman, but Fearmonger's voice stopped her.

"Uh, uh, uh. No moving unless I say so. This is my classroom, my rules. But I see you've seen my other student. Julia's a little sleepy right now, too, but she'll wake up soon and then the real lesson will start."

Julia. She'd found her sister. And now they were *both* in deep trouble. Fearmonger apparently read her thought process in her wide eyes. He laughed again.

"Why are you doing this?"

He pulled a folding metal chair from the corner and set it in front of her. Maggie winced at the scraping sound it made, echoing in her pounding head. "Because I knew you'd understand."

"Understand?" *Understand what, freak?* She wanted to yell at him. He was being so calm, as if her life, and her sister's life, weren't in jeopardy.

"It's just like us scholars to want to explore why people do the things they do. Like what I said about fear."

"Us scholars? This really is some stupid lesson to you, isn't it?" Her mind balked at his delusion.

In classic Fearmonger style, his mood shifted like a weather vane in a tornado. His eyes grew hard. "It's so much more than that. It's justice, too. I've fantasized about teaching my parents, and you, this lesson for a long, long time. Fantasy has always been better than reality, unfortunately. My parents' deaths weren't nearly as eventful, as prolonged or as painful as they deserved. But you, Maggie—I'm confident your death will satisfy my every fantasy." He rose and walked to the corner, where he drew back his leg and kicked Julia in the stomach.

"Stop it!" Maggie yelled. Julia didn't seem to respond, but Maggie thought she saw her sister flinch before she'd covered it.

Fearmonger waved the knife at her. "Keep your voice down or I'll kill her. And that wouldn't be much fun after

all this buildup, would it? It would totally ruin the lesson.
But then, we don't have a lot of time."

Stall.

Maggie watched Julia, but there was no further movement. She thought she'd seen her sister's fingers flex, though,
so maybe she was awake, but biding her time, just as they
should, giving Ethan a chance to get here.

"Get up, bitch!" he yelled, kicking Julia harder. She
moaned and he laughed. "I know you're faking. Stop stall-
ing. I'll kill Maggie now if you don't move."

Julia gave up the attempt to appear unconscious and
struggled to sit up. No easy feat with her hands tied behind
her back and her mouth gagged. And her abdomen had to be
hurting after those kicks. But her eyes glinted with determination in the white warehouse lighting as she met Maggie's
gaze. Her sister had stayed strong. Maggie tried to convey
her support with a look. Then she remembered she wasn't
the one who was gagged.

Screw monster man. She would say what she needed to
say, since they might not make it through this.

"I'm proud of you, sis. I love you."

Julia's eyes filled with tears as she nodded.

"Awww," Fearmonger said, his hand over his heart.
"Touching. Now get up. We're moving. Time to get to class."
His knife at Maggie's throat, he shoved a stumbling Julia
in front of them. "To the van right outside. No fast moves."

As they stepped outside, Maggie recognized the brick
buildings. They were on the grounds of the furniture factory, less than a mile from the bar. And Ethan had already
been suspicious of J. P. When he realized the man had gone
missing at the same time she had, the SSAM team would
hopefully track her here.

But her hope sank as the monster shoved them into a
white van with no rear windows and slammed the door shut.

There were no handles that would allow her to open the van from the inside. They were leaving, and Ethan would have no way to track them. Unless he came in the next few seconds, she might never see him again.

"Can't this thing go any faster?" Ethan urged Noah, who ignored him. Okay, so his nerves were on edge. He was being insane. Love did that to a guy.

Love? Ethan pondered the word for a whole second.

Yes. It was definitely love. Nothing else would make his insides quiver when he was around Maggie, and shake with terror when he knew she was in danger.

"We're almost there. But we're waiting for backup."

Like hell, Ethan thought. Noah could sit and wait for the cavalry to arrive. Maggie's life was in danger. They pulled up in front of the brick building, which looked innocent in the evening twilight. It was anything but. It had housed a vicious murderer. It had given him sanctuary, a place to indulge his madness.

Noah had just called Damian, who'd located the home address of the owner—Mr. Thomas Armstrong—and had sent SSAM agents to the house.

But what really scared Ethan was that Fearmonger had to have known that they'd find all of this information soon. That they'd be closing in. He had nothing left to lose. He only had to complete his final pet project. Maggie.

Ethan leaped out as soon as Noah stopped the car on the warehouse lot.

"Ethan!" Noah hissed, but he was ignored. "Shit."

Ethan heard Noah's feet crunching on the gravel behind him as he secured his gun in his holster, preparing to scale the chain-link fence that surrounded the property. He could see two more buildings, similar to the one he'd already been in but larger, in the back.

Trying for stealth as well as speed, Ethan scaled the fence and waited as Noah did the same. Together, moving forward in a crouched position, they approached the first of the two back buildings. There was only the sound of birds, the hot breeze in the trees, and the gravel that crunched underfoot as they neared the door. With guns drawn, they communicated silently.

Noah moved his head to indicate he would take the lead. Ethan allowed it, only because the other man was more clear-headed at the moment, while Ethan saw everything through a haze of red. He tried to focus on good things, to regain his impartiality. But Maggie's gentle, knowing smile was the only good thing he could think of. And thinking of where Maggie currently was made him insane.

So he centered his thoughts on the asshole who'd taken her. The fake cowboy. The wannabe fear expert. He imagined evoking fear in the man himself as he ripped him apart.

The first warehouse was the smaller of the two buildings and was packed full with finished goods. Noah squeezed down an aisle, heading toward the back, and disappeared from view for a moment before he returned, shaking his head.

Nothing.

They immediately moved to the other building, approaching in the same manner. As they entered, their echoing steps were drowned out by the sound of an engine starting. Bypassing caution, they ran full-out toward the back. Light streamed from an open door that led to an empty room. It had probably been an office once upon a time, if the ancient filing cabinet in the corner meant anything. The light came from the window inside. The skid of tires on gravel grated on Ethan as the two men ran to the window just in time to see the blur of a white van as it disappeared.

"Shit," Noah said before flipping out his phone and dialing.

Ethan gestured to the numerous padlocks on the office door and Noah nodded. Someone had really wanted to keep people out of here. Or keep them in.

Noah spoke into the phone as someone picked up. "Maria. He's on the move down the back alley, heading west. We'll double-check he didn't leave anyone behind. White van. Didn't get the plates. Had the name of the furniture place on the side, Custom For You Furniture."

Jesus, Ethan hadn't even noticed that—through his red haze and all. *Fuck.* He had to focus, or he'd be no good to Maggie. But his blood was boiling. They'd been so close. Only seconds behind Fearmonger.

"Give me your keys," he growled.

"No way." Noah surveyed Ethan's face. He no doubt saw the crazy desperation lurking there. "No. We go together. I've got police watching for the van. It can't be far away. Meanwhile, think about where they could be going. Maria said Becca regained consciousness at the hospital. She's giving them hell right now. Wants to get back into the action." Ethan hadn't even thought to ask about Becca. Remorse stung him. Noah seemed to notice his anguish. "You're upset. I get that. But we can help you. You're not in this alone. So just trust me, okay?"

He laid a hand on Ethan's shoulder. "We'll find Maggie and Julia. This is actually encouraging. They've got to be alive, otherwise he would have left them and run on his own."

Ethan jerked a nod. Yeah, they were probably alive. But what did Fearmonger have planned for them? And how long until the killer realized he could run faster by himself and decided to get rid of dead weight?

* * *

"What are we doing here?" Maggie felt her chest tighten as Fearmonger touched the tip of his very large knife to her shoulder, prodding her to follow Julia, who was still gagged, her wrists bound behind her, as they entered the dark abyss of the tunnels beneath the university. Dark, small, unfamiliar places were not at the top of her list of safety zones. Especially when she was stuck with a murderer who had a long, sharp instrument in his hand.

She pressed the anxiety down, however, ignoring the pain behind her breastbone as she focused on Julia's ramrod-straight back. They hadn't been able to communicate since he'd forced them from the van, but she sensed that her sister was ready to run if the chance presented itself. But could she get very far with her hands restrained?

As for Maggie, fear for her sister overcame fear for herself. The ache in her chest was bad, but hadn't gotten worse, and the drugs seemed to have worn off. Until the monster decided to whip out another one of his special syringes. He'd left her untied, at least, and that was a blessing.

"We won't be in the tunnels for long. Just long enough to get to where we're going. Just think of it as a little field trip." He waved the knife in front of him in excitement. "I always wanted to be a professor. A medical professor, actually. But thanks to you, I won't be." In his other hand, he held an electric lantern high. The light cast large, eerie shadows on the tunnel walls.

Thanks to *her?*

"Apparently you, dear Maggie, didn't believe I had the brains for it." His voice had turned hard, his eyes black as the tunnel walls. "You and that medical school board, marking me down because you couldn't recognize true genius, which isn't measured by numbers and letters. You're just like my parents."

Maggie made a sympathetic sound, but her focus was on memorizing where they turned, the number of footsteps before they changed direction, and anything else that would help them get away. Dear God, where was he taking them? And if he blamed her for his failure, what would he do to her?

Ahead of her a couple yards, Julia stumbled and fell to her knees. Her gag muffled her cry when she couldn't catch herself with her hands bound behind her. Fearmonger pushed past Maggie and put the knife to Julia's throat.

"Get up."

"Don't hurt her," Maggie yelled as he yanked Julia to her feet and shoved her against the wall. Julia grunted from the impact. Maggie resisted cursing at him. He wanted to see her upset. He thrived on any sign of fear. She forced herself to sound calm and reasonable. "She doesn't need the gag anymore, does she?"

He eyed her as if evaluating what she could be up to. Her breath came out in a rush as he nodded. "I'll take it off. But if she talks, she dies. If she screams or shouts, you both die." Julia met Maggie's eyes with a silent thank-you as he took the gag from her mouth. Her sister had to be thirsty as hell, but she didn't complain.

"And the wrist restraints?" Maggie pressed. "You've got the knife and she has nowhere to run."

"No. She stays tied up. What, do you think I'm stupid?" His eyes flashed in the light of his lantern as he stalked back to her.

No. He wasn't stupid. Just crazy. But she detected a definite pattern here. The guy didn't like to be thought of as stupid or inept. Even when he'd called in to her show, he'd only become angry when she'd seemed to refute his point of view. And he obviously wasn't happy about not getting into medical school. Perhaps she could use the information to their advantage. Rattle him a bit. Of course, rattling him might prove even more dangerous. But hell, they had nothing to lose.

"You say you know human behavior," Maggie said, struggling for some semblance of respect. The man clearly wanted to be seen as a scholar. Could she possibly use logic to reason with him? "There are so many facets to it, though. Why focus on fear?"

"Because fear is everything. Only fear makes the world go 'round. Only fear truly motivates us to survive. Stop here," he told Julia, then gave the lantern to Maggie before he moved ahead. He pulled a key from his pocket to unlock a doorway, shooting a warning look over his shoulder.

She thought about running for all of two seconds. But he still had the knife. And it was painfully evident that Julia's options were limited with her hands bound. Dousing the lantern would only make it more difficult to get away. Sure, he wouldn't be able to lash out with his knife as well, but in the narrow tunnel, she wasn't willing to take that chance. Even without the threat of a weapon, they wouldn't get far in the pitch black.

When he swung open the door and flipped a switch, dim light filled a large room. *A basement?* At any rate, it was a rarely used room, if the number of cobwebs and mold growing on the wall were any indication.

He shut the door behind them and nudged them onward. "Keep going. There are stairs at the end of the room. Follow them up to the third floor. Room 303."

Maggie's head whipped around as she gasped. "We're in the medical-school building?" *No. Oh, no, no, no.* She hadn't come back here since…

His grin was lethal. "I'm surprised you didn't figure it out sooner. You know what I do with my victims. I help them face their greatest fears. And now, it's your turn."

NINETEEN

"THE ARMSTRONGS ARE DEAD," Noah reported as he hung up his phone. Every bent head around Sullivan's corner table—Maria, Damian, Lorena and Ethan—looked up. The rest of the bar had been emptied of patrons. Police were down the street sweeping for clues in the warehouse where Maggie and her sister had recently been, in the bar's restroom where Becca and Maggie had encountered Fearmonger, and everywhere in between, searching the alley that ran behind Sullivan's as well as Custom For You Furniture.

Ethan gripped his hands together to stop from punching something. Every lead they gained seemed to be useless.

Noah sat down hard. "The officer on the scene forced his way in, upon Chief's orders. Found Mr. and Mrs. Thomas Armstrong dead. Probably been dead a few days."

Damian shook his head. "Not surprising, but still tragic. Any sign of their son?"

"None."

"At least we have a name now. Christopher Armstrong has to be Fearmonger. I'll call Catherine and have her cross-check that information with the database of people who attended or worked at the universities at the times of the other crimes."

Maria's phone rang and she immediately picked up with a glance at Noah. "Yeah….Where?…Good work. We'll be there soon." She hung up and smiled. "They found the van."

Ethan felt a tiny ray of hope. But finding the van didn't necessarily mean finding Maggie. "Abandoned?"

The look in her eyes was full of empathy as she nodded. "Yeah. But it's where we found it that'll help."

He stood as adrenaline kicked in. "Where?"

"The university."

"Let's go."

The entire team moved, sirens wailing to part the Saturday night traffic, to the Chicago Great Lakes University campus. Officer Lewis gladly stepped aside as Noah and Maria took over the security office to serve as a base of operations.

"What'd I miss?"

Ethan looked up in surprise as Becca strode in, a white bandage at her temple. He scowled, but her smile only brightened. "Shouldn't you be at the hospital?"

"They can't force me." She put a hand on her hip. "And neither can you. I'm in this until the end. Besides, I'm fine."

Worry about Maggie kept him from ordering her back to the hospital bed. He could use all the help he could get right now. And as much as he hated to admit it, Becca's head—wounded though it was—was functioning more rationally than his at the moment. He took a deep breath, telling himself for the hundredth time that charging through the tunnels after Maggie was no use to anyone at the moment. Drawing on his training, he steadied his emotions.

"Fine. You're in." He gestured to Lorena, whose FBI training might come in handy in the field this time. "You and Lorena start at the psychology building where Sharon's murder occurred." Ethan tapped his finger against a point on the blueprints. "I'll work my way through the tunnels from the dorm where Fearmonger first entered. Noah and Maria will enter the tunnels at the opening nearest where the van was found."

Officer Lewis cleared his throat. "What about us?"

Ethan's gaze roamed over the three uniformed men who'd been called in for added security since Sharon's murder. At least, with darkness falling and evening classes out already, the campus was near to empty. "I want one of you at the library and one monitoring the dorms, in case Fearmonger does something unexpected. We want to keep the students safe." He didn't want anyone else going through what Maggie and Julia were.

Ethan's hands curled into fists and he forced them to relax. "Besides, if we trap him, he might try to escape by blending in with the student population." He looked at Lewis, whose wrinkles and deep-set eyes showed confidence and experience. "You come with me and stay at the entrance to the tunnels where we know Fearmonger's gone into the dorms before. He may try to enter behind me."

As Ethan's focus returned to the blueprints, the taller, rail-thin security officer spoke up. "There are some areas that aren't on there." All eyes swung sharply to him and he cleared his throat. "I used to go to school here, and some of us snuck down to these tunnels. There are a couple of maintenance rooms and storage areas that I think were added during construction, after these blueprints were drawn up."

Damian stood from where he'd been leaning against a desk in the corner and stepped forward, handing the man a pen. "Mark as many of those rooms as you can remember on there. He may be holed up in one of them. We'll get copies for everyone going down there to search. I'll be here in the security office, coordinating everything."

"As will I," Bellingham said, entering the already-crowded room. "I've spoken to the police commissioner. More backup is on the way. And I've placed the library and dorms in lockdown mode until this is over."

"Thank you for your cooperation," Damian said. "It could save lives." He moved away as his phone rang.

"This bastard thinks he can come in and take over my campus and frighten my staff and students," Bellingham continued. "Well, he'll have a reality check real soon."

Ending his call, Damian moved toward Ethan as everyone else left to get flashlights and their copies of maps and tunnel blueprints. "Ethan, can I speak with you?"

He was itching to get out there and look for Maggie, but he sensed Damian had something important to say. Was there something he hadn't shared with the group? "Yes?"

"That call was from one of my private investigators. He found the missing guard's body. She was killed, swiftly and efficiently. No message about fear."

"He's cleaning up his loose ends because he knows he doesn't have much time left."

Damian nodded. They both understood what was at stake. Fearmonger was a guy with nothing more to lose. "You can do this, finding Maggie. You know that, right?"

"Of course."

"I just wanted to be sure. I hope you know I wouldn't have hired you unless I knew you were capable of the job."

Ethan rubbed the back of his neck uncomfortably. "Three years ago, most people were calling me a washout," he said, looking away. "I never did understand why you called me with this job, but I'm thankful."

Damian smiled grimly. "I'm not looking for thanks. I'm looking for results. I know a good person when I see one, and I know you've got it in you to get those women back safely. *You* just need to know that you have it in you. No more letting the past cloud your mind."

"I won't." Maggie's life depended on it. "And thank you, sir, for the vote of confidence."

Damian clapped him on the shoulder. "I was always confident in you. You just weren't ready to believe it."

Ten minutes later, the team split into groups and moved toward their assigned areas. Ethan jogged beside Officer Lewis to the dorm building that led to the tunnels, feeling the familiar weight of his weapon in his shoulder holster. He'd discarded the suit jacket in favor of comfort and maneuverability. Still, sweat trickled from his temple. The sun was setting, but the heat wave hadn't let up.

At the tunnel opening, Lewis waited while Ethan proceeded into the dark, musty tunnel. The beams of his flashlight flickered over metal pipes and trailing cobwebs as he swept them over the passage ahead.

Except for the heartbeat resounding in his ears, there was only the sound of water dripping from somewhere farther along. A faint whistle of breeze came from the tunnel, brushing his cheek and offering some relief from the heat, lifting the hair from his forehead before gently setting it down again. Maybe Becca had opened the doorway from the psych building, several hundred yards distant and out of sight, creating a breezeway. Or maybe another door was open, perhaps around the right-angle bend ahead, where someone else hid.

Fearmonger had marked this tunnel with Sharon's blood days ago, and the words were still there, reflecting the light as Ethan swept the beam right to left, left to right. The shiny, once-sticky surface of the bloody letters increased the sense of urgency within Ethan as he thought of Maggie and how he'd first seen her scrubbing blood from her living room walls.

Would Maggie's precious lifeblood decorate some forsaken tunnel several feet beneath the university? Had Fearmonger brought Maggie through here? Had she seen the walls? Was she having an anxiety attack even now, when he couldn't get to her?

Moving more quickly, he made his way the hundred yards to the corner and turned, then went farther into the dark depths. It sloped downward for a little ways, but evened out again. Finally, he came to a door. One he hadn't noticed on his previous exploration because the bloody words had only been in the first length of tunnel. Here, there was nothing. Only quiet. And the door the security guard had marked on Ethan's map.

But it didn't budge. And a closer examination with the direct light of the flashlight beam showed indications the door had not been opened in some time. Probably fifty years.

Another hundred yards down the tunnel, he came to another door. If the map he held was correct, this one led to the basement of the psychology building. He shoved it open, noting someone had oiled the old hinges. Probably Fearmonger. He pushed through and came face-to-face with the barrel of a gun.

The third floor of the medical-school building was as familiar to Maggie as her own home. She'd spent about as much time there. But she hadn't been back in a year. Not since Brad had died here, just inside the doorway of Room 303, where Maggie had an office for supervising med students interested in practicing psychiatry. And where she'd held a grant for performing outpatient therapy with low-income patients. Patients like Deborah Frame.

Fearmonger shoved them into the room, and Maggie took a place next to her sister. Julia's eyes widened as she glanced at their surroundings.

"Is this where…?" Julia's voice trailed off as she gulped.

He chuckled. "Ding, ding, ding. She gets a prize. Welcome to the place of Brad Levine's final moments." He grinned at Maggie. "And where Dr. Margaret Levine learned her first lesson in *true* fear. I thought it would be an appropriate place for your final lesson."

He pulled a podium from the corner. It hadn't been there during Maggie's occupation of the office, but it looked familiar.

Following the direction of her gaze, Fearmonger smiled. "Nice, huh?"

"It looks just like the one in my classroom."

"Because it is just like that one. President Bellingham ordered a couple dozen for the university and I made and delivered them. That's how I got the keys to these tunnels." He chuckled again, obviously pleased with his cleverness. "I doubt Bellingham even realized they were on his key ring when he lent them to me. Nobody pays close attention to blue-collar workers, after all. It was a piece of cake to have a few copies made."

He sneered. "People can be so trusting. Those other girls, years ago…they were trusting, too. All I had to do was deliver some furniture. Get the layout of the house. Give them a smile or two, and maybe say something flattering." His eyes darkened. "They thought they knew everything and flaunted it at students they deemed inferior. I had to show them they were wrong to underestimate me."

He seemed to shake off his musings. "Now where did we leave off?" He moved behind the podium. "Only fear makes the world go 'round."

Maggie felt her heart pounding. He'd killed so many innocent people, and he waved it away as if it were nothing or as if they deserved it for thinking so little of him. She pressed her lips together. She glanced at Julia and gave a small, hopefully reassuring smile before stepping away from her sister. She wanted the monster's attention on her and only her.

He wanted an active participant? Then, okay, she could play along. "Only fear?" she asked, tilting her head to the side as if in thought. "I'm still not convinced. True, fear makes your heart pump and motivates some actions, but what about love?"

His face grew taut. "Love is only the fear of being alone. It's something people make up to soothe themselves when they don't think they can make it through life by themselves. Like a lullaby. I don't need it to survive."

"That's not true." Maggie knew what love could do. Her family had shown her. And Ethan had shown her. "Love is the most potent emotion on earth."

"Except for hope," Julia said, her voice scratchy and dry behind Maggie. They were the first words Maggie had heard since their exchange at dinner, forty-eight hours ago, and they were like beautiful music. Over her shoulder, she exchanged a soft look with Julia, who nodded. Neither of them was going to give up hope.

"No. No. No." Fearmonger stalked forward the few feet that separated him from Julia, spittle flying as he got in her face. She cringed but didn't back away. "Hope is the thing that makes fear all that more powerful. A catalyst, if you will. If one hopes, then one has more to lose, and that feeds fear. But it all still comes down to fear."

"Bullshit," Maggie said, hoping to draw Fearmonger's attention again. It worked.

He swung to her, a feral grin lighting his face. "Really? Right now you're hoping someone will come to your rescue. And he will, Maggie. I'm counting on it. Because, you see, I've done *my* homework. I know how much you and a certain SSAM agent have grown to *love* each other. And I know what it would do to you to watch him die. Right after you watch your sister die." Fearmonger's grin grew wider. "Then, we'll see who's right."

A breath of relief whooshed out of Ethan as he noted who aimed the gun at his head. "Stand down, Becca."

She lowered her weapon, then pressed a hand to her chest. "You startled me."

He didn't point out that *she* was the one with the deadly weapon pointed at *his* head. "Sorry. Didn't want to yell ahead in case Fearmonger was around," he said in a low voice that nevertheless reverberated throughout the basement. He gave a wry grin. "At least you were ready for me." He frowned at the bandage at her temple, noting the red stain. "You've started bleeding again."

She shrugged. "A bit. I'll live." She didn't have to add that Maggie and Julia might not. They were both well aware of the stakes.

As they walked beyond the empty concrete chamber where the tunnel ended, they entered another room that was clearly still in use, though apparently had not been occupied for some time. It held old aluminum chairs and beat-up desks. A row of battered filing cabinets, standard 1950s office equipment, lined one long wall.

"No sign of Maggie or Fearmonger, then?" he asked, the feeling of urgency still pressing on his chest. He wondered if this was what Maggie's panic attacks felt like. Becca followed on his heels as he made his way up the stairs and out of the basement.

"Nothing." The disappointment rang clear in her voice. "Lorena is hanging out near Maggie's classroom. You know, in case Fearmonger takes them back to the scene of the original crime."

Indeed, they came upon the SSAM mindhunter roaming the hallway outside the classroom as Becca spoke. "Though some serial killers go back to the scenes of their crimes, I don't think he's going to show up here." Her dark eyes were troubled as she frowned.

"Then we need to think of other options, fast. Talk to me, Lorena. This is your specialty. Help me think this through."

Ethan fought to bring organization to his jumbled thoughts. "All along, Fearmonger has been talking about fear, and how important it is. He wants to prove it to Maggie. And it looks like he brought her to the university to do that."

Lorena nodded. "Most people go where they're comfortable, and he's killed here before. He seems to know the tunnel system. It makes sense he would come here again. Besides, he has fantasies of being a professor, of being in charge, of proving he's worthy to others."

"But what if it's more than that? What if it's about the fear?"

"About Maggie's fear, you mean. What does she fear most?"

"Losing her loved ones."

"But he already has them. So we assume he'll make her watch as he kills her sister."

Ethan felt sick to his stomach. But the adrenaline rush pushed it to the fringe. They were closer to catching this guy than ever before. He could feel it. "This is his last stand. What would he do to make the event even more profound?"

"The first victim, years ago," Lorena said, "was found in her apartment. She'd been strapped to the bed and covered in spiders before he'd sliced her up. The second victim had been burned, but only from her waist down. So that he could keep her alive and conscious longer, I suppose. The third was drowned. She still had cuts all over her body, but the ultimate cause of death was drowning. Spiders, death by fire and drowning must have been their greatest fears."

Lorena continued to play out the theory, pacing now in the hallway. "So with the twin sisters, he strapped them to the walls opposite each other, made them face each other, and made them watch each other die. Slowly."

"And in the apartment where they lived together," Becca

added, having remained silent until now, content to watch them work out their thoughts.

"Of course," Lorena said, her words picking up in tempo. "The location is just as important to him as anything else. With the twins, he'd evolved. Their greatest fear could have been being separated, and living without each other. But performing his act in a place that was so personally important to them would heighten the emotion."

"That sounds plausible." Ethan was pacing the corridor now. "So what place on campus, other than her classroom, would Maggie feel personally connected to?"

"She didn't go to school here, right? So what other areas has she worked in?" Lorena asked.

Ethan's heart pounded in his throat. "The shooting. It was in her office in the medical-school building." She'd told him herself how her brother had been standing in the doorway when Deborah had seen them give each other an affectionate goodbye. Her office, which she would once have seen as a safe haven for herself and the clients she treated, would have become a symbol of fear after what Deborah did. Fearmonger, having done his research, would surely know that.

"That's where he must have taken her," Becca said.

"Lorena, call Damian and find out where, exactly, in the medical-school building Maggie's office was." Ethan began down the hallway at a trot, Becca following on his heels. "I'm heading over there."

"Be on your guard," Lorena called after them. "Fearmonger might have discovered a thing or two about your past that he can use. Fear is his weapon, and he's learned to wield it well."

Picking up speed, Ethan ran outside into the warm summer night air. There was little breeze to cool the sweat on his brow. Becca was right behind him, following as he veered to the right where a large brick building loomed. He recognized the bench where he'd found Maggie and Damian sitting on the morning they'd discovered Sharon's gruesome murder. She'd never said anything then about the significance of the other campus building. But then, she hadn't shared the details of that particular personal tragedy with him yet.

He only hoped he'd have many more chances to talk with her, share with her, after tonight.

The knife hovered at Julia's throat, but Maggie kept her focus on Fearmonger. If she looked at her sister, she'd lose her battle with anxiety. And she knew her sister was fighting her own inner battle. She had to help Julia.

I am in control. Her mantra helped her remember to breathe in and out.

"Come on, Maggie," he urged. "Give in to the fear. I know you want to. I can see the panic glazing your eyes."

His teeth glinted in the low light of the camping lantern as he smiled. She tried not to think about what he intended to do with them in this small, dark room he'd led them to. A room just off the tunnel by which they'd left the medical building.

"That's not panic," she said through gritted teeth. "It's determination."

Fearmonger laughed. "Even as you pretend to hold strong, Julia here is quivering in my arms. You see, like every noteworthy scholar, I'm a very thorough researcher, and I found out Julia's greatest fear. Small, dark, enclosed spaces. Isn't that right?"

Julia whimpered.

"And what are you afraid of, Owen?" Maggie prayed she could distract him from torturing Julia further. "Being a nobody? Being *stupid?*"

His smile slipped, and Julia hissed out a breath as Fearmonger jerked her head to the side, exposing her tender throat to the tip of the knife. It pressed precariously close to a vein pulsing at her neck. With her arms still tied behind her and Fearmonger holding her off balance, Julia could do nothing to fight back.

"Call me Fearmonger," he told Maggie in a hard voice. "I'm not Owen or J. P. or Christopher Armstrong."

"I think you just answered my question. You're pretending to be someone you're not. Someone smarter than you are."

"No!" he roared, his face reddening in the dim light, making him look like the devil he was. "I'm not afraid of who I am, or my bastard of a father. He was weak. He exploited his physical prowess. He wouldn't know what someone with a functioning brain looked like."

Maggie scoffed, adopting on a blasé attitude she didn't feel. Not with that knife still aimed at Julia's throat. "Like *you* do?"

He waved the knife at her and Maggie sucked in a breath. For the moment, her sister wasn't the target. "Yes. Like *I* do. I use my intelligence. I got you two here, didn't I? I got to those other women and taught them their lessons, didn't I?"

"And the way you overpowered and killed them didn't require your physical strength? You're such a hypocrite."

"Don't mock me!" His voice was as loud and sharp as a slap. Maggie prayed someone outside could hear them. But who would be in the dark tunnels underneath a university on a hot summer night? Fearmonger seemed to think Ethan would come for her—indeed, he seemed to relish the thought of killing him in front of her—and she knew Ethan wouldn't hesitate to come if he knew where to find them. If someone tracked the van, or thought about Fearmonger's old hideouts, maybe they'd be on campus. And maybe they'd guess he'd taken them to the tunnels. But it would take them forever to search all the dark passages.

"I'm not mocking. I'm just telling the truth."

Suddenly, Fearmonger smiled, an unholy light in his eye. "Well played, Maggie. You almost had me losing control. But you're the one who'll be losing the control you prize so highly. And it won't take much. You're already feeling the fear, aren't you? Pressing on your chest, making it difficult to breathe?"

Maggie struggled to ignore the squeezing in her chest that his words created. She focused on her breathing. *In. Out.*

Fearmonger was smiling again. "It's *only fear,* Maggie. Isn't that your attitude? That you can conquer it? We'll see. You've been to the place where your brother breathed his last. Where your hope for mankind led to your downfall. I'd hoped to finish things for you there, after you watch your sister's greatest fears come true."

He shook his head as if disappointed. "But that's the first place they'll look for you, if they have any brains." He shrugged. "Intelligent people adapt. As you listen to your sister's dying breaths, I'll be hunting down another present for you. You've fallen for Agent Townsend. I could see it today." His sneer turned feral. "And he'll die for that."

She couldn't breathe. Julia. Ethan. They were going to die if she didn't stop him. And her parents might never recover from such a loss.

As her breathing continued to hitch and her vision swam in the dim light, Fearmonger continued speaking in a singsong voice. "I'll bring him to you and we'll have a little reunion." He jerked Julia up and back, choking off her air. "In the meantime, you get started on the party without me. Welcome to your own private hell."

Before Maggie could understand his intent, he shifted the knife in one fluid motion from Julia's neck and stabbed her forcefully in her side. Julia's mouth rounded in a soundless O as Fearmonger released her and she slipped to the floor.

His laughter echoed off the walls as Maggie's knees gave out and she sank down beside her sister. "No!"

"Excellent, Maggie," he said, raising his lantern to look in her eyes like a doctor would. "You're getting there."

Taking the light with him, Fearmonger rushed from the room, his shadow cast over Julia's body. The shadow grew and turned to complete blackness as the door slammed shut. She heard the grate of metal on metal as the monster locked them away. Gritting her teeth, she squeezed her eyes shut against the overbearing darkness, pretending it was dark because her eyes were closed.

Maggie fumbled on the floor in the pitch black, crawling forward and reaching for where her sister had fallen before the lights went out for good. She felt something warm and wet. Blood. Julia's blood. Trying to control her racing pulse, she forced herself forward until her fingers brushed sticky, wet fabric at her sister's waistline.

"Julia?"

No response. She refused to think that her sister was dead. People survived knife wounds all the time, didn't they?

One hand felt for a pulse at Julia's neck, but in the blackness, found her sister's chilled lips instead. But—thank you, God—there was an exhale of breath coming through them. She felt a little further down, following her neck until she felt the thready pulse there.

Alive. Definitely in trouble, but not hopeless yet.

She gently probed for the edge of the warm wetness on her sister's shirt and found where blood seemed to be issuing forth. She pressed her hands there as she said a prayer.

The monster had locked them away in a tomb. Away from help for Julia. Away from Ethan.

TWENTY

"WHAT WAS THAT?" Ethan whispered into his cell phone.

On the other end of the line, Noah, who was down in the tunnels while Becca and Ethan scouted out the medical building, wouldn't have reception much longer. Ethan knew from his previous experience in the tunnels that once he moved more than fifty yards into the ground, all connection to the outside was lost.

They were in Fearmonger territory.

"Sounded like metal creaking and banging," Noah said in a hushed voice. "But it's hard to tell down here how far away it was. Maria and I are heading in. We're about to lose contact with you."

"Got it. I think we're closing in. I feel it in my gut." And his heart told him he was close to Maggie. God, he hoped she was okay. But if the maniac was on the move, and there was no other sound than the opening and closing of doors, his brain told him maybe it was too late.

"Mine, too. Be careful, man."

And then the phone was dead.

"This is the number Damian gave us, 303." Becca's voice was barely audible as she approached the room that had once been Maggie's office. The threshold where Brad had lost his life. And an office Christopher Armstrong probably associated with failure. While crossing the campus, Becca had received a text from Catherine that explained Fearmonger's connection to Maggie. A Christopher Armstrong had indeed attended various colleges in the vicinities of the previous murders—and had flunked out of all but one. The period when he hadn't been torturing and killing innocent girls was the timeframe when he'd earned his Bachelor's degree. Apparently buoyed by that success, a Christopher Armstrong had applied to medical school at Chicago Great Lakes University a year ago and been denied. And Maggie's name had been on the committee that had denied him.

As a team, Ethan and Becca moved quietly, but no sound came from within the office. There was no reason for stealth. The room was empty, the door standing wide-open.

"What's this doing here?" Becca asked circling a wooden podium that stood in the middle. "Odd place for a class, don't you think."

"But not for a lesson," Ethan added grimly, crouching down beside it. He found the logo he was looking for. Custom For You Furniture.

"They *were* here."

"And we're still playing catch-up." He ran a hand over the back of his neck. "There's got to be a tunnel leading into this building. We didn't see them leaving as we arrived."

She nodded in agreement. "Must be in the basement, like the ones that lead to the other buildings on campus." They took off at a run down the stairs.

"Julia?" Maggie's voice was hoarse with unshed tears. She was beginning to shake, but not with fear or anxiety. With fatigue. The muscles in her arms had been pressing firmly on Julia's side for what seemed like a long time now. It had probably only been a few minutes, but in this unending darkness, who knew? It messed with your mind.

She gritted her teeth against the urge to give in to panic. Not yet. She had to keep it together for Julia.

I am in control.

It was only fear, after all. An emotion. She could control it—or at least her reaction to it.

It was just darkness. She imagined herself lying in the dark on a featherbed with Ethan's arms wrapped around her. They were making love. Slowly. And he was whispering words of love and encouragement in her ear.

She wanted that so badly. That future with Ethan. She had so much to live for. And Julia would be proud of her for choosing to reach out for it, she thought, choking down a sob.

"I'm not giving up hope," she told her sister.

She had to get Julia out of here. The regular rise and fall of her chest as she breathed had turned irregular.

Maggie squinted into the bright light that appeared as the metal door squeaked open again. *Ethan?* Her heart leaped, then plummeted as she recognized the lantern Fearmonger had held before.

He was back to finish the job.

She continued applying pressure to the wound at her sister's side. The bleeding had slowed, but she still needed a hospital, fast.

"Time to go, Maggie. It's time for the next lesson."

"No. I'm not leaving her."

Fearmonger held the lantern up a little more, throwing his features into frightening patterns of light and shadow. "Then I'll finish her for good." He stepped forward and the blade of the knife caught the light. Parts of it were dark, and Maggie realized it was her sister's blood that stained it.

Saying a silent prayer for Julia, Maggie rose on shaky legs and held out a hand protectively over her sister, as if she could ward off evil. "No, wait. I'll come with you."

He glanced down the tunnel as they heard a noise that seemed far away. Another door? Hope soared, even as the knife in Fearmonger's hands had her heart pounding harder.

He'd used it on her sister, and she had no doubt he'd use it on her. Or, worse, on Ethan.

"Walk." He waved his lantern toward one direction of the dark tunnel.

Was it the direction from which the noise had come? It was hard to tell. The acoustics in the tunnel distorted sound and other sensations. But somehow she doubted he was leading her toward safety. No, it was more likely he was setting the trap for Ethan. With her as bait.

Was that a flicker of light ahead?

Ethan motioned to Becca to stand still behind him, then switched off his flashlight to hide their location and stood still, holding his breath as they listened. The light farther down the passageway seemed to grow stronger, but then it went out completely. The tunnel was deathly silent.

A long, low, bone-chilling laugh replaced the quiet. "E-than. I know you're out there somewhere," a voice said. Fearmonger. The way sound carried in this place, he could be anywhere. "We'll be waiting."

Ethan said nothing, only walked a little faster, a little less cautiously as the man spoke. He heard Becca's light footfalls right behind him, her hand resting lightly on his elbow so she could feel when he moved. Choosing speed over stealth, he risked turning his flashlight on, realizing it could be more dangerous to them to run in the dark.

"What's that?" came Becca's whispered question.

Guns drawn, they approached the metal door that stood ajar. No light, no sound came from within. There was only the stillness of a tomb.

Ethan signaled to Becca to stay back as he checked it out. His flashlight swung across the interior, then lower. It stopped when he spotted a still form on the ground. His breath caught and held until he stepped forward and realized it wasn't Maggie. But Julia was in obvious trouble and needed medical attention fast. He knelt and felt the bleeding wound his flashlight had illuminated, and immediately applied pressure.

"Do you get reception here?" he asked Becca, keeping his voice as low as possible in case Fearmonger was nearby.

She checked her phone and shook her head. "Not enough, but the tunnel entrance from the medical building wasn't too far back." Every second counted, for both Julia and Maggie.

"Go back and call Damian. Tell him where Julia is and that we need an ambulance. Then get back here. Fast."

Becca took out her own flashlight from a loop at her belt, switched it on and took off at a run. Ethan was left with the warm, sticky feel of Julia's blood under his fingers, wondering what Fearmonger had in store. The killer knew Ethan was here. Had called him by name. Which meant Fearmonger must have guessed how important Maggie was to him.

The question was, how did the monster plan to use that information?

Maggie stumbled and Fearmonger cursed, kicking her in the leg. Her cry of pain echoed down the silent, dark tunnel.

"Shut up and keep walking. Faster."

She didn't know what was better—the calm, philosophizing Fearmonger, or the tense, desperate Fearmonger. She fought to keep her breathing and pulse under control as she continued along the tunnel, pressing her hands against the walls every so often for balance. And to leave a handprint in Julia's blood. He seemed to believe her fumbling act. Either that or he didn't care if Ethan tracked them. He'd already admitted he had plans to kill Ethan while she was forced to watch.

Like Julia.

She hoped to God Ethan was getting help for Julia at that

very moment. The rest of the SSAM team couldn't be too far behind. Even her captor had known they were coming, taunting Ethan. But that also meant he had something planned.

"Through there." Fearmonger nudged her with the point of his knife toward the door on her left. For good measure, she stumbled again, using the door to pull herself upright. "Now!" He pulled the door shut tight behind them.

"Good girl, Maggie," Ethan whispered, finding her handprint on the door to his right. Forcing himself to slow down and be more careful had paid off. Sweeping the flashlight from side to side had revealed a bloody handprint. He was sure Maggie's hand had left it—with Julia's blood. At least, he hoped Maggie wasn't bleeding as well. With Becca's return after her phone call to Damian for help, which she'd assured Ethan was only seconds away, he'd relinquished his position at Julia's side to her and taken off after Maggie. Still, he estimated he was about ten minutes behind them. Of course, Maggie might be slowing Fearmonger down.

Becca had cursed at him as he stepped back out into the tunnel, telling him to wait for backup, that it would be there any second, but he hadn't listened. How could he, when every second that passed, every heartbeat, meant risking Maggie's life?

The squeak of rusty hinges sliced across Ethan's taut nerves as he pushed open the ancient door. The maze of tunnels beyond the door wasn't marked on the map. And he could deduce why. This tunnel appeared unfinished. It didn't have the echoing concrete of the other passageways. Instead, a warm, moist earth smell swamped his nostrils as he tentatively poked his head around the doorway, listening carefully for any sign of a human—or in the case of Fearmonger, perhaps *nonhuman* was a better description—presence. Something dripped and echoed in the distance.

Cautiously, Ethan entered the tunnel, one step at a time. Instead of the sound of footsteps, his foot met soft dirt. Definitely an unfinished tunnel. Would his backup be close behind? He hoped to God they'd found Becca and gotten Julia to safety first.

A whistle of air brushed past his head, lifting a lock of hair, then stopped. Someone had opened a door on the other end of the tunnel, creating a brief draft between the ends. And now the door was closed again.

Deciding to go with his instinct and throw caution to the wind in favor of speed, Ethan's long strides ate up the distance as he broke into a jog. His flashlight, in one hand, pointed straight ahead. In the other, he held his gun.

A minute later, he halted, his light bouncing off another metal door. Taking a moment to catch his breath, he holstered his gun and dug the tunnel blueprints out of a pocket, aiming his flashlight beam at it as he tried to judge where he was. But the darkness had been so disorienting, he couldn't be sure. He thought he'd jogged due west, toward the edge of campus, but at some point, the floor had sloped and curved gently. He couldn't be certain he wasn't just linking up again with the same tunnel, with Fearmonger creeping up behind him. But it didn't matter what danger awaited him if Maggie was on the other side. He'd walk into certain death for her.

"Holy shit," Ethan breathed. "The radio station."

If he was right in his calculations, that he'd headed due west, he was now near the building on the edge of campus that housed the radio station. It made sense that Fearmonger would take her there. It was meaningful to him since their dialogue about fear had begun in that setting, but what if he guessed wrong? Time was of the essence.

Heart racing, he stuffed the map back into his pocket and drew his gun again, pushing open the door and finding himself with a choice to make. Right or left. There was no sound or light from either end.

An examination of the floor gave him his answer. The moist dirt from the older tunnel had stuck to someone's shoe, just enough to leave a faint outline of a shoeprint. It had to be Fearmonger's. Leading toward the left. Toward the radio station, he surmised.

Adrenaline pumping through his system, he raced in that direction.

A few minutes later, the oiled door at the end of the tunnel didn't squeak as he pushed it open. It had clearly been used more recently. He entered a cement room in a basement he didn't recognize and halted when he heard voices ahead, just past a doorway.

"And what are you afraid of, Fairy Princess?" That had to be Fearmonger, only this time his voice wasn't echoing off tunnel walls. Ethan had finally caught up to him.

Fairy Princess?

"I guess I'm supposed to be afraid of you," the princess returned, sounding breathless. *Becca.*

Shit. Somehow she'd found Fearmonger first. She must have run across campus the moment help arrived for Julia, guessing where Fearmonger was headed. Was Maggie there, too? He couldn't see around the edge of the doorway without risking exposure. Ethan edged forward quietly until he could see the room. Fearmonger had Becca in a corner, a gun aimed at her head. Her gun? How had he gotten it? And how had she figured out which building he was in?

He tried to see Maggie, daring to peek around the edge of the doorframe as Fearmonger's back remained to him, not twenty feet away.

There. Maggie stood near the wall, not five feet from Fearmonger and Becca.

"I'm the King of Fear," Fearmonger said, leaning toward

Becca. "I'll help you face your fears, embrace them. I'll set you free."

Ethan felt some pride for his trainee. Even in her trapped position, she was staring the guy down. Blood now streamed down her temple past the bandage that had once been white, as well as from several scrapes on her arms. She had put up a hell of a fight, but somehow the monster had gotten hold of her gun.

"Dr. Levine is the healer," she said. "You're just some little boy playing with fire, pouting because he didn't get into med school. I figured out you were heading to the radio station. How long do you think it'll take Ethan and the others to find us here?"

"That's so sweet. You're worried I'll get caught." Fearmonger laughed.

"Hardly." Becca's chin jutted out.

"Let her go," Maggie said, stepping toward them. She swayed a bit and clasped a hand to her chest but kept going. Ethan stifled the urge to run to her and hold her back. "It's me you want, anyway. She has nothing to do with this, with your *lessons*."

"It's Ethan you really want," Becca added. Ethan thought her glance flickered his way ever so subtly, but he couldn't be sure. Did she know he was here, flat against the wall on the other side of the doorway, under the cover of darkness?

"And where is the man of the hour?" Fearmonger asked, glancing up the stairs just beyond Becca.

"Right behind me. I just run faster. Once help arrived for Julia, I took off," Becca said, effectively letting Ethan and Maggie know that Julia was safe. "But he'll be here. And you're going to jail. You may take one of us down, but you'll never get us both."

Ethan winced at her taunt. She was keeping her cool, but he wished she wouldn't push Fearmonger's buttons. Of course, he probably would have done the same thing in her situation. It would keep the man's attention on her, and allow Ethan to take a shot.

But could he take that shot?

Fearmonger stood almost squarely between Becca and Ethan, but what if Maggie moved to the side, even a couple inches? Or what if the bullet went slightly right and hit Becca? Or what if it wasn't enough to stop Fearmonger, and he got to Becca or Maggie before Ethan could save them?

As the old doubts plagued him, the image of the little girl he'd failed filled his mind. Her eyes looked up at him as she lay on the grassy lawn where she'd fallen. *His fault.* He'd made a choice and defended Mallory, and Bethany had paid the price. What would this choice cost him?

"You're right, you know," Maggie said, stepping a little closer to Fearmonger.

Ethan bit back the urge to shout at her to stay put. Her comment, and the way she seemed to approach him rather than cower, drew Fearmonger's attention—and kept it away from Ethan and Becca. She didn't think twice about drawing the danger to herself if it meant helping others. His chest filled with love for this brave woman. *His* woman.

Fearmonger tilted his head in question.

"About fear," Maggie continued. "You were right when you said it can take over your mind, your heart, your soul. My panic attacks are proof enough of that. But you're wrong about something else."

The gun shifted a bit, ever so slightly off of Becca. Unfortunately, it shifted toward Maggie. "No," Fearmonger said, his voice hard. "I'm not wrong."

Maggie shook her head, and the gun inched just a little more toward her. "If there's one thing you've taught me, it's that people *can* take control. They can face their fears. If not, why else are we on this earth? God gives us what we need to cope. He gives us the strength to deal with our fears."

It was as if she was speaking to him, Ethan thought. About his past. Did she know he was there? Was she ready to get to safety if he moved in?

Her next words confirmed it. "Your theories are *bullshit*."

Fearmonger's roar of anger snapped Ethan into action as the killer swung his gun to aim it directly at Maggie. Ethan caught the flash in Becca's eyes as she signaled to Ethan. It was now or never. And they were counting on him. Ethan took a step forward, feeling the comforting, familiar grip of his gun in his hand.

Fearmonger shook his head, his body quaking with his fury. "You can have this conversation with God, if He exists, shortly. You won't be on this earth for very much longer. But first…" As Fearmonger moved to aim again at Becca, she ducked and Ethan put the man in his sights and fired.

"Get down!" Ethan yelled to Maggie as Fearmonger fired his gun, the loud report reverberating off the thick basement walls and drowning out his warning. But she'd already dropped to the floor and was rolling away from the danger. Ethan's bullet connected with Fearmonger's back and he crumpled to the ground. Fearmonger's bullet slammed into the concrete where Becca's head had been just seconds before. Ethan propelled his body forward and kicked the gun away from Fearmonger's hand, sending it skidding into a corner. But there was no need.

"He's dead," Becca said, checking for a pulse and taking the knife from the scabbard at Fearmonger's belt as Ethan kept his weapon trained on the monster.

"It's okay," Maggie said.

She had risen and come to his side, but he hadn't noticed. He didn't want to take his eyes off the bastard. She guided his hand down, lowering his weapon. Holstering his gun, he reached out and grabbed her to him, loosening his hold only when she moaned slightly. He pulled back and ran his hands over her, searching for wounds. If that maniac had hurt her, he'd shoot him again.

He cupped her face in his hands—hands that had been steady only moments ago but now shook with emotion. "Did he hurt you?"

She shook her head, but her eyes sparkled with unshed tears. "Not me. But Julia…"

"Damian's got her to the hospital by now," Becca said. "I'm sure she'll be okay. I'll go upstairs and make a few calls. See if I can find out the latest."

Ethan turned to Becca. "You did good, Agent Haney."

She grinned. "Thank you for noticing, Agent Townsend."

"But how did you figure out where Fearmonger was taking Maggie?"

Her grin widened. "There were only four places he could exit the tunnel he was in. One was the medical building and we knew he didn't go that way since we came from there. Another was the area he'd parked his van, which he had to suspect had been discovered since we'd tracked him down. When I saw one of the other exits was the radio station, I knew that was a logical place to take Maggie. It was a place that linked them."

"Great work."

"Except…" She hesitated. "He got the jump on me. Got my weapon."

"He threatened to slit my throat unless you tossed the gun to him," Maggie exclaimed. "What else could you have done?"

Becca grimaced. "I should have been prepared. I should have had a Plan B."

"Next time." Ethan clasped her on the shoulder. "This

was your first big assignment. You survived. You learned. And next time you'll be more careful."

She nodded but was clearly still contemplating how she could have been better. "I think I'll give you two some time." She jogged up the stairs and out of sight.

"I guess that means we have her stamp of approval now," Maggie said with a grin.

Unwilling to go any longer without her body against his, he pulled her close, wrapping both arms tightly around her. His throat worked as he swallowed the lump there. "God, Maggie."

She squeezed him back, her arms circling his waist. "I know. But we're okay now. You did it. You got the monster."

"I got my life back," he whispered against her hair. "When I saw what he'd done to your sister, and thought about what he would do to you… I don't know what I'd do without you." He pulled away to gaze into her dirt-streaked face. She'd never been more beautiful to him.

"You've got me now," she assured him, leaning up until she was a breath away. "Show me what you'd do *with* me." The tenderness in their kiss made his chest swell and ache. She tilted her head and he followed her lead, deepening the kiss, reaching for the passion he knew they shared. The sound of several footsteps at the top of the stairs had them reluctantly pulling apart.

Ethan leaned his forehead against hers and sighed. "We'll finish this later."

Noah, Maria and Lorena came rushing in at almost the same time, from the direction of the stairs leading into the rest of the building.

"Julia?" Maggie asked.

"She'll be okay," Noah assured them. "Just heard from the hospital. She lost a lot of blood, but she got there in time."

"Thank God. Do my parents know?"

"They're with her at the hospital." Noah looked at Fear-monger's body lying sprawled on the ground. "Looks like we have several things to be thankful for tonight."

The summer night wrapped around her like a warm blanket as Maggie stepped through the hospital's automatic sliding doors. She'd needed a moment to herself, to absorb what had happened in the past few days. She felt her heart pumping but embraced the feeling. The awareness of this ordinary function of her body was no longer solely linked to anxiety but now a reminder that she was fully alive.

As was her sister, thank God. Julia had come out of surgery and was recovering in intensive care. The prognosis was good. The desire to hear Ethan's voice, and to share her relief, was so intense it almost knocked her knees out from under her. She leaned against a concrete pillar and stared across the dark parking lot. She had to stand on her own. Ethan was busy, anyway, answering questions and helping to process the scene back at the university. Thanks to Damian's insistence, the police had agreed to delay her questioning and let her go to the hospital.

A niggling of doubt picked at her. Now that the danger was over, would Ethan still feel connected to her? Their passion had been intense and sudden. But it had also felt right.

She blinked as the form of a man emerged from the darkness, weaving between the cars. She'd know that swagger anywhere. He headed for her and she straightened, swallowing as he came up to her, his gaze sweeping over her body. She felt the heat of his look all the way to her toes.

Tucking her hands into her back pockets, she fought the urge to reach for him. She wanted to give him some space. Let him make the next move. Danger did things to people, made them more vulnerable in so many ways. Perhaps when he'd declared his desire for a future with her before, he'd been under the influence of adrenaline or something.

"I have that answer for you. To your previous question," she continued when he didn't say anything. He just stood there, looking at her with an odd, intense expression on his face. She resisted the desire to shuffle her feet. "You know, about our future."

Oh God, what if, now that it was all over, he'd changed his mind?

She almost backed away. But no, that was the old Maggie. Hiding from her fears. The new Maggie stood up to them. The new Maggie claimed her right to live life to the fullest. And she was certain Ethan had to be a part of that life to make it truly full.

I am in control.

For the first time in a long time, she believed it.

She swallowed. "If you're, uh, still interested in something long-term, I'd like to give it a try. I think we should be together."

"Bullshit."

"What?"

"I don't *think* we should. I *know* we should be together, and you do, too."

She sucked in a breath, her heart pounding as she reached into her front pocket and pulled out a piece of suturing thread she'd found on a supply cart in the hospital. She handed it to him.

"What's this?" he asked, his look of confusion comical.

"I told you there were no strings attached. But now I want them."

"I don't think it's long enough," he said, his lips curving into a grin. "I plan to be attached to you for a very long time."

The earth shifted as Ethan pulled her to him and embraced her as if he'd never let her go. She sank into him, savoring the steady heartbeat beneath her palms. She felt him breathe in and out before he spoke again.

"I thought you were gone forever. I thought I'd lost you." His hands came up to frame her face. "God, I never want to feel that way again," he whispered. It was a prayer.

"You won't have to." It was a promise.

* * * * *

REQUEST YOUR FREE BOOKS!

2 FREE NOVELS
PLUS 2 FREE GIFTS!

MYSTERY WORLDWIDE LIBRARY®

Your Partner in Crime

YES! Please send me 2 FREE novels from the Worldwide Library® series and my 2 FREE gifts (gifts are worth about $10). After receiving them, if I don't wish to receive any more books, I can return the shipping statement marked "cancel." If I don't cancel, I will receive 4 brand-new novels every month and be billed just $5.24 per book in the U.S. or $6.24 per book in Canada. That's a saving of at least 34% off the cover price. It's quite a bargain! Shipping and handling is just 50¢ per book in the U.S. and 75¢ per book in Canada.* I understand that accepting the 2 free books and gifts places me under no obligation to buy anything. I can always return a shipment and cancel at any time. Even if I never buy another book, the two free books and gifts are mine to keep forever.

414/424 WDN FEJ3

Name	(PLEASE PRINT)	
Address		Apt. #
City	State/Prov.	Zip/Postal Code

Signature (if under 18, a parent or guardian must sign)

Mail to the **Reader Service:**
IN U.S.A.: P.O. Box 1867, Buffalo, NY 14240-1867
IN CANADA: P.O. Box 609, Fort Erie, Ontario L2A 5X3

Not valid for current subscribers to the Worldwide Library series.

Want to try two free books from another line?
Call 1-800-873-8635 or visit www.ReaderService.com.

* Terms and prices subject to change without notice. Prices do not include applicable taxes. Sales tax applicable in N.Y. Canadian residents will be charged applicable taxes. Offer not valid in Quebec. This offer is limited to one order per household. All orders subject to credit approval. Credit or debit balances in a customer's account(s) may be offset by any other outstanding balance owed by or to the customer. Please allow 4 to 6 weeks for delivery. Offer available while quantities last.

Your Privacy—The Reader Service is committed to protecting your privacy. Our Privacy Policy is available online at www.ReaderService.com or upon request from the Reader Service.

We make a portion of our mailing list available to reputable third parties that offer products we believe may interest you. If you prefer that we not exchange your name with third parties, or if you wish to clarify or modify your communication preferences, please visit us at www.ReaderService.com/consumerschoice or write to us at Reader Service Preference Service, P.O. Box 9062, Buffalo, NY 14269. Include your complete name and address.

WWLI1B